Predication 2012

www.predication.info

by

Richard Barker

Predication 2012

A CIP catalogue record for this book is available from the British Library.

ISBN 978-0-9571933-0-7

Cover design by Bobby Grindrod

Dedication

This book is dedicated to Anita Brownrigg, Pat Piper and my mother Ruth all of whom are no longer here to read it but whose love, kindness and selflessness continue to inspire me.

Acknowledgments

I believe in smart strategies. I have partnered with a number of exceptional people in the production of this novel, most notably my father, Prof. Barker, who taught me to think for myself; Vivienne DuBourdieu, as editor, for her suggestions, encouragement and continuity, and without whom I could not have taken the book to market; Harry and Bobby Grindrod for marketing and original artistic contributions; Jeff Thomson as mentor and narrator; and Liz Justice for her guidance and ear. To enjoy the creative journey with such inspiring genii has been an amazing experience for me.

Chapter One

Friday, 14th December, 2012
The Murray Institute, Birmingham University, England

Time is an illusion; we create our own reality.

It is mid December 2012 and the festive season is well underway. This year, however, there will be an ending like no other...

Slumped forward on her desk at the university, Jean, the cleaning supervisor of Birmingham University, dozed off on the last shift of the week.

As exhaustion gave way to slumber, a tall, shadowy figure slid through the office doorway and crept across the room. Dressed in double-denim, he looked freshly shaven and wavy, dark auburn hair brushed against his collar. Beneath his jacket, he wore a checked flannel shirt. He looked more late 1980s than early 21st century. Not what you would expect of a professor; but then Murray was no ordinary professor.

Seeing that Jean was in a deep sleep, he relaxed, reflecting on his wait and the countless journeys he had made to get to this point. It was not just any 'old journey.' Murray was not on a quest or a soul-searching venture to Thailand - the sort his students waxed lyrical about. But yes, this moment had certainly been a long time coming; it had taken countless trips in fact.

Jean looked very different from the girl he had lost many years ago, and was clearly unaware of the gift she possessed, or what was at stake. "Just innocence," he said softly. As he stepped forward to look more closely at her, a tendril of hair unwound out of the tight chignon it was bound into. The flaming red locks, freed from restraint, cascaded across her neck, Murray's hands twitched slightly as he reached out towards her. But then, in a moment of grace, he turned and slipped away, murmuring under his breath, "I'll be back..."

He returned to the doorway and stepped into the corridor, not wanting to be caught when Jean woke. The patter of raindrops on the skylight had already threatened to awaken her from uneasy dreams. A moment or two later, Jean, unnerved by her dreams, cried, "Let us out of here!"

In her dream - or nightmare - Jean was in a basement containing cages of files; some sort of stock room, she deduced. Deprived of air, the place stank of musk; and the sounds of the street above were merely whispers. It was not Smethwick, and definitely not the West Midlands. Perhaps it was a foreign place, or even a fictional place like a movie set. Yes, that must be it. But who was she talking with?

"A man..." she said in surprise."I *know* this man. Oh, so handsome! He must be an acquaintance, but maybe not. Well, no closer than that anyway... and yet I know him well." Her eyelids flickered. "How well?"

Jean flung her arm out in a frustrated gesture. They were prisoners, shamed and desperate. Why? She spoke aloud again. "If I recognise him, who *is* he?" Abruptly, the door opened to their prison and she was falling. "Arghhh! I've gone over the edge," she cried. "I'm falling into water and looking at..."

"Woo hoo! Look at that view! Amazing!" Awe-struck, she drank in the Pacific rollers and the crystal blue ocean beyond them. The mass of water came closer and closer, frame by frame, as if in slow motion, and she was falling towards the Bay below. "Brace," she told herself, "brace against the crash."

She stirred, nearly waking. "But what's this? A plane...

"I've never been in a plane," she protested, and harnessed her reason for long enough to notice that everyone on it looked odd. They might have been airlifted from an eighties' party. The women with big hair, massive shoulder pads and shiny, blue eye-shadow. Nightmare, that's it, it must be a nightmare a cocktail of indigestion, overtiredness and TV drama all mashed up into one. "Oh, I really must stop watching TV so much!" she scolded herself.

"Damn the TV..." she said distantly as a new scene played out. Jean's heart was racing, her pulse pounding. Then inexplicably, her breathing slowed down again. What a beautiful park. There's that wonderful view again with the bridge spanning the Bay and the twinkling lights. But who's that man, that man in the green car?

"Oh no, not him!" She gulped, "I must get away. The bike, take the bike. But, I can't ride a bike..." Regardless of her skills, suddenly she was on the bike and gunning the engine. Her voice croaked, "Faster, faster, drive faster, get away from him. It's the only way to get control!"

Crazy as it seemed, something in her knew she had to go over the edge. "Faster, faster, turn towards the edge."

Momentarily, another part of her stepped in, terrified of driving into the Bay, "No, no..."

Jean woke up with a sharp jolt. "I'll die!" she screamed.

She was in her office, and had no idea what she had just witnessed - a nightmare, perhaps. She brushed her hands down her body to check and, yes, she was undoubtedly alive. She had better compose herself, then. What if the new professor walked in and found her in this state?

"Hmmm. A little shaken, stirred even, but I'll live," she told herself. She sat quietly for a while. I have to stop going on those big nights out with Paula, she reflected. It's doing me no good. She remembered the story of the man whose drink had been spiked at a party with acid. He took a trip, and never came back.

Jean wondered if her weekend revelry was creeping into her working day. Flashbacks from one gin and tonic too many kept creeping into her mind. She had always thought nightmares were a reflection of her mental state but, then again, maybe not. If her dream was a reflection of her life, maybe she needed to take a break.

As she calmed down, her breathing became deeper. She was puzzled and disorientated, but the confusion cleared as she took in her surroundings. The cocktail of chemical aromas seeping in from the university labs steadied her nerves. She almost laughed because the lab smells usually got up her nose.

Gradually, Jean's sense of alienation faded in the familiar environment; and so did the unpleasant images she had brought back with her of something happening outside time.

"Snap out of it Jean, come on," she said, taking charge of herself. "Let's finish the day, lock up and get out of here. It's the weekend."

Jean rarely wasted time in chewing over the past. Today, though, she felt a little odd. The dream hung around disturbingly; if it was a dream. Fragmentary visions floating around her head had nothing to do with any life that she had lived - well, not consciously.

As with all optimists though, Jean rallied swiftly. Forgetting her earlier intentions of researching elements of the dreams, she bounced back with a spring in her step. "Another adventurous weekend!" she grinned, dramatising a reality that scarcely matched the interlude she had just experienced.

In fact, her weekends were usually far from adventurous and, for a feisty woman like Jean, just a bit too inclined to melt unnoticeably, one into another.

"Reality..." she sighed in a bemused way.

It didn't take a medium to predict the future. Coming on 41, Jean's life was similar to that of a zillion other women: her life ended at 40 it seemed the fairly dreary weeks of work stretched to the horizon. Even so, Jean did her best to liven things up outside the 'everyday box'.

At university, people generally saw Jean as a stout-hearted Midlander: not a woman to be crossed. She was physically petite, busty, and slightly plump around the middle - alcohol was unkind, and she had too much of it at times. All the same, she had kept her looks and basic figure.

At work, however, Jean wore a stern aura over that comfortable appearance. She had a reputation for not suffering fools gladly. She could be sharp-witted, and was sometimes vehement. Yet even at work, despite her stern air, Jean was intrinsically kind-hearted, warm and caring. She had the capacity to be generous in all things.

In her private life, the picture was slightly different. Jean talked! When people first met Jean socially, most were overwhelmed because she had opinions about *everything*. Those who gave her time, though, slowly became aware of a softer side; a vulnerability that everyone warmed to. She was a stalwart friend and confidant: never judging, always listening.

Nonetheless, life had given Jean an unorthodox character, and she sported a unique dress sense to match it. Often ahead of the curve, she read up the latest looks from the catwalks of Paris and Milan, and made her own predictions about where fashion was heading. With a miniscule budget, she spent hours trawling charity shops and retro clothing outlets to make her salary stretch further. She took a girlish delight in the compliments received from friends and colleagues.

Jean had been divorced so long, she thought of herself as a 'single mum' although, admittedly, her darling Sue had left the nest. That left Jean poised on the edge of a new chapter in her life.

She paused to reflect on the decisive battle at home in her early years. She rarely looked back for long but the recent dreams had made her wonder whether her genes went through some mutation in her youth.

She chuckled to herself and pondered on her youth, "What youth?" Although barely a teenager, she had flipped when her father, Joe, lashed out at her in a drunken haze. Overcome with rage, she found herself shouting at him, "You bastard! You bastard!"

Her mother, Hope, the reluctant accomplice, tried to intervene; and justified her part in the abuse by the feeble attempt to help Jean. "If she wanted to 'help'," Jean told herself, "she would leave Joe." And this time, she fought back.

"No, Father! Stay away from me, stay…"

Jean had put up a front, and he hated her attempt to regain control of what was 'his'. Energised by his anger, Joe hit Jean hard enough to send her flying across the room. The fall winded her. Then he pushed Jean into the ground. It was not just the air that he expelled that day but her confidence and self worth.

Under her breath, she swore, "Nobody tells me what to do or how to live my life; you'll never touch me again!"

Having minimal control or security in her home life meant that she sought significance at school – at least, she did when she turned up. Most of the time, she attended the first lesson at school and then went truant in town for the rest of the day with Paula, her best friend and fellow miscreant.

Paula was a little older than Jean, and had been around from the very beginning. They had grown up in the same estate together; and excelled in sharing pranks.

"I've got a double maths at 11am but it can wait. Shall we go to town instead?" Paula would say.

Jean would need no persuasion. "Well, I can't catch up on my grades now. Let's face it, maths don't light my box."

To the dismay of the headmaster, one of their milder sins involved changing road signs and redirecting the rush hour traffic through the school. They became more reckless still; in one incident, they left the Bunsen burners on and unlit in the science lab overnight.

When the chemistry teacher, a Mr Burns, switched on the lab lights next morning, the lab exploded like a small bomb. The force was so great that he flew through the door into the assembly hall, over the heads of a line of second years. There would have definitely been a fatality if the lines of first year pupils had not broken his fall as they fell about like skittles.

"Jesus, Paula! What are you thinking? This is going to end badly!" Jean exclaimed as the boom knocked them both flying; their crimped hair standing on end as a light coating of soot and dust rained down on them.

The explosion had taken out most of the science block but, by some miracle, no-one died.

"Burns' Burners Go Bang!" screamed the banners for the local rag. Burns retired after that. The press revelry was the final straw for him but, needless to say, the governors were none too pleased at losing a good teacher or at the huge bill for the replacement science block.

Jean and Paula did feel sorry for Burns – for a millisecond – but then, it's difficult to change habits; is it not?

Always where the action was at school, Jean quickly spotted that the *main* action came from being where the boys were. She took to following Ted around as he was captain of the soccer squad. He was a local rascal, but handsome and athletic, with dreams of becoming a professional football player.

Jean's pain was so great at home that she engineered a completely misguided romantic rendezvous. A baby, to her, would be a ticket to social security. It was freedom, whatever the cost: a passport out of the living hell that was her family.

"We could be good together, you and me," she said to Ted.

"Is that right?" he asked, staring down at her. He liked the love she gave out; he could feel it in her when she was close, and loved the connection, which was something he had never had before. Life had been tough for him, too.

The son of a miner, Ted made opportunities where he found them. His father spent most of his time and money out of the pits in the boozer or fronting the picket lines, on strike. Ted knew this from talking to his mate's dad next door, who was a 'Bobby'. The sensible policeman bought a boat with his overtime and named the boat Maggie, in deference to the Prime Minister of the day who had sanctioned the extra hours.

They were two boys from the same street, same school: similar folks but with very different outcomes in life. Ted knew that life wasn't fair, but he still had his dreams.

"Fancy being a footballer's wife," he asked Jean? She nodded. They crept upstairs, and Sue was conceived. When she found she was pregnant, Jean calmly presented Ted with the facts of life. Not yet eighteen, his dream of a professional career as a footballer was rapidly diluted by the prospect of fatherhood.

They needed each other for the wrong reasons, and by the age of nineteen, Jean had jumped out of the frying pan and into the furnace by marrying Ted. Perhaps the relationship was doomed, everyone said so, but all the same, they walked up the aisle with their toddler, Sue, clinging to

Jean's legs. It was exciting in the beginning, of course: lots of attention was not something that Jean was used to; and she lapped it all up.

After the birth *and* then the wedding, the reality of marriage hit. The responsibilities of raising a child, and dealing with Ted's bouts of drinking drove Jean back into a miserable place.

Ted realised that football was not going to be his saviour – somehow pint after pint and line after line hampered his development - and he turned to Jean for comfort and the future that he foolishly denied himself.

"Just one more match," he would say. "I've got a sure thing on the next 'Wednesday away' at Nottingham." The team members were fine. Direction from their captain was what was missing. It was the same with Ted's marriage.

"All care and no responsibility," Jean muttered on a daily basis. Life was controlling her again. Her dash for freedom had become soured by the constraints of her relationship with Ted.

"You must be joking. I'm not staying in," he would say. "I work all day, and now I'm going to relax. I'll be in the pub; won't be long, love."

One drink in the pub would lead to the whole night and he rarely returned after the pub closed. She would wait up, worried about him, and clean the house as the hours passed by; and then clean it again. Then she would put on a movie and fall asleep.

The final straw was when he turned up after 'a heavy one with the local lads', replete with the word 'loser' freshly inked on his chest. When rumours of his antics reached the team's sponsors, his career came to an abrupt end.

With his dreams smashed, Ted had nothing to look forward to and, although he didn't say so, he blamed Jean and his daughter for it. He would never leave her, and always came back before dawn, but that made it worse: it was a half-life, a life without meaning or purpose for either of them. The only plus was that he never hit her.

She felt herself slipping into the stereotype: effectively, a single parent. Time passed and the pressure of having a teenager in the prime of her life became overwhelming. Ted was absent from the household on wild, drunken binges ever more often. It slowly dawned on Jean that she had, unwittingly, recreated the family she had been so desperately trying to run away from.

Bad habits and patterns in life can change, though, and Jean's life changed in an instant with just one phrase; a small sentence that pushed her mind into the realms of possibility after a decade of painful, compromised parenting.

It came when her eleven-year-old daughter, Sue, enrolled Jean in an amateur theatrical production. She was terrified when the big day arrived! As she waited to go out on stage, the adrenalin flooded her brain. For a few seconds at the beginning of the performance, she knew she would either succeed or fall flat on her arse. But she had practiced, she was confident; and she came out with a song and a dance.

"You come to me... come to me, wild and wild..." She was concealed behind an umbrella and then dropped it for the big reveal. The timing was impeccable. Something seemed to take over inside her and a personality that she could only show on stage - funny and fun to experience - came to the fore. She connected with herself and her audience.

"Tear us apart, baby... I would rather be dead... ooh you're the best!" She belted out her Tina Turner tribute to rapturous applause. Afterwards, though, she just couldn't believe they loved her, really loved her.

I'm sure Tina Turner would have something to say about it, Jean thought later, but then her story was similar: love and violence rolled into one toxic relationship.

"You were good today, Jean!" the director said warmly, remembering the scenes with a telling smile. Then, looking closer at her wide blue eyes, he added incredulously, "But you don't believe it, do you?"

The penny dropped: she *was* gorgeous, she was beautiful, she could be loved and she deserved to be happy. It was time for a revolution. Jean had stolen Ted's dream of playing in the Premier League, and now Jean showed Ted her own red card, confining him to the bench at the prime of his life. She had resolved that history would not repeat itself. There would be no more passing of the behavioural ball to her precious daughter.

She began divorce proceedings to regain control over her life; and surgically removed her partner. "Goodbye and good riddance," she declared triumphantly.

Once rid of Ted, Jean pulled herself up by her bootstraps. She did a great job of bringing up Sue, who, at the aged of eighteen, renamed herself Ocean as part of the punk image she sought to affect. She had pink hair, piercings and tattoos and did exceptionally well in her schooling. Ocean went on to university and became a social worker; a good one. In a strange way, Jean had subconsciously impressed upon Ocean the person she had always wanted to be, but given up on.

With her daughter off her hands, and successful in her own right, Jean now manically played 'catch-up'. She put balance back into her life by projecting her wonderfully caring soul and energy into work and those people who, to her perception, needed it most. In the past, she had always put others first, to the detriment of herself, but now her actions were no longer to her detriment.

-

Back in the present, Jean deliberated the notion, 'Be careful what you wish for' and wondered what the world would be like if we actually lived our dreams. Jean had a cleaning job - well a bit more than cleaning job. She didn't realise how far her influence stretched.

The cleaning job was 'a natural career' after years of almost obsessive clearing up after Ted, who hadn't shared Jean's high standards when it came to housework. After the divorce was settled, she presented herself at the local university with a single-minded vision and the energy to see it through.

Jean climbed easily to the position of Hygiene Supervisor at the Murray Research Institute. She was a domestic domo oiling the wheels of academia. Her aim was to ensure that standards were met - hygienically and ethically. She had a private mission to correct the dubious nature of those around her. Single-handedly, she projected her vision of a joint initiative between the cream of the academic world and the captains of industry; and she had the determination to make it happen.

She always thought that professors and business professionals were an unlikely but symbiotic partnership, each relying on the other for survival. Birmingham University, a red brick university that received its Royal Charter in 1900, had achieved a string of notable research fellows; and it was an active contributor to the technological changes of the last century. In fact, it claimed to be the historical residence of several Nobel Prize winners.

Traditionally, Birmingham University had focused on chemistry and biology. The focus had changed this year, though. When its latest laureate arrived, they renamed the department in his honour. After all, Professor Murray from Berkeley, CA, *had* been awarded a prize for his controversial contribution to psychokinesis, and they hoped the kudos would rub off on their students.

Jean felt strangely drawn to him. It almost seemed as though her place at the Institute was no accident. Of course, there was no possibility of them being anything but acquaintances; university life was like 'Upstairs and Downstairs' - a polite exchange of niceties and a few jokes, nothing more. All the same, were her intuitive feelings right?

Psychokinetic abilities include the reading of minds, conversing with those who have passed over, feelings of déjà vu, a collective consciousness and even conversing with the creator. The next time she saw Murray, Jean took a deep breath, and fronted him directly.

"What made you choose psychokinesis, Prof?"

"Have you got time for a coffee?" he asked.

Over a thermos flask of fairtrade in his office, Murray told her these experiences were commonplace to people across the globe.

"Actually, Jean, my PhD theorised that world religions have often been based on 'mystical states'. I proved scientifically that this phenomenon could be achieved by *anyone* in a particular state of openness.

"In other words, it became evident to me that much of what existed in people's daily reality *was* grounded on numinous experiences that could only have come from *shared* psychokinetic phenomena."

"You mean," she said slowly, "mystics thought ideas that came to them unbidden were divine but, actually, they were sharing them with other people on a higher level than usual?" She wrinkled her nose cutely.

Murray looked at her in astonishment. "You've got it in one, Jean!" A smile streaked across his face. "That's fascinating..."

A day later he told students and the media, "The next evolution in human beings will be cerebral." Murray knew these experiences became more acute as each generation passed. As an aide memoire for his followers, he recycled a common term, 'the generation gap', as the 'generation bridge'. He knew the university's hygiene director was a particularly interesting example of this development.

On another occasion, stumped for a clue to the project that demanded much of his time, Murray had artlessly puttered over to her side of the faculty and asked her, "What would you do about the time problem?"

"Oh, fold it!" she said without any hint of hesitation. He pondered that for quite a while and, eventually, discovered she was very close to the mark.

They developed an almost playful relationship. "Prof," she would call him, bringing him down to her level.

One day, with a quizzical little laugh, Jean cornered him near the lab. "If you don't mind, Prof, please could you let me know the lottery numbers for this week's draw? It's just that the gas and electric have gone up, I need a new look for the new season ahead, and Jimmy down at my hairdressers doesn't come cheap. It's a challenge keeping up appearances these days."

Murray, a wry smile on his face, tried to ignore her pantomime, but took in every word.

"And if you could let me know who shot JR," she added, "then it would put us all out of our misery."

Always making light of his project, Murray loved Jean's dry sense of humour; and the way she brought him back to reality.

Along with Murray, Jean knew very well that what is commonly known as 'a woman's intuition' is real; and that was another thing that Murray had shown to be scientifically certifiable. Although *how* they could do that, she was not at all sure.

"They could have saved themselves all the bother and just asked me!" Jean exclaimed, after hearing the official news of that discovery. Well, Jean *had* been sniffing out the weasels in her life for years with intuition as her guide; she often seemed to see things coming before others did but downplayed the ability.

"Does everyone think like me?" she asked Paula, wondering what life would be like if she could see the future.

Paula replied, "I wish!" and ordered another drink.

Chapter Two

Wednesday, 18th December, 2012
Manhattan Island, New York, New York, USA

Evil is all in the mind.

"Your incompetence is not my concern," the Watcher said coldly. It was just before midnight, and the entire office heard his icy tones. Uninterested and aloof, he gazed at the array of twinkling lights making up the mass of Manhattan skyscrapers, with the statue of Liberty standing like an avenging angel beyond them. He owned most of the real estate on the island; and the final coup of his growing empire was only days away.

He lowered his head and began reading a fistful of papers, ignoring the problem he had been presented with. His travel director came back, looking tense.

"You're asking the impossible! We can't shift another 100,000 people before the end of the week," he said wearily. "There's no room at Oasis," he added.

The Watcher heard the note of helplessness in his voice and looked up, not amused by the negative response. He did not like being challenged, especially by someone who palpably cringed in his presence.

"You still here? Trouble-shooting's what I employ you to do! Plenty of others would be happy to take your place, or have you forgotten that?" He snapped, "I suggest unpaid guests bunch up. I want another 100,000 there. Make it happen."

The executive had forgotten what he was capable of. It had been a stressful week and everyone was at breaking point. Nobody had slept for days, but it wouldn't matter soon. He capitulated. It was easier.

"Of course, Sir, I'll make it work. You can count on me." The man departed without his boss acknowledging, or even seeing him. He had other things on his mind. To be accurate, he had a vision: a woman in an office and a man with her.

A shiver ran down The Watcher's spine. Details emerged: an oak panelled room with a skylight. A woman was slumped over a mahogany desk: not as grand as his, but quintessentially English.

"That's her, she's nothing special," he growled.

He assumed the woman he saw was ordinary, and no threat to him. The man though... he recognised him. Where were they, though? He felt the tension and tingling in his forehead, again.

"That's odd. Surely it was a random connection? But why; why now?" That was when he realised it was important.

"Timing is everything," he noted. He hadn't felt this feeling for a long time and it unsettled him. Then his beleaguered travel director came back again. The sudden blank look and gazing into space was out of character for his boss.

"You okay, Sir?" There was no reply so he continued, cautiously. "The extra non-payers are on their way. Is there anything else you want?"

There was a slight pause as The Watcher processed the question.

"No, that's all."

He picked up his phone to his PA's office. She was also doing the midnight shift.

"Yes, Sir, how can I be of assistance?"

"I want a file with photos of all US professors currently residing in the UK, and I want it on my desk within the hour. Get our man in the US state department to help you."

The Watcher mumbled to himself, "If I can just get rid of her, I'll get control of him."

Chapter Three

Friday, 14th December, 2012
Murrays Lab, Birmingham University, England

What you think, you become.

At day's end, it was Jean's responsibility to see that the cleaners - over 100 of them – were out of the building. Then she made a final inspection, turned out the lights, and headed home for the weekend. Jean told herself she had a vibrant social life, and that the late shift on a Friday got in the way. That slightly exaggerated her social reality, though.

Jean habitually used the last shift of the week as an opportunity to snoop around. It kept her informed. She liked to know what was really going on in the university; and much preferred other people's tittle-tattle to creating gossip of her own. She used it like a litmus paper; to check her own hunches.

This Friday seemed no different to any other. Jean paced the floors to inspect the work of her domestic division; a route she had been down a thousand times before. Her eye for detail soon spotted any anomalies. Her team joked - in front of her - that she could spot dirt at one hundred metres. When she saw the door to Prof Murray's tutorial room was ajar, she stopped dead, and murmured, "That's odd, the door shouldn't be open..."

Thinking the professor might be working late, Jean popped her head around the corner of the long, oak-panelled tutorial room. She sensed he was there, and relished the thought that he might be working late. That might mean an opportunity to talk with him.

Straightening her dress, she inhaled deeply before forging forward, as if 'on a mission'. She enjoyed her conversations with Murray. He was not just a curiosity, he was a deep mystery. Other than the gas board's ability to multiply units like mice mating in a lab, when it came to heating her home, mysteries were small cheese in her life. Prof Murray gave her a chance to stretch her imagination beyond the known boundaries.

The talk of the university was that Murray could have gone anywhere with his credentials, so why Birmingham? If Harvard, Berkeley and Oxbridge were in the top league; comparatively speaking, Birmingham was well down the ladder. Nobody knew much about him, but Jean knew more than most. She took pride in extracting information painlessly from the cleaners who worked under her. Piecing together these titbits had given her a fairly comprehensive picture of Murray.

She relished their chats, which she told herself were 'strictly professional' ones. But occasionally Murray asked Jean loaded questions; and the way he did so always made her feel significant because he listened so attentively.

Walking into the laboratory with its long benches and tables extending either side to the end of the room, Jean looked down hopefully towards Murray's grand writing desk. Disappointingly, the room was empty.

"That's odd. I could have sworn I heard someone moving around," Jean said crossly to the only resident, a surprisingly quiet parrot found by the professor on the banks of the Titford Reservoir. She had been focused on Murray being there, and felt confused to find the room empty. "Naughty boy, naughty boy..." the parrot twittered, displaying some prescience.

The smell of chemicals ruled and Jean got high on the energy permeating the room. She almost felt possessive about the marks made by generations of students on the wooden benches. They appealed to her sense of history, time and space. Many life-changing ideas had been nurtured here.

An anteroom ran off to the left of Professor Murray's desk. The room had originally been a store for the bound theses of past students; and cleaning the room was forbidden. The resident professor would evaluate and make recommendations on each student's PhD, then store the work in this dusty room. Many theses stored here originated from the USA, and were stamped Berkeley, CA. This rarely visited 'trophy cupboard' really bugged Jean's cleaning obsession.

The room, however, had recently undergone a partial conversion. A door had been added to a covered walkway for Murray's personal use, and the opposite end of this was connected to private labs where major research projects were undertaken. Only Murray and his colleagues had unfettered access to the area.

"Hmmm..." Jean assessed and justified her next step. "Someone could be in for the chop for leaving the door open." She had better check that the other rooms were empty before making a full report. She knew the rooms beyond were out of bounds - even to her - but, as usual, temptation won the toss.

In her official capacity as 'last person out', the opportunity to thoroughly examine the empty labs was something that Jean rarely passed up. Although what she did may have been against university policy and procedures, they could hardly fault her official role - even if a large portion of the research was sensitive in nature.

These academic types were notorious for not emptying their recycling bins and leaving all manner of documentation hanging around; material which should be shredded before departure.

"Quid pro quo!" she stated self-righteously, cloaking herself in the garb of an unremitting mission to find contraband.

Occasionally, Jean came across papers left on a desk or a PC that had not been shut down. She would confiscate any written material to her handbag, pending an opportunity to hand it over to the proper authorities, or she would lock the PC and leave the offending student an officious note. Jean would cite security as the reason for confiscation. Once any documents were in her safe hands, she would skim their contents before locking them securely away in her lost property cupboard.

Over the years, she had seen everything from adulterous emails to top-secret files, and much more. She often felt that she had the firm basis of a doctorate, herself. Sometimes, she contemplated - with an element of fun - the notion of being Doctor Jean.

Nonetheless, the chance to peek into this prestigious, restricted area was rare. Ethan Murray was a meticulous, almost regimented sort of man, and certainly not prone to forgetfulness, so Jean was alarmed over the open anteroom door. She stepped cautiously inside. At this juncture, she suddenly remembered a particularly vivid dream she had experienced. She ran it again through her mind.

Jean had been in a bar with her best friend, Paula. Well, where else would she be? That part was true enough. With Paula, she was always in one kind of bar or other.

Anyhow, she was describing the man she was falling in love with to Paula. They were walking in a park: San Francisco in the US. She recognised the distinctive red suspension bridge. Then... she was trying to escape. Escape from what? She leapt on someone's motorbike, but found herself falling; falling down a long way...

After this, came a feeling of walls collapsing in on her in a strange room where she was incarcerated; it was deep below street level and she was not alone.

Jean had woken up, on the verge of screaming from a sense of dread that foretold death and destruction. She could not reconcile it with any feeling she had ever felt before. Worse, she had missed a crucial detail, but had no idea where to find the missing clue. "Another flash-back! I really must stay off the gin," she grumbled, her heart racing.

Right then, a motion sensor kicked in, lighting up the white, pearlescent passageway ahead. Jean had a strange sense of déjà vu, but dismissed the instinct.

She said aloud, "I've never been here before." Well, surely she would have remembered it. But wait, that déjà vu moment. Was it a dream, or was it real? "Oh dear, now I'm going loopy!"

On another level, though, she had an uneasy sense of being watched; not that it stopped her wandering eyes. What Jean saw next completely mystified her. Directly ahead was a plain white room with a metal box inside. She assumed it was a machine, although there were no obvious panels, buttons, knobs or flashing lights; and there did not appear to be any obvious kind of power connected to it. For all she could tell, it might be a hollow shell.

Once again, she had the strange sense of déjà vu. She had been drawn instantly to the machine, but there was nothing she could see to help identify its purpose. As she moved closer to the box, or whatever it was, she noticed something strange about the metal. Its skin contained thousands of tiny dots, similar to the pixels on a computer screen. And it only appeared to be metallic in nature.

"Odd!" She gazed almost trance-like at one side of the box. Then she noticed something very strange indeed. She had seen it before in a magazine: a 3-D picture embedded in a sea of dots, which, to the untrained eye, is merely a pattern of dots. The action of looking at the dots induces a gentle trance. In fact, it requires a significant amount of concentration to extract the image lighting up the frontal lobe, which makes your brain tingle.

As Jean tried to figure out what this particular image was, she felt a fierce tingling behind her eyes; and a shiver went down her spine, as if someone had walked over her grave. Then an image began to emerge. It was a circle, with the capital letter 'M' in its centre. Must be for Murray, she deduced, but why would he put a stereo on the side of a quasi-metal box? A sharp searing pain knifed through her forehead.

"Ouch! What was that?"

Jean felt another brief, shooting pain; and then a third, the last one more of a pin-prick. She looked around, troubled, once more feeling as if someone was reading her mind. It made her feel vulnerable; and she wanted to protect her secrets.

She told herself it was all too ridiculous. "I certainly don't want people to know my business, but that's just a machine." Then she heard a movement on the other side of the walkway. She turned abruptly and walked away, closing the door behind her.

She could hear footsteps marching inexorably towards her. Probably security; she was in for it now. Running across the Air Bridge, and back into the anteroom, she peered round the doorway, checking if it was security on her tail. The fear stemmed from a dread planted in her childhood about being told off. Caught by fright, she took one look out of the anteroom, ready to embrace the crippling disapproval she was certain would come. There was nobody there. She would have sworn someone was there!

Relieved, she shut the door behind her, made her way back down the long office, and out into the corridor. What a narrow escape! She dwelled briefly on how professors managed to get huge amounts of cash for such silly experiments. Stereos: whatever next?

Jean was completely unaware of what she had just done, or what the consequences would be.

Chapter Four

Saturday, 15th December, 2012
172 Marion Road, Smethwick, England

A collective consciousness is a part of us - in our language and culture; most of us choose to ignore this natural instinct.

It was Saturday morning, and Jean was tucked up snugly in bed. An estate agent might call her house 'a typical two-up, two-down terrace, with original features intact.'

It was a small but pleasant dwelling. The interior was a projection of Jean's artistic creativity: her safe space, where she curled up like a butterfly in a cocoon. She had different colour schemes in every room, and objects were placed purposefully. The whole effect was a harmonious slew of silky pinks, blues and purples with swags, glossy tails and pristine ruches.

Built of brick in the 30s, Jean had inherited the house - like her name - from her grandmother. It had a large glass veranda out the back where she could sit all year round, sunning herself. There was a small garden with a garage at the end, housing a vintage Morris Minor, which she occasionally drove on Sundays.

There was still a strong presence from Nanny Jean, and her grand-daughter found this hugely comforting. Whether it came from associations with the good times Jean had there as a child, or there was something supernatural going on, she could not say.

These rows of terraced houses, with a passage running in between, were originally built for Midlands metal workers when Birmingham, her home town, was the heart of an industrial metropolis. Nan's house had survived a bomb, which took out the house fronting her back yard.

The flattened house to the rear had belonged to Nan's nasty neighbour, Audrey, who died from a direct bomb hit in WWII, considerately leaving Nan with a lovely view. Nobody ever reclaimed the land so Nan built a garage on the section with the bricks that were left, and boasted a slightly larger garden than those of her neighbours.

She always said she had seen the German pilot flying overhead in a Messerschmitt, and asked him to release its payload over her neighbour's house; it seemed that Nan had developed the habit of creating her own future.

"Drop your bombs on that bitch, Audrey's house, and make me a happy woman," she begged the bomber. "But," she added as an afterthought when an image of Audrey's Golden Retriever flashed into view, "save Flossy." Flossy had a wonderful temperament, despite provocation from her owner. Anyway, it seemed to work: Nanny Jean's mystical conversation with the German bomber rid the neighbourhood of a troublesome resident.

Nan had emerged that day from her Anderson shelter to find Flossy sitting on a pile of rubble. They never found Audrey, and Nan became a bit of a legend after that. She always thought she was psychic in some way. Buoyed up by this, she honed her 'psychic art'; and had some success doing card readings at fairs. This strand of her career ended abruptly, though, because she was blunt to the edge of tactlessness; and caused a ruckus when one of her customers ran out screaming. "

"What do you see?" the woman asked.

"Ahh... I see the Devil and Death in your present and the Fool in your past," Nan reported with rare interest. She added, "And I see betrayal and infamy."

Nanny Jean could be a tad dramatic. She continued, she was on a roll tuned in to the spirit world "I see a man called Dave. He's kissing a woman who has blonde hair in a bob, and she has a limp." She paused briefly. "Oh! What's this? Does Bognor mean anything to you?"

That was apparently when Nan's client screamed, and began weeping. "Dave's my husband," She wailed. "He met the blonde piece when we were in Bognor on holiday!"

Mystic Jean asked for confirmation, concerned that the woman might have got the wrong end of the stick. "How do you know it's the right woman?"

"His tart has a wooden leg!" Grabbing her hat and coat, the woman was out the door in a flash and, needless to say, forgot to pay her for the session. Unfortunately, everyone at the fair thought Nanny Jean had deliberately terrified the woman; and it seemed a good day to give up fortune-telling.

Jean was disturbed by a dream. "Nan, Nan! Is that you, Nan?" Jean was one of life's dreamers. When she woke up to a new day, she was often unsure whether she was awake or dreaming. The fact that she was also something of a grafter may have had something to do with her difficulty in separating dreaming from reality.

Inevitably, Jean was tired and groggy from her hard working week. In that environment, she pushed herself as far as she could but, once it got underway, the weekend was different. Flicking with her remote, she clicked on the TV at the foot of her bed, and prepared for her first sin of the day: bacon and poached egg muffins, as well as compote of soaked muesli. Then she settled back into bed, half-hypnotised by the worst of the week's gruelling TV schedule.

It was the same crazy content as ever: wars, crises, and a smattering of reality TV - the twenty-first century, with all its extremes. As she listened to a report of another shooting, Jean murmured, "There might be more diversity and choice than ever before, but standards are slipping."

Recognising the backdrop, she realised it was less than a few hundred yards away. A young hood, only 17, in with a bad lot - drugs and guns - was to blame. She looked out of the window to see plastic tape at the end of the street. It was emblazoned: "Police Line. Do Not Cross."

"Better put a brick in my handbag when I go out tonight, just in case," she told herself. The area she lived in was not the best, and opportunists always prey on those who show weakness.

In Jean's view, petty crime was simply a matter of people trying to make a crust the only way they knew how; and it was often fuelled by drugs. She blamed the generation born of 'free love' for taking over the reins. In her view, that was compounded by a slew of The Eighties' 'help yourself' ethics.

The future was looking so hopeful at one point, but she believed the next generation had been dealt an ill-fated set of cards. Every generation believes they can better the one before. In her view, any real hope was the young people around her at university. Being on the edge of an information and communications revolution gave them an edge over those who preceded them.

"Noughties' babes - they're our future," she sighed, reflecting that it was a generation defined by 'values rather than things'. Paula always disagreed with Jean on this. She insisted that revolution was a fallacy.

"Most people can't see beyond the sound and video bites," Paula stated fervently.

"There are opportunities for everyone," Jean always argued. "People simply need enough insight to reach out and grab what they want."

Having put the world back on course, Jean settled back against the cushions and pillows for her favourite soap. This week's story went into the technicalities of gays having a baby. It was followed by a serial killer on the romp: he had buried a string of ex-lovers under his patio. In her opinion, most people would like to see their ex under a patio.

She remarked with feeling, "I wish I could stay in bed all morning!"

Then something odd happened. She felt a strange tingling sensation in her forehead, but was unaware of the impact of her intent on the present. Responding to Jean's intent and words, the silver machine in the professor's lab pulsed with a bright white light. An iridescent wave rippled out, and the metal box put on a mind-blowing display of brilliant lights. Jean had no idea that she had shifted through time. She shuddered, and the room became blurry.

"What's that strange sensation in my forehead? I must be coming down with something," she remarked in worried tones. She decided it was safest to stay in bed a little longer. "I'll need all my energy if I'm meeting Paula for lunch."

Until then, Jean had almost forgotten her regular commitment for Saturday lunch. She reached for the white Teasmaid next to her bed and poured herself a cup of the ready-made brew: everything ordered and as it should be. From her viewing position, Jean failed to see the brilliant flash of light, and a slight change in the sky outside. The day had become just a little darker.

"Hold on!" she cried in a startled voice, 'I've seen this episode before - literally, moments ago." The soap appeared to have begun from the beginning, once again. Did she accidentally click the remote by mistake when she reached for her tea? Jean struggled to justify the anomaly in her 'soap viewing'. It was odd that the remote was nowhere nearby. Perhaps there was a fault with the player or something. Technology had never been Jean's strong point.

She fast-forwarded the programme. This was getting irritating! She was viewing the wrong episode, and back-tracked to the last part of Friday's drama, settling in for the last few minutes. How very strange. She looked up at the ceiling, again.

"What next?" There was no response, and Jean yawned. "Better get up, I suppose: things to do." She looked at her watch, racked with guilt about all the jobs to be done.

"That can't be so!" she said disbelievingly, running through her recent actions. "I set the alarm for 9am, but it's only 9.30. So how come I just watched two hours of TV. Bizarre! These gadgets are great until they go wrong."

She pondered for a moment, wondering if there might just be another reason for the odd leaps in her morning, but that was too fanciful. She dismissed it out of turn.

Saturdays were for fun. Normally, Jean met Paula for a cocktail down at Brampton's; and anything was possible from that point on. Paula, who was Jean's oldest friend, was slightly off-the-wall. A fellow drinker, and a party person with attitude, Jean loved the free-wheeling adventures that drinking with Paula provided although she abstained, and was remarkably diligent during the week. It was party time. And it was time for Jean to look at her wardrobe.

What to wear? The retro 80s 'crossover' dress in autumnal colours showed her curves off nicely, and stopped just above her knees, which were clad in mustard, gold-patterned tights. Her 'green' boots - in the vegetarian sense - were a take on the glorious cowboy boots of the 80s. They had filtered back into the present as if they had never been away. A full-length, fake tiger overcoat provided winter cover, and a broad-brimmed, black felt hat sat atop the electric shock of loose red curls.

"Faboush," she said, looking at herself in a self-supporting, long mirror angled for flattery. "Perfect for the reveal." By that, she meant the impression people would get when she took off her hat and coat. Jean knew that first impressions were essential; the way you presented yourself on the outside gave people a sense of who you were on the inside. Her sentiment might have been right, but something always went awry.

Put it this way, Jean was always trying to meet Mr Right, but she usually ended up with Mr Wrong, probably because she looked in all the wrong places. On weekdays, Jean had one persona, at weekends another; and this was her curse.

Jean sauntered onto the street for the short walk to Brampton's. She was not due to meet Paula until lunchtime and, thanks to the technological error in timing, she was scrubbed, perfumed, dolled up, and feeling a million dollars. As she walked down the road, she attracted glances; some startled, some admiring.

"Oi, Grandma. Where'd ya' get yer' outfit from? Jumble sale?"

They were pretty accurate. In her eyes, however, the fact that she was not wearing the latest copy from a Milan cat walk was a positive attribute. Jean was different; she always had been. and enjoyed the sense of significance given by the image she projected: it pressed the point home that she was, every inch, an individual.

By now, it was late morning, and Brampton's did not open until midday. She decided she might as well pop in and pick up a lottery ticket.

"Morning dear," she said at Arkwright's Occasional Store, slipping into her weekend persona. "Can you order me a vegetable and fruit box for next week, please; and I'll take The Guardian and a Hello."

The right balance of serious journalism and celebrity tittle-tattle was, of course, essential. "And if you could find a pen for my lottery slip, I'd be most grateful."

Jean – like her grandmother before her - liked to call on her inner resources when deciding what numbers to go for. On this occasion, though, she was blissfully unaware of the full impact of her focus, which was far more vivid than usual. In her mind, Jean simply imagined watching the monitor in Brampton's that evening.

The silver machine pulsed for a split second, and a bright, white, bow wave of light filtered out into the atmosphere.

Jean entered into a trance. Mute, and adrift from the present, she felt like a passenger in a stranger's car. Images and sounds bombarded her in a cacophonous blur. Then, suddenly, there was clarity. Seeing the numbers nine, twelve, fifteen, twenty-three, forty-five and forty-seven emblazoned on the lottery balls, she promptly wrote them on the lottery slip. Then she handed her lottery slip to the assistant, who tapped the numbers into the computer.

"You have to be in it to win it," the assistant declared. Jean took the Lotto slip and pushed it into her pocket, paid, turned, and marched out. She was feeling peculiar, with that tingling sensation in her forehead again. All the same, she felt very good about herself today.

Somewhat contemplative, Jean reflected on her life as she walked, and Brampton's was upon her in no time at all. They were just opening the big wooden doors as the clock struck midday. The place looked as if it once had a significant makeover, and a loving owner had ploughed funds into it, but it was now tired from the constant revelry taking its toll within.

Brampton's had two endearing factors. Firstly, it was cheap. Secondly, Jean and Paula always, without fail, had an experience to talk about after the evening had been played out. It was a 'people's pub' and they loved people.

"The usual please, Nathan," she said, and winked at the barman. A jug of Long Island Iced Tea turned up promptly. "I must pace myself," Jean told herself.

But her subconscious cut in. "Don't be sensible, darling, let your hair down - it's the weekend. You haven't retired!" 'Fun' won out every time, and Jean took a sip of her magic beverage while she focused on the TV, which was fixed to the wall.

From the corner of her eye, Jean caught sight of a dishy individual on the newsreel. She was proud of her ability to sieve out handsome young men from the rest of the pack; a natural instinct she had honed over the years.

Like Professor Murray, Dr Stuart T. Richanti was another mystery in Jean's life. In his late thirties, and owner of one of the largest private companies based in the US, he had grown up on the cusp of the USSR, and might have been Albanian in origin. His chiselled good looks and extraordinary physique made him both a man's man and a ladies man.

When he arrived in the West, Richanti took an Italian name to appeal to the public. There appeared to be no family records to identify him; this particular émigré was just another enigma in a long line of them from the East.

During the break-up of the Soviet Union, Richanti picked up a number of state contracts in Azerbaijan, and now owned an oil empire. After feeding the West with cheap fuel for a while, he used the profits to invest in media, construction, security and heavy metals. Trading globally, the empire had been split into seven regional corporations. These were subsidiaries of the enormous Demran Corporation, an offshore entity with bank vaults in Switzerland. People were often mesmerised by Richanti's personality, position, and power. Either that or they had an urge to take him down a peg.

As Jean watched, a naive reporter thrust a microphone into Richanti's face, and asked, "Dr Richanti, can you comment on the accusations made against you?"

It was impossible to dodge the question, so Richanti composed himself. The cocky reporter would be out of work for life before the bulletin hit the secondary stations. Jean however, was probing her brain over where she had seen this deeply handsome man before. She knew she had, but where?

"He's a public figure, I suppose, but it's a long time since I first saw him," she mused. She had a wonderful instinct for people. Give her a picture, a bit of speech and behaviour; and Jean had the talent to tell you anyone's life story. In most cases, she 'read' people better than they understood themselves.

Jean put it down to her upbringing. Defensive tactics were part of the self-preservation and conflict-avoidance tactics she employed from the age of around thirteen. For years, she had to be on her toes: always ready to predict the next move. She was an adaptive child; and had built-in these strategies to survive. Yet, conversely, she had spent a lot of time in her head dreaming.

Prophecy, insight, call it what you wish, Jean had 'the talent'. Steadily, she observed Richanti as he spoke convincingly to camera.

"I care deeply about the Middle East; and I have invested heavily - at my own risk - to rebuild these important nations. If there was no other contractor for the government award, it was because nobody applied."

Calmly, he continued, "The fact is, we've managed to turn reconstruction into a profitable business. This testifies to the fantastic efforts from those staffing Demran's regional offices. Look at the services that are now in place: hospitals, motorways, airports and transit systems." It was plausible stuff.

Then abruptly, Richanti changed tack, and challenged his interrogator. "Would you prefer we hadn't completed these projects?" The reporter backed off, unable to compete with his argument or energy. Richanti went in for the kill. "Does the BBC have any doubt in their mind, now, that these contracts were awarded fairly?"

"That's him!" Jean shouted.

Nobody else but the barman was in the pub yet. The barman shouted back, "Yes of course Jean... he's the one. We've heard it all before." He smiled at her in the way that professional waiters so often do when they intend to humour a good customer.

Jean ignored him, transfixed by the images she was seeing.

The interviewer mumbled a few words, and faded out. Another camera followed Richanti as he moved to a sleek black, chauffeured car, caught moments later disappearing into Demran's offices.

Meanwhile, the report had dissolved to a chart showing the record profits of the Demran Corporation. It was one of the largest construction companies on the planet. They also showed a fly-by of a brand new city that the Demran Corporation had created somewhere between Baghdad and Basra, on the plains of the Tigris and Euphrates rivers. As Jean looked at the city, she had the strangest feeling that she had seen it all somewhere, before.

"How very odd," she noted, filing it away in her mind. She was, undoubtedly, having a strange day. Then a second comment tumbled out of her lips as she sat looking at the images of Richanti's city. "The Oasis!"

She had no idea where the name came from.

Richanti picked up his iPhone 5 and called the media desk at one of his news stations. Hearing the distinctive ringtone, the editor's heart missed a beat; then it started racing. When he saw the number come through, his fears were confirmed. It was Richanti.

He picked the phone up and the tycoon, without bothering to introduce himself, barked, "I've just done a piece for BBC News, and nailed the reporter.

"Buy the coverage," Richanti ordered. "Run it on every station: every hour, on the hour, for the next two days. Throw up a pie-chart of our charity contributions after the interview. It's important that we be seen positively in the Middle East. I want this story challenged, and then dropped.

"Oh, and put out a writ to stop them showing coverage of the city. It's off-bounds until later in the week. We've kept it quiet this long; and Baghdad will help us… possibly even threaten to throw the BBC reporters out of Iraq. Make sure the item's erased from the News Company database at the media centre! "

"Is that it, Sir?" It was too late for an answer: Richanti had rung off.

"He's a liar," Jean said flatly. Her instinct was strong; and she sensed that Richanti was not telling the truth. She could see right through his façade. She had a dark feeling about the man. His seemingly perfect persona was what made him so disturbing. On the face of it, he appeared trustworthy, even adorable, but beneath the surface he was poisonous, manipulative, and dangerous.

Another image sprang up in Jean's mind.

She saw a long, winding queue of people, with smiles on their faces. They thought they had survived, but from what? Jean sensed hope; and then they were gone, lost into the fire. An elevator shaft to hell itself, apparently. Incinerated!

If she had not been confused before, she certainly was now. Jean had always been disturbed by the influence that some individuals had on international events; and she often wondered who really ran the world.

"It's not the politicians, that's for sure!" Jean asserted to her small audience.

No, the real power brokers in the world were hidden; and she sensed invisible influences manoeuvring the Masters of Mayhem.

What else could account for the warped reality in which we lived, where common sense was absent from our life experience? She always sensed that she had a part to play in the grander scheme of things, but, on the other hand, she had always dismissed the thought as some inexorable dabbling of her own personal psychosis.

Jean realised that while she had been lost in thought, she had been sipping on her Long Island Iced Tea and almost finished off the jug - a moment marked by the arrival of Paula. It had always amazed her how time seemed to speed up when you were enjoying yourself. That's drink for you: hours squashed into seconds.

Other punters were filling in the space around her when Paula bounced into Brampton's. She was half-cut already from the half-dozen Buck's Fizzes since breakfast. She glided in towards Jean, who always wondered how she did that: turn heads with her energy, posture and panache. After sizing up the whole room, and pausing for a split second to check out a group of rugby types, Paula turned her gaze to Jean.

"Thank goodness you're here," Jean said gratefully. "I've had the strangest morning. There's something not quite right; and it's to do with that man! I don't trust him," Jean said, gesturing towards the TV screen.

Paula looked towards the TV, where the news had been followed by Football Focus and a commentary on England's 2012 highlights.

"Yes, I see what you mean," Paula replied, somewhat bemused. There was an image of John Terry on the screen. Paula, unsure of Jean's state at this point, felt compelled to placate her. She went right along with her, surmising that it was Terry who Jean was talking about.

"He's not the right man for the job, is he?"

"He's going to commit mass genocide of some sort," said Jean, not realising the news piece had ended.

"That's a little strong isn't it?" Paula laughed. She looked down at the empty jug. Perhaps the booze was to blame for Jean's attack on John Terry, although she was hardly one to criticise.

"Sure he's had his share of scandals, but genocide?" Paula had to stifle her giggles. People do get passionate about football, though. She thought it best not challenge Jean on this point at the moment.

Paula was an interesting character. She had amazing genes, a striking jaw line, and a concrete constitution. In her prime, she was the epicentre of the local social scene. Before Facebook, information percolated out into the ether through her. For years, she had been a social hub; *The Stage* for non-thespians.

Unfortunately, even good genes are no guard against the ravages of time. Paula's figure - once an enviable one - needed a few tucks: everything was heading south. A serious amount of substance abuse, late nights, and Special Brew had left her middle-aged. She had lost her confidence. Now, although she would never admit it, Paula found young people and politicians equally hard to comprehend.

"Hey Nathan. Another jug of Long Island Iced Tea, please."

Paula turned to Jean and smiled, adding, "You've already downed one, I can see. You *were* up bright and breezy this morning."

"It's been a very strange day," Jean replied, composing herself. Paula's presence had grounded her. She started again from scratch, smiling with genuine interest at her friend.

"How's life, dear, what have you been up to?"

"Drinks, guys, and The Guardian - you know, the same as usual," Paula replied.

Changing tack, she added, "How about you?"

"Term's almost out so things should get much easier from next week," Jean stated.

Paula had no real interest in what Jean did during the week. She assumed Jean had the same persona, day in and day out, rather than working highly respectable weekdays with an edge of debauchery at weekends. If Paula brought the worst out in Jean, she was consistent in herself. Her outrageous personality shone twenty-four, seven.

The two friends polished off their next jug. A three-course lunch followed. This included a bottle of Australian Cabernet Shiraz with a 13.5%

alcohol count; enough on its own to knock the average female flying. Deep in conversation about themselves over lunch, they eventually focused their mellow attention on the rest of the room, and the talent around them.

By now, it was late afternoon, and the bar was filling up nicely. Paula's 'relationship radar' kicked in, and she decided that the company of three rugby lads half her age deserved her attention. Usually, Jean pursued Paula, hoping to pick up the scraps. Paula's cast offs were often the nice ones!

Today, though, part of Jean's mind was elsewhere. She only made half-hearted efforts to follow the badinage; just enough to seem friendly. If the boys were a little disconcerted by their middle-aged gatecrashers, they calmed down when they decided the two women were simply hell-bent on having fun; as they were.

Paula retold the story of her brief sojourn into stardom as a glamour model, almost convincing the guys that she was a child star; and probably a pin-up for their dads. Of course, the debauchery didn't stop there: this particular bar was famous for its liberal approach to a good night out.

Quite how it happened is hard to tell, but Paula and Jean - who always followed in the footsteps of the femme fatale - had, along with the three guys, mounted the bar. They were raunchily strutting their stuff when, suddenly, Jean had that strange feeling of déjà vu again.

She looked up at the monitor and forgot all about the dancing. It was eight o'clock and the lottery results were being drawn.

"Nine," Jean muttered under her breath, and hopped down to the floor for a better look at the screen. Unable to hear over the din, Jean lip-read the words, "And the first number for tonight's rollover Lottery draw is the number nine."

Jean went white. Even the self-obsessed Paula saw something was not quite right.

Jean said, "Forty-five." By this time, she was rigid with excitement. Paula clambered off the bar, too. She couldn't understand why Jean was glued to the screen: she never won, nobody ever won the lottery; everyone knew that. "Fifteen," Jean said loudly. Now Paula *was* worried. "I've won. I've won the Lottery, Paula!"

"Forty-seven," she continued sotto voce, and reached for her purse, pulling out the winning ticket. "Twelve." Jean handed the Lotto slip to Paula and they began chanting together, "Twenty three."

Both women were still fixated on the screen when the boys were pulled off the bar and manhandled out of the premises by the bouncers, and the music was switched off in an attempt to contain the riotous revellers. As the TV audio kicked in, Paula looked at the ticket, then again at the monitor, and compared the numbers.

"Nine, twelve, fifteen, twenty-three, forty-five and forty-seven are this evening's Lotto wins," repeated the presenter.

"You've won my dear. You've won, you've won. You're a millionaire!"

Jean and Paula didn't notice the doormen coming up behind them.

"You're barred," retorted a stocky. but handsome bouncer.

Jean looked back at the TV as the bouncers attempted to escort her and Paula from the premises. She fell, slipped, and saw Richanti flash up again on the TV as they re-ran the clips from earlier in the day. This time, she noticed a difference. The clip was now edited. It showed Richanti putting down the reporter, and then some stats on his charitable donations.

The news ran into a piece on the Processional Equinox in less than a week's time. Thousands were flocking to Stonehenge for the Winter Solstice.

"A sham", she shouted, "it's all a sham. Richanti's a sham!" She thought about the strange dreams she had been having, and started humming to herself, "I'm going on a jet plane, off to San Francisco with a flower in my hair." She was definitely a little the worse for wear. It was all too much. Jean passed out as she hit the deck, although her mind was not asleep. There was a meditative smile on her face.

She was, once again, in a timeless state, but this time it was not one of clairvoyance, but detective work. Piece by piece, as her unconscious body lay on the floor in Brampton's, the day played over and over again in her mind. She relived the entire morning, including the lottery win that she had engineered, herself, and her instinct about Richanti. She was seeking an explanation.

Suddenly it hit her. Of course, that was it - her meddlesome visit to the 'holy of holies' the day before at the Murray institute: that machine.

"I wonder..." She mused some more. "I wonder... Murray, Richanti, Precession, Murray, Richanti, Precession." She hummed her new 'favourite tune' once more, and focused her attention on the lyrics: "I'm going on a jet plane, off to San Francisco with a flower in my hair."

The silver machine pulsed once more with a bright white light - brighter even than before, if that were possible.

Observing the event at Brampton's, the machine's inventor smiled: his secret creation was a success. Although it meant that he was not so much an inventor as an operator. You can't invent what already existed.

His parrot chuckled: "Jean for Queen."

Chapter Five

Saturday, 15th September, 1990
British Airways flight 285, San Francisco International Airport,
California, USA

Failure is part of success

Touch down. As the hostess's ran around tidying up the plane, the captain thanked them for flying with British Airways. Jean looked through her fuzzy window as the hulk of her Jumbo landed at San Francisco International. An alien skyline lay ahead, while a string of hotels, car rentals, and parking lots spread out below her.

The eleven hour flight seemed a short one, given the soporific effects of Jean's first class flow of champagne. And that wasn't all. After taking a voluntary downgrade in exchange for some friendly faces, she shared a volatile mixture of G&Ts, then Martinis, with her flighty friend, Ada, while they swapped diet advice and life experience.

Although she had no idea how it happened, Jean had somehow translocated herself into a 747 Jumbo jet en-route to San Francisco; and an old one, too, by the look of things. Maybe she had fainted. Yes, that was it, she fainted after the lottery win; and now she was hallucinating. She began to recall the events and strange time shifts of the day: first, the extra long morning, and then the strange vision in her local shop, when she tried to visualise the winning lottery numbers.

She looked around, speechless, her mind busy processing the new environment. She wanted to say it was 'yesterday' but was not quite sure when yesterday was. In fact, it looked more like 'tomorrow' to her. Perhaps it was daylight, but not in the future; a tomorrow in the past, if that made any sense.

As Jean looked down at the smooth skin on her hands, her eyebrows rose in surprise. She was young again; in her early twenties. Then she remembered getting off the bar to look at the TV screen properly, the bouncers trying to get her and Paula out of Brampton's, and her thoughts about Murray, Precession, and Richanti.

"Of course!" she thought. "I have to warn Murray about that man. About Richanti!"

San Francisco was where Murray had come from; he told her once. Apparently, he started his career at Berkeley University. That explained all the PhD papers stored back at Birmingham Uni.

Entering into a trance-like state, Jean separated her mind from her body. Pretty soon, she saw flashes of Murray in danger; and it wasn't just him. There were the screams of lost millions in her head: spirits of the dead pushing her to save them from an elevator to hell. What was all *that* about?

Her instinct had brought her here, wherever *here* was. She decided to co-opt the help of British Airways to confirm her suspicions because it was disconcerting to not know exactly *when* and *where* she was, to say the least of it. She called over the airhostess.

"Excuse me," she said politely, "what date is it today?"

"15th September."

"No sorry, I meant what year?"

The air hostess looked puzzled, "1990, of course; all year. She looked closely at Jean who felt more than vulnerable. "Are you feeling alright, madam?"

Jean stared blankly, trying to process the information. Then she nodded thanks to the hostess, who was looking worried. When she slowly pulled out a sick bag from the back of the seat in front, the attendant smiled sympathetically, and backed out of range.

"Come on," Jean told herself with a frown, 'pull yourself together." There was only one possible explanation: time travel. She had, somehow, shifted back decades into a different time and space. How on earth she could have been zapped from her local bar to a jumbo jet. like slipping in and out of a dream, was something that made her feel decidedly queasy. She fumbled with the sick bag. And what about her lottery win? Were the numbers picked by chance, chosen from memory, or picked by actually seeing them in the future?

Confused, but ever the adventurer, Jean fixated on her crutch of choice. Why not make the best of the opportunity at hand? True, the flight attendant did look at her oddly when she got on the plane, but that was not surprising: she was gawping into space, and gazing around her as though she had never been aboard an aircraft before. Well, true enough.

Flying had not been part of Jean's freefall through life. But British Airways' stalwart service accounts for all eventualities so, when First Class stewardess, Nancy, briskly approached her somewhat odd passenger, she dutifully asked, "Can I get you anything madam? A drink, perhaps?"

"A glass of Champagne, please?" Jean gulped. Then, gathering confidence, she added with a winning smile, "In fact, could you make that a bottle...?"

As the hostess opened a baby bottle of Moët with a linen napkin, Jean tried to process the weird feeling that she was meant to be meeting up with Murray in 1990. But surely that was a bit OTT, even for her on a day off. All the same, she had a sense of needing to intercept him at Berkeley University. Quite where it had come from, she had no idea. Perhaps she had seen his original PhD at Birmingham University. That made sense.

Another pressing thought disturbed her: Richanti. What was his part in all this? She shivered a little and shook her head. The champagne bubbles must have made her fizzy, but at least she didn't feel sick any longer.

Jean had initially been in First Class, but there was too much 'bling' and bad manners for her taste. A rather nasty couple carrying a painting worth more than she earned in a year sat hogged to the window seats, and exuded disapproving looks. Behind her were a smelly politician and an off-duty airhostess who didn't quite know whether she should join in the frivolity, or tow the company line.

After the first couple of champagne freebies, Nancy, the friendlier of the three hostesses (and an even prettier male attendant) had suggested Jean moved to Economy. "It will be much more fun and I'll make sure you're sorted for free Champagne." A few hours later, Jean discovered that complimentary champagne meant "six baby bottles, precisely."

"That's the limit," the frosty airhostess in Economy said crisply, but Jean managed to negotiate more, on the basis of "slumming it from First".

-

Back in Birmingham, where Prof Murray had been hosting a garden party for sponsors of the department, one of whom was named Richanti, his parrot managed to knock over a bottle of champagne and drink some of it. "Jean... (hic)... Jean... (hic)." He took the befuddled bird inside, laid it on a bed of straw in its cage, leaving it to sleep, and looked thoughtfully out the window. Something was happening; and he needed to be in the right place to meet destiny, his plan was working it seems, the future having an impact on the past and his reality in the present.

-

After a few hours Jean had to move back to First for landing. She and Ada said their goodbyes, and swapped numbers, although quite how Jean was going to call her, she had no idea: Jean would be several decades in the future when *she* eventually got back home. She got up to compose herself after the long flight, and made her way back to her original seat.

Dropping into the First Class toilet on her way back to the upper deck, Jean was startled when she looked in the mirror. This led to several revelations about herself. Now a young woman, she was stunned at how beautiful she was with pale, flawless skin - all the wrinkles ironed out from her face - and beautiful auburn hair down to her waist.

She began to cry. Why had she devalued herself when she was young? It was those around her who made out she was ugly when, really, she was pretty. It was their jealousy that brought her down. They needed to control her. There were also tears of happiness, though. Now, she understood that all the counselling had only scratched the surface of the beliefs that limited her. The truth was there before her: beauty, reincarnated.

For the first time, Jean was living life the way she was always meant to live, and everything seemed totally congruent. She was comfortable in her skin, had unbounded energy; and every possibility lay ahead of her. It was only herself and the beliefs she had held about herself that had been holding her back; it had been like running through life with a ball and chain. The difference, now she had dropped the shackles, was truly exponential.

"Mind-boggling," Jean muttered, thinking over the last couple of hours... seven, eight hours... this was the adventure of her life. Now that she was back in First for landing, she stretched her legs out and sighed.

"Excuse me," she said pleasantly as the air hostess tried to sneak past, "more champagne, please." The addictive side of Jean had come to the fore with all the complimentary booze; her mind was in overdrive. The fizz and time travel had gone to her head.

The hostess said with a sly grin, "Sorry darling, that busy drag queen has locked the box, he insists complimentary means six."

"No matter," Jean replied, still a little tipsy from everything she had already drunk in Bucket Class, "How about some water... and a piece of barley sugar?"

Life had to be real otherwise it wasn't worth living. If Economy appealed to her working class roots and sensibilities, First was fine with her as well. But better than all of that, she was going to enjoy being young again.

Chapter Six

Wednesday, 18th December, 2012
A little later, Manhattan Island, New York, New York, USA

Trust your instincts; they come from a place of absolute truth.

The Watcher stirred. A feeling had surfaced that he had not felt in a long time.

A handsome man, he was a master of manipulation. He pulled social strings, moved markets, and nurtured news stories that enhanced his prestige, or gave him an advantage. To most people, he appeared to be trustworthy, honest and likeable. This was how he liked to present himself. Of course; it was just one mask of many.

He reflected on what people wanted to see in him, and how it made him invisible. He was a caretaker of secrets passed down from the beginning of living memory; unchanging from generation to generation. He had always been this way: an invisible puppeteer in a population of puppets.

Now, he realised his master plan was at risk, although he didn't yet know why. This alarmed him considerably. He acted quickly on his instincts, and made a call.

"Cover all the airports. I'm looking for an auburn-haired young woman in her early twenties - female - she's a foreigner, and arrives today at San Francisco. Tag them all! I want a report on my desk by the end of the day."

Chapter Seven

Saturday, 15th September, 1990
Customs Hall, San Francisco International Airport, California, USA

Learn to enjoy the journey; it is all about now.

Irritated by the queues in front of her, Jean wished she had chosen another mode of transport to the US. "Quite why did I arrive on a 747 with all the hassle and stress of American Customs," she grumbled quietly to the beagle dogs sniffing around her suitcase. But she didn't wish too loudly in case she found herself on a 19th century clipper instead.

Jean had not yet had much chance to practice her new 'time talents'. She was struggling to comprehend that, merely by thinking about being in the Nineties, she was able to temporally transport herself; then and there. Or was that 'here and there'?

Her penchant for positive thinking had come to the fore, though. Jean considered the notion - picked-up somewhere during her eclectic education - that 'sometimes the *journey itself* was more fun.

"More fun than the instant gratification of time travel...?" she mused aloud. "Ah yes," she sighed "The journey; not the destination."

She was all 'attitude' in Arrivals: a perky derby hat atop her wildly flowing auburn hair, tweed jacket over a peasant blouse and wide pants with soft leather ballet shoes.

The cute, moustachioed Customers Officer said, "Your passport, Miss." That pulled her up slightly. She smiled uncertainly at him, and wondered how it got there. No offence was taken, though. She definitely needed a passport, and was glad he had it. She was impressed at the level of organisation on this trip, but exactly who was taking care of the details?

For a woman on a mission, the world had provided plentifully for Jean. She found a purse when she pushed her hand into her handbag. Not only were there quite a few dollars inside, there was a wad of traveller's cheques, and a ticket on BART, the Bay Area Rapid Transit, which would take her across the Bay to Oakland.

Walking out from the terminal building into an autumnal haze, Jean was getting the feel of her 'new skin'. She needed to practise her role. It was important to *behave* like a young woman going to Berkeley University, California. She not only needed to *look* like a 'fresher', she also had to remember that the year was 1990, not 2012.

It was challenging enough to unnerve a fully-fledged graduate, she noted in passing, let alone someone as untraveled as she was. Yellow Cabs flashed by, airport car rental buses touted for business, and empty limos stretched in front of her - their drivers eagerly swarming around her, and offering to take her to the Moon. Ignoring them all, Jean made her way to the BART terminal, and got straight onto a train for Berkeley.

"Back in the Nineties, again," she grinned to herself. "Such fun!"

"Dum-di-dum, dum-di-dum"– the noise of the track below the train – rattled merrily through her brain. Jean stared into the black, hostile eyes of an African American beauty. Getting no response, she gazed at a zoned-out Irish-American woman. America, ever the contrast! Always inquisitive, Jean struck up conversation with the second woman.

"Hi, my name's Jean. Where's the action in Berkeley? Any ideas? I'm starting college there today."

"Hey sister, you wanna get outta that neighbourhood to get yourself some fun. The Haight's where it's happenin'. Berkeley's full of preppy, classy bitches an' yo' don't look like no classy bitch."

Was that an insult or a compliment, Jean wondered briefly. Zoned-out Marge was on pot or some other recreational supplement, and had eyes like saucers. She was drifting in and out of reality so nothing she said made much sense. There were lots of disconnected and disparate thoughts resting on a spiky bed of paranoia.

Speaking of paranoia, suddenly Jean had a sense of someone watching her. It was her turn to clam up. Inwardly, she contemplated her look and image, noting that she *had* to get in and out of Berkeley at the earliest opportunity. Subways were strange places. Everyone forced in together, with just a few people conversing, but all of them exposed to each other's lives and energies.

The probing sensation came again - of piercing eyes somewhere on the crowded train. It was probably just the negative energy in the subway, she thought, and focused instead on her journey; imagining the adventures that were soon to come.

Emerging from the subway, Jean pulled out an address she had found in her handbag. It was in a letter which granted her admission to Berkeley. First, though, she needed to check in at 171 Berkeley Studios; this was a furnished flat just opposite a set of very grand, intimidating gates. After dropping off her bag, Jean walked up to the huge Californian campus that sprawled before her gaze.

"Arrival time," she gulped nervously. "This is my chance. Win, or lose everything!"

The first day of a fresher's week could be just as daunting as the first day at primary school. Jean was distracted from her purpose by some amazingly good-looking guys; and there were lots of equally attractive, but intimidating, girls. Full of themselves, they were parading around with egos the size of elephants. Most of them sported bottomless wallets. They had come for freedom from their former, well-behaved lives, and were primed to try the unknown; to seek adventure amongst their peers.

Jean had to think on her feet. Here, she was neither the brightest nor the best-looking female on the planet, so she formulated a familiar strategy.

"Get tipsy and go for the cutest." She had always used alcohol that way; to give her confidence.

Across the crowded room, as if by magic, a man with big ears appeared. This slight imperfection was balanced out by dark auburn hair, like hers. Jean felt an instant connection with this tall, handsome man and observed that he had wonderfully deep brown eyes.

"Pools of passion," she murmured, "windows into his innermost self." Already captivated, Jean allowed a pent-up breath to whistle out of her body. That must be him.

It transpired that his name *was* Ethan Murray and, after a few enquiries, Jean had engineered a conversation with him. She knew the meeting was significant; and if she had any doubts, the now familiar tingling sensation down her spine gave her a nudge in the right direction. Always led by her instincts, Jean moved in.

"Hi. My name's Jean. Gosh, I just love your accent. Are you from Australia?"

"Gee, no," he replied, and smiled encouragingly at her. His accent may not have made him sound like the brightest of students, but nonetheless, he enchanted Jean. Fate had a way of attracting you to the people important in your journey through life.

Ethan was from the 'deep south' Savannah, and had a broad accent. Jean swiftly discovered he also had a surprisingly broad perspective on life.

"What about you?" he asked.

"I'm from Great Britain," Jean replied. "From the Midlands, actually. It's my first year in the USA. In fact," she confided, "it's my first time away from home." Well, that was more-or-less true.

"We have that in common," said Murray.

"So, what are you studying?" Jean probed.

"Physics. I got a scholarship. My father was an inventor, but not a very good one, so we never had any money; however, he did give me an inquisitive brain. I began to experiment from the age of three." Jean choked a little and Murray shrugged, grinned. "While the other boys were out playing football, I read about relativity, and gorged on encyclopaedias."

"Good for you, Ethan...!" Jean did her best to look both interested and intelligent. 'Relativity...' she pondered. What's that, then? Perhaps she would find out tomorrow. There was a lecture on scientific cosmology in the morning. Thankfully, she was a natural at maths. She had discovered this by doing an IQ test during her counselling period and, subsequently, taught herself maths and accounting.

Jean didn't need to ask Murray any more questions because he was off on an Olympic run. He talked and talked and talked, having found that rare thing - a female who actually wanted to listen to him.

"Space, time, and the meaning of our true nature fascinate me," he enthused. "There's so much more to us than our physical bodies. Our physical nature's just an illusion: a field of energy, a vehicle for one moment in time."

Whoosh! Murray's scholarly comments went straight over Jean's head, but alarm bells rang in her mind. Space-time, she thought. Does this have a bearing on my time talents?

Breaking the spell, Ethan suggested they head for the student reception in the main Berkeley Hall. It was all Californian Cava and bonhomie between professors and tutors, who vied with each other to woo their prey for the year.

As she reflected on the reason for her trip, Jean was briefly alerted to her moral mission. She recalled someone called Richanti; someone who was a danger to the world. Unfortunately, her focus on the wider purpose of her visit to Berkeley soon faded. When you're young, your focus tends to be more in your pants than your maths. She didn't worry as she slipped selfishly into the moment. One glass followed another, and Jean was totally absorbed by Murray. And her co-dependent nature successfully drew him in.

"Hey, why don't we get out of here", Jean suggested as the competition to inveigle students into this group or other grew more fierce. "I heard that the Haight was the place to be. "In truth, the college environment was a little uncomfortable for Jean. She was eager to find herself in ground that was more familiar; and to connect on a different level. Hormones!

"Sounds good to me," Murray said. Had she been looking, Jean might have noticed a certain glint in his eyes; he was smitten by his hormones, too.

The promise of another booze-crazed evening meant that Jean, for the second time that day, had missed the main feature in favour of fun. For all his country bumpkin references, Murray seemed to know his way around the campus, and before long a group of them were ready to venture downtown; beyond the 'relative' safety of the Oakland suburbs.

The two other girls, Caroline and Julie, were less predictable than most of the females Jean had noticed on campus; and Jean took to them straight away. They reminded her of Paula. Not quite a match but pleasant enough company were Murray's two geeky friends from his Physics group. Naturally, they wanted to tag along too. They were a little unworldly, but Jean guessed they could be led astray.

Their small group got off at Market terminus to catch the downtown tram. To their surprise, a Mardi Gras was in full swing. They glimpsed The Parade mincing its way up Market Street. Leather-clad guys with hairy, muscled torsos, and big line dancing bears, surged forward alongside fierce, drag queens with funky street cred and bulging handbags. Jean danced her way in, and the others followed.

The girls mirrored the hip gyrations of a couple of go-go boys, who wore little more than a smile. The tagalongs felt pushed-out but stiffly got into the groove. They walked alongside floats that made their stop-start way up Market Street, marvelling at the sights. A set of muscle boys in Speedo swimwear held a banner emblazoned with 'Dive Bars'. South of Market

(SOMA) Bay area mommas pushed prams alongside their lesbian and gay offspring with pride.

The staff from The Creole cafe melted around a sweet-looking drag queen who was rising majestically out of a cup cake every thirty seconds, to the crowd's delight. A set of line-dancing queers dressed in backless, cowhide chaps marched ahead of them. Jean thought the whole scene was an absolute joy to behold – it was a statement of freedom and personal expression – and she knew it could only happen in a place as socially liberated as San Francisco.

Murray and his friends were looking uncomfortable. They were just getting used to the idea of sex outside marriage, let alone sex with the same sex; and as for boys dressed as girls, that was pushing it.

In an attempt to normalise the situation, and make her straight mates more comfortable, Caroline suggested they all take a trip to The Haight and find their inner selves – 'trip' being the operative word. Jean had always been opposed to drugs. Quite why, when she mixed alcoholic beverages in a highly eclectic manner, was beyond her; and she was aware of the irony.

They followed the parade for a while longer before a party of rather grizzly-looking bears started to prey on the preppies: not an ursine attack, it came from an overzealous group of hirsute leather guys, so they peeled off quickly to make their escape.

The six intrepid social explorers ventured out further away from Castro, and its colourful men and women, and found themselves walking up towards the corner of Haight and Ashbury. Here, they hit a bar to extend their evening of adventure. The bar was typical of the area: wood panelled walls with a pool table at one end and a string of bar stools stretching out along a sea of optics at the other. Draught beer decorated with every brand you could imagine adorned the venue: an iconic American advert.

Murray set the tone, inspired by his new-found buddy. Before anything was said, there were six Bourbon shots and beer chasers lined up on the bar before them. One of the geeks placed a twenty dollar note to cover the tab; and before long, the six new friends were in full flow.

"Now we'll show you how we drink shots in the Deep South" one of Murray's now braver friends piped up, a little relieved to be in familiar surrounding rather than the alien parade a few moments before. All six shot glasses were emptied in unison and refilled at the bar. Jean led the pack; her purse seemed to be packed full of dollar bills, which she found quite a novelty.

Murray engaged Jean in conversation, trying to draw her attention away from the others.

"So tell me about England, Jean. I've heard so much about it! I'd like to visit some day."

Jean felt disconcerted trying to explain England as it was in the Nineties. It had not been the best of times for her. Worse, the feeling that someone was watching her had returned. It was more intense than before, and out of keeping with her environment.

"Hey, can we go outside, Ethan? I feel a bit strange," Jean said, making an excuse. "Maybe it's the Bourbon." Disturbed by the energy in the bar, they slipped out. Murray suggested they sample the sights of the city and, as they walked in the fresh air, Jean picked up on his earlier question.

"The city where I live has lots of industry: mainly metal and cars," Jean remarked. "It's not pretty, and nor is the new fashion for clearing slums and throwing up concrete blocks. But all the same, I love Birmingham. It's home; and it has a beauty of its own." She added, "It has an inner beauty."

It sounded glamorous to Murray, but then he would be captivated by whatever Jean said. She could have said she lived on a dilapidated dung pile, and he'd still have been enchanted. Not only was she remarkably attractive, she had a mind. He had never met a woman quite like her before.

They walked further up Ashbury, entering the edge of Golden Gate Park as twilight fell. They continued on slowly, towards the bridge, taking in the twinkling lights of distant Sausalito and the prison island in the Bay. Hand-in-hand, they contemplated their luck at finding each other. They were alike in the sense that they were both slight misfits, trying to conform. It was only natural that they began to plan their future time together.

"We could travel the world!" said Jean enthusiastically.

Abashed, but exhilarated, Murray replied "Okay! Where to, first?"

"Who cares?" Jean answered with a cheeky grin, completely given to the moment. "It's pretty good right here." She was at peace.

Time stood still as they lost themselves in fresh love, before finally flagging a cab to take them back to the reality of their temporary homes in Berkeley, CA. Murray was a gentleman, and dropped Jean at her door. There was a moment of awkwardness, and then he began to lean forward. Unsure of himself, but sure of her, he found his lips puckering. Terrified, in the way that only love can make you, he prayed she would reciprocate. Jean answered his prayer, and placed her lips on his.

Locked in a passionate embrace, their sense of time vanished once again. Jean finally pulled back, visibly shaken by the sensations of bonhomie washing over her.

"Can I see you again?" he asked.

"Of course." She smiled at him, "I'm attending a science lecture tomorrow morning - intro to cosmology. Let's hook up then." He looked at her in surprise and admiration as she headed for the doorway. "Physics," he grinned. Another connection!

"Until tomorrow," Jean said, letting herself in and closing the door behind her. She was in a rather gothic looking entrance hall. The stairway immediately ahead had a brass balustrade which led to her studio above. She saw the concierge in the hall, who seemed to have nodded off. Tip-toeing past him, up to the floor above, she opened the door to her studio.

She scooted through the bathroom, and fell into bed, soon to be lost in a deep sleep.

Chapter Eight

Early hours Tuesday, 18th September, 1990
171 Berkeley Studios, Berkeley, California, USA

Addiction is part of our biology.

The stranger let himself into Jean's room. A handsome man - military fit - there was a hint of sadness about him. He was a mercenary recruited to execute the will of others. He focused quickly on his mission and, moving towards Jean's bed, stood and looked down on her. He wondered how this young woman, just out of her teens, could be a threat to national security. The world grew stranger; and his assignments matched as each year passed. He thought about the new boss who had just turned up from nowhere, pulling rank on everyone.

How could he just appear like that? What explanation was there? He had caused chaos; everyone was running around on edge. There was an associated name mentioned in despatches: The Oasis; something to do with a future project, and a scientist.

The mercenary's plan was simply to squeeze a few drops of the drug into the water by the side of her bed. "What an interesting day she'd have shortly after she woke-up," he mused. On the way out, he dropped a packet into her handbag, and closed the door. Then he tipped the concierge a hundred dollar bill, and flashed his badge. Emblazoned in bold lettering was the stately acronym: CIA. The three digits on the bill, and the three letters on the badge, should be enough to keep the concierge quiet.

From afar, The Watcher sensed that the timeline had turned back in his favour: a job well done. He put out the call. "Is it done?"

"Yes, it's done but how do you know? We haven't even picked her up yet."

" You will. I want you to burn the file and take a vacation when it's finished; don't contact me again."

It had been easier than he expected. "She's not much of an adversary, after all," he said sardonically. "It's like getting candy from a baby, or picking fish from a barrel." He had never come across anyone so oblivious to his plans before.

Chapter Nine

Tuesday, 18th September, 1990
171 Berkeley Studios, Berkeley California, USA

Lose your focus on life and you'll drift like a bottle in the ocean.

When Jean awoke in her bed the next morning, she smelt something strange: the unmistakable, musky pheromones of a man's scent. It unnerved her slightly, filling her with an unwelcome sense of confusion.

"What's that smell?" she asked, frowning. Her curiosity didn't plague her for long, though. The memories of her romantic encounter with Murray the night before came flooding back, and she felt like an old soul in a young body - she had been given another chance at life; a chance to do it all again, this time the right way. In the heat of the moment, and the warmth of her memories, her desire to warn Murray about Richanti faded from sight. She was too busy kindling the feeling of new love. Jean was smitten.

She reached out for the glass beside her, and gulped the water down in one toss. It had an odd, chemical taste. She must remember not to drink from the tap; that's a very English habit. she chuckled. Here, the water was obviously full of chemicals.

Jean thought nothing more of the incident as she unpacked her things, showered and busily prettied herself, her confidence renewed by her new body. Suddenly, though, she felt a different kind of high and her mind worked overtime to piece together the last 48 hours. It must be the effects of the time travel, she thought, as she flipped in and out of reality.

At last, she was ready to take on the new day, and opened the door to the outside world. On the way out, she passed a very sheepish concierge who refused to look her in the face.

"What's wrong? "she asked.

The man gave no reply and retreated back into his office.

That, she found very odd. Then, suddenly, she felt a rush of warmth overcome her. However, this time, it was not the comforting kind that romance might bring. This was unwanted, and uninvited. Barely unable to step outside to the street, Jean's vision clouded over. Her hearing went wild. Alarms and cymbals crashed in her ears. The whole experience created cacophony in her brain. Highly sensitised to light, sound, colour, and shapes on the busy street, Jean told herself to get a grip. But what was happening?

"Never mind!" Her higher self took over for a moment. "Just focus on the mission: get to Murray."

Despite the heightening synaesthesia that was taking over her mind and body, Jean put everything she could into finding her erstwhile employer. Her urgency - verging on paranoia - was fuelled by the images of Richanti on TV the day before - the day she won the lottery - and the genocide he was to be responsible for. Meanwhile, it seemed that someone had spiked her drinks last night. The vision of many, many corpses burning made her shudder, and nearly retch as it tore into her mind; the result of a doomed Earth that had been ignored by its own superpowers.

Heart racing, Jean anxiously, if bravely, launched herself into the street; she rose above everything. But she was starving: a result of the alcohol from the previous day and the early morning acid. She bobbed into a bakery on the sidewalk to grab some breakfast. While she queued, she swirled like a washing machine on full spin; around and around.

Reaching the counter, Jean attempted to order coffee and a pastry, but nothing came out. She was totally mute.

"Can I help you miss?" The baker said politely, even though Jean's head had a slight rotating motion, her eyes were dilated, and she was unable to focus on anything.

"A coffee and a pastry," her mind dictated, but her mouth did nothing. She tried once more. During Jean's excruciatingly long attempt to explain what she wanted for breakfast, the face of the baker morphed into a shade of blueberry, not dissimilar to the muffins in front of her; and at that point she found her voice. A scream broke the silence.

By now, the baker had lost his patience and was tapping his foot wildly. Frustrated, Jean pointed at the pastry, and passed over her purse. Disdainfully, the shopkeeper took a few dollars and ushered her out while heads in the cafe turned, agog, in unison. Jean tripped her way inelegantly out of the shop, and back up the street.

Finding a bench, she scoffed her breakfast, feeling as though she might easily have died of hunger. Normality seemed to return for a while; long enough for her to make it through the university gates and into her first lecture. Staggering late into the lecture hall, the door banged behind her.

"Sorry I'm late!" Jean blurted out.

Everyone turned around. Her eyes squinted, and she wobbled on her heels, then she spied Murray two rows from the front with a geeky friend from the night before. She slowly tottered to the front - one step, two steps, every inch an effort in concentration - oblivious to the mass of people watching her. She stopped beside Murray.

The lecturer was speechless, but everyone else applauded except for young Murray, who was looking down at his lap in shame. Buoyed up by the attention, Jean stood, turned, and returned to the top, where she delighted her audience with a twirl at the top of the stairs, then repeated her entrance. Sirens were heard outside, as if the whole performance had been planned. It was a tad dramatic, even for the San Francisco Police Department (SFPD).

Two burly policemen ran into the lecture hall. The timing was perfect. Just as Jean was about to topple head over heels down the stairs, she was saved by the bigger of San Francisco's finest, who grabbed her handbag. She swung, turned and embraced the remaining officer, while the first went through her handbag. Triumphantly, he pulled out a packet of white powder.

A subdued "aaahh" interlarded with "dope" crept through the lecture theatre, passing downwards towards the podium, row by row. Murray looked up towards Jean in dismay.

"Looks like cocaine, plus some wraps of LSD," the first cop cried out triumphantly.

The other unwrapped Jean's arms from his neck, and barked, "Take her in!"

Scarcely aware of the handcuffs being applied to her wrists, Jean calmly asked, "Why are you all wearing pink today? And who are the two fairies trying to steal my handbag?"

Then she screamed, as the lecturer turned into a blueberry.

"I'll get you all back. I'll get the wizard to turn you *all* into blueberries, and then you'll be sorry."

Despite Jean's considerable distance from sobriety, she felt that her remarks were not quite appropriate, but she carried on regardless.

Murray ran out of the theatre while his friends looked on with smarmy looks on their faces, giggling uncontrollably. His heart was broken, and he felt completely betrayed by his drug-addicted darling.

Jean was aware that Murray was important, but she didn't help matters by screaming again, pointing at Murray, and shouting, "Murderer! That man's murdered all the fairies! That's why I'm being attacked. Murderer! Murderer!"

He looked back at Jean briefly, only to see her pass out, collapsing onto the floor with limp limbs, leaving Murray nothing but shattered dreams. She closed her eyes, and was gone.

The machine gave out a pulse of pink light, with a touch of blueberry.

Chapter Ten

Wednesday, 18th December, 2012
Manhattan Island, New York, New York, USA

If you want an extraordinary life, then raise your standards.

The Watcher, *the master manipulator,* smiled as he saw that his grand plan was back on track. He always succeeded. No-one ever got in his way. In his view, everyone had their price. The human race was so easy to lead astray: always bending the rules. They compromised themselves, and lowered their standards; this made them fair game. They were such pushovers.

"What next for her?" He thought for a moment. "I know, why not give her what she's always wanted? How kind and generous I am!" He intended to pay Jean off, and seduce her soul, just like all of those before her.

Chapter Eleven

A different reality altogether on Friday, 15th December, 2012
Stone Manor, Gloucestershire, UK

Material wealth is no substitute for happiness.

For a split second, as Jean engaged the silver machine, there was a burst of bright white light, but someone interfered with her intent. She fell short of her target.

Jean woke abruptly, catapulted into a different reality. She was in a grand porch; a perfect fit for carriage and coachmen. A camera lens greeted her; and people were milling around her. Greeting guests, with her back to Jean, was her daughter Ocean. She was now in her mid 20s and, bizarrely, wearing a wedding dress: French couture with conch shaped sleeves, with a train draped around and laid out in front of her. Two adorable children held the ends of it.

What had happened to the pink punk-rock hair, the pins and the tattoos? Strangely, Ocean now looked more like the Sue that Jean once expected her to be... but who was that with her? Her son in law! Jean felt astonished at the prospect. What was this place? She pinched herself.

"Ouch!" It was real alright. She looked at her skin. "Ohhh..." she sighed sadly. Jean was middle-aged again, and dressed in middle-aged beige. "Beige...?" She shuddered, "I wouldn't be seen dead in beige!" She had, it seemed, escaped the clutches of the San Francisco Police Department only to be chased by the fashion police.

"How timely, how convenient, and how different from the Bay," Jean rued, feeling grief-struck at the loss. Berkeley may only have been seconds ago in her memory, but it was decades distant in her past.

Ocean and her husband were barely an hour into their new life together. They were mingling with guests in the grand entrance hall of a 19th century, Victorian mansion. A dramatic staircase swept up from the Great Hall, where exotic palms were interspersed with occasional tables. An ornate, carefully positioned vase caught her eye. This was home.

"All of this belongs to me," whispered Jean in awed tones. Then it struck her. "Oh, it must be another lottery win!" It seemed she was lucky in life, no matter which life she was living. There was her family; and her former husband, Ted, apparently no longer a 'former' husband. To add to her surprise, there were two grandchildren.

Ted was handsome, respectable and respectful; not a role that Jean was accustomed to. He was dancing attendance on her and the children while Ocean posed for the cameras. One of the twin toddlers looked the image of Jean; and the other, a boy with sweet blue eyes and blonde hair, could have been Ted when he was younger.

Jean had been catapulted forward in time from the 90s to a different present; again, not the one she knew. It offered a better outcome for her and her family, well at least on sight. But something was radically different; something had changed. Where was the other Jean, the Jean with a bohemian, single parent lifestyle? And was it true that Ocean, her daughter, that crazy punk, lesbian, rock chick, was now a mum with her own family?

Jean noted wryly that all the interesting details of Ocean's personality had been erased. Moving on naturally from there, she wondered, "Could I really be a grandma? And be with Ted?" She recoiled at that. How could it possibly have worked out with him? In search of explanations, she tried to get Ocean's attention.

"Ocean, darling..."

"Mum! You know nobody calls me Ocean anymore; it's Susan. *Please* remember."

"Of course, darling. Silly of me. But what *did* happen to all the pins and pink punk? And you were a lesbian, if I recall. What straightened you out?"

"Just a phase, Mum, you know that; they wouldn't wear pins and punk at RADA. It had to go. 'It narrowed your options in life,' they said. "And now I really must get on with the photos!"

RADA? Ocean went to RADA? As in, the Royal Academy of Dramatic Art? The best acting school in the country! Jean was seriously flummoxed. She wanted to ask, 'What happened to the social work, then? And to being an individual? What about individuality?'

Sure, she realised actors were no less worthy than other people in pursuing their dreams, but this conventional little marriage scene was not Ocean's dream, although it may well require acting ability. All the same, it felt as though her daughter was bowing to pressure, to celebrity, and to society.

As she watched the posturing around her, Jean began to feel quite disturbed about the house, the grandchildren, Ocean (now a first-rate snob) and Fitz, not to mention Ted; all elements in the grand scheme of things. It also appeared that Ted had finally made it as a football player, and a celebrated one at that, which explained the serious amounts of cash; although no doubt Jean's networking skills and contacts had helped along the way.

A butler appeared. "Ladies and gentlemen, dinner is served. Please make your way to your tables." There was a baronial table laid out at the top of the room, with strategically placed guests. Additionally, there were five or six round, linen-covered tables, each containing a dozen people. Adorning these were faux antique goblets in gold plate, golden cutlery, and pearly white china plates on golden platters, not to mention over-the-top arrangements of flowers: lilies and orchids swimming in a sea of ivy. Jean hated ivy; it was considered bad luck, for a start; and as for the vulgar gold...

Jean murmured to herself, "Well, let's hope the guests are honest, or they'll be walking out of the door with cutlery in their handbags."

To her delight, a friendly face appeared: Paula. "Come on dear, take your place on the top table. And thanks for sitting me with the football team; bless you." Some things had not changed. Paula was still single; and still getting attention from the boys.

A smile flickered across Jean's face. She noticed Paula carefully altering the name tags to place the most celebrated and well-muscled closer to her. Evidently, she planned to work outwards from a central position, using the latest West Ham programme as her guide. Well, at least Paula had stayed true to her own personality. No matter how eccentric, drunken, creative, or self-centred she could be, she was comfortable in her own skin; and everyone flocked around her because of it.

Whispering in Paula's ear, Jean asked, "What's going on?"

"What do you mean, 'what's going on'? It's your daughter's wedding - the happiest day of her life. You have a family; and a life that most people can only dream of." Paula looked fondly at Jean. "Oh, and I'm your best friend; lucky me."

Jean thought on her feet. "I know what you mean, Paula, of course... But I just can't believe how things have changed since we were young. That's what I meant to say. Imagine going straight from the council estate to being a footballer's wife, in just a few easy steps. Just remind me, how did I get all this?" She waved her arm vaguely around, and pointed at the golden array on the table.

Paula gave a considered reply. "Well, yes. The opportunity was there; and you believed in it enough to seize it. Your lovely daughter started the ball rolling properly by persuading you to join that silly drama club; and success changed you in an instant. You created this wonderful life for yourself. Standing up to Ted like you did! Look at Ocean - sorry, Susan - and your focus on getting her into RADA. After that, you steered Ted towards his first break with a First Division Team. You created it all, Jean, you know you did!"

Paula looked oddly at Jean, who looked back at her with a thoughtful expression.

"Sometimes I don't think I know you at all," Paula grumbled. Then, shrugging her shoulders and smiling, she swanned off to attend the squad that quickly assembled around her for kick-off. From Jean's observation point, Paula, wasting no time, assumed the captaincy of the group, accompanied by the sound of corks popping as the free champagne flowed. And she would make sure her boys were kept 'topped up'.

Jean wondered whether she really did make all of this happen. She was capable of it, she knew that. But had the mere thought of the life she wanted made it so? She moved to the top table, and sat next to her husband. Ted looked at her indulgently; he was different, somehow. He obviously adored her and, in hindsight, it seemed he had a lot to thank her for. He *was* handsome, she thought, and started to feel fond of him, again. It was funny how you could forgive a decade of abuse in an instant, but then she always was a good judge of character; she could see that his intentions were now honourable.

"Ted...?" She grabbed his attention, still somewhat wary. Old habits die hard.

"Yes, Jeanie?"

"Why did I decide to stay with you?"

Ted, looked puzzled, but replied, "You threw me out, remember?"

"Ok, so why did I take you back?"

Ted continued, "You managed to get that job at the newspaper as a PA; and they persuaded you to stay with me. They paid for a counsellor when they found our marriage was on the rocks. Remember that lovely Pat from Greenwich? We have a lot to be thankful for. You even invited your boss to the wedding, Jeanie. Surely you remember? Maybe you've had too much champagne, love. Take it easy."

Fear hit Jean; for a moment, she was blind with panic. It made her contemplative for a moment, but she shut her mind to the alarming, intrusive sensations beating on the back of her eyeballs. It took a few, sizeable gulps of champagne to face down the ghosts of the past before she settled into her new-found role as head of a matriarchal dynasty.

Smiling affably at family and guests, she knew how lucky she was to have all she ever wanted. Jean almost purred. How easy it was to be seduced by fine clothes, celebrity friends, and a properly functional family. She might just as well stay here a while. It seemed a fun place to be. And imagine what damage she could do with credit cards that had no limits!

"It's easy to slip back," Jean told herself, "but it's much harder to forge ahead. I deserve it; I'm going to keep it!"

Before long, the wedding reception was in full flow. There was much joking and laughing; and she enjoyed catching up with people whom she once despised, or who had despised her, now seeing them from a different perspective. She gathered information about her new life from people she barely knew, but who treated her like their best friend.

Ted's remark had given her the first clue; she had been PA to the boss of a large media corporation, and worked her way up through the ranks into journalism. Her contacts were the perfect complement to Ted's ambitions as a football player. She dried him out, and confiscated the drugs, so that he started to focus on his next addiction: football and fitness. He rose through the ranks at a crazy pace, and was soon playing for West Ham.

They had a home here in Gloucestershire, and a warehouse apartment in East London. They also had a boat, a Bentley, and a rather repulsive brand of perfume called Jeanie, while she - astonishingly - was the face of the year for a leading French fashion house. Dowdy old Jean, a fashionista... Who would have believed it?

She seemed to have many friends, but to be honest, not many of them seemed that genuine. She preferred the 'old faithful' who were still around, and could cope with her success. It was hard to believe that she was the same person in such a different life.

After a few hours, Jean was comfortably chilled; and acting as though she had always been a rich, powerful matriarch. Only those closest to her knew the truth about the real Jean; the loving and giving Jean; the shy Jean of the past. She listened to everyone's speeches intensely to find out more about herself; and how others reacted to her.

What odd circumstances to find herself in. At the same time, she felt quite excited about her new future. And, after a while, she began to understand what was going on. That was important; she really could get a glimpse of who she was in this celebrity reality. It was like looking in a mirror. If only she had noticed, watched and listened before!

Ted was finishing his speech.

"... We are blessed by this wedding, by our beautiful daughter, Susan, our new son-in-law, Fitz, a wonderful family and friends, our amazing careers, and this beautiful home. It wasn't always like this: a chance meeting changed the course of our lives."

Ted launched into one of those predictable wedding speech monologues. "Some people float in and out of your life; others change its course..." Jean was learning more and more about herself.

"However, I'm not sure that Ted wrote that," she demurred. It sounded as though it had been edited and enhanced. Jean assumed they had speechwriters. It all sounded a little fake to her.

Ted continued, "We'd like to thank a very special friend who has honoured us with his friendship, and is responsible for the confluence of our two lives. He came when we were struggling to hold our heads above water, and helped us to bounce back; to swim against a foul tide."

"Please be upstanding, Stuart. Everyone, raise your glass to our friend, Stuart. Most of you know him as the CEO of Demran Corporation. I give you Dr Stuart Richanti."

How could she have missed that? Jean felt uneasy and looked over to the other side of the room. It was the man from the TV: Richanti. How could he be here? Had she somehow attracted him into her life? She did not understand what was going on. Yes, she had an idyllic life, but why was Richanti intimately connected with it all; and why was Ted praising him as changing the course of their lives? That wasn't real, it couldn't be right.

Jean was overwhelmed with sadness, again, thinking of Murray back in the 90s; her abrupt exit; and how she stopped focusing on the task she had travelled back in time to do. She was stricken at losing the promise of someone who truly understood her. Murray was her soul mate.

She looked over at Ted, at Ocean, and her husband, Fitz; and she deliberated long over her two delightful grandchildren. Everyone looked so happy, so content. There was a side to Ted, now, that reminded her of the early days when they first met. The old feelings washed back over her again. What would happen to them if she left? Or was this some kind of dream?

She needed an answer, and cautiously approached Richanti.

"Stuart..." She made the assumption they were the best of friends in 'this life', thus translocating into a tempting and false reality.

"Yes, Jeanie?"

"I can't believe you could make it; so good of you to come."

"I wouldn't miss it for the world." He spoke with a sense of profound satisfaction.

"We've come a long way, haven't we, since my PA job at the paper?"

"Yes, *you* have," he replied.

"So, what's next?"

"Funny you should say that. I have an opportunity up my sleeve for you, Jeanie. There's a political job that I've had to turn down, but I think you'd be interested in. Fancy being an MP? It's a safe seat in the East End. With Ted in West Ham, and your name already in the public eye from your compassionate work with orphans, I'd like you to run as an Independent. After that... we can get you into government with whichever party gets in. It'll be a hung parliament, this time round."

Leader of the Just Jean party, she thought incredulously. How did he know that? "Hung parliament?" she asked aloud.

Richanti looked at her oddly. She reflected that he wasn't the first person to look at her *oddly* today, but he continued his tack urbanely.

"Yes, I've been working on it for a while now, Jean. I thought I'd discussed it with you before. You don't *really* think politicians run the country do you? Far from it. It's the money men who do that, Jean; always has been, always will be. Politicians, let's say, are at the delivery end of the business; and we're always looking for new recruits."

Jean choked on her champagne, and the bubbles rocketed up her nose. She spluttered out... "Delivery end of the business? A sort of midwife?"

Richanti was uncomfortable. She had been so malleable up to now. Sensing a change in her attitude, he tested her. "Of course, Ted's up for renewal at West Ham this season. The governors were going to give him a captaincy, but, if you don't want to stay in the East End, then we could take the pressure off Ted to allow you to do something else."

Jean played along with his game. She was a master manipulator, too. She had to be to survive when she was younger; and it seemed she still had to survive in the shark pond.

She took a deep breath for the performance of her life, quite literally. "Yes of course Stuart, darling, I would love to. The East End fits with our portfolio perfectly: all those real estate opportunities to sell off council estates in order to develop offices, and top end apartments. I'll have it. In fact, I'll take two," she chortled. "Haw, haw, haw... you're so good to us!"

Making her exit, she thought to herself, "What an awful man. If this was her life, she didn't want it; and she didn't want it for her family, either." She thought of Ted, Ocean and Murray. She made a decision that she had to go. To be happy and have a family was all she wanted, but not if it compromised everybody's integrity. It was fake. There was no value in this charade whatsoever. It was someone else's life, not theirs.

"Be an individual: be true, be honest!" Jean resolved quietly. "I must go, but go where?"

She reflected on the mission in life that took precedence over family. Jean had a higher purpose, which trumped her own personal gain, or that of her family. It involved self-sacrifice. It rejected all of this fluff, this detritus. She didn't need it, and she couldn't understand why anybody else would think she needed it either. It was a luxury, obviously; but not essential to her wellbeing. She felt good to be free of the burden.

Returning to her seat besides Ted, she hugged him and said, "You know, Ted, I always loved you; and I always will. Just remember this moment, Ted, and put it ahead of all others; even if I appear to do you harm."

She was crying, and Ted was puzzled by it. Jean knew where she had to go, and what she had to do. She had a wrong to right. She closed her eyes, and welcomed the tingling sensation in her front lobe.

The silver machine pulsed with a brilliant light, and Jean was gone, leaving her alter ego to finalise the celebrations.

"Teddy darling what are you doing? We haven't got time for this?" Not used to affection, Jean pushed him away, oblivious to the double who had taken her place for one brief moment. "Let's get on with the party; go on with the show." She walked over to Richard, who was apparently more important than her husband was. What kind of woman had she become?

Chapter Twelve

Another chance at Sunday, 16th September, 1990
British Airways flight 285, San Francisco International Airport,
California, USA

The world we are used to seeing is a world of illusion limited only by our beliefs.

For a split second, the silver machine pulsed with a bright white light.
Touch down! She was getting used to time travel.

Jean looked left as the hulk of the jumbo landed at San Francisco Airport, California. There was the alien skyline with its strings of hotels, car rental firms, and parking lots spreading out beneath her. She thought of Murray, and looked forward to meeting him again. She was over the moon, in fact. The airhostess in First Class shouted, "Champagne!" over the noise of the engines.

Jean smiled, and declined firmly. "No thank you."

The queue through US customs went quickly, for the second time. There was time to formulate her strategy. Go with the flow: watch, wait, listen and learn. Be open to new ideas, but question yourself whenever something seems too comfortable. For good measure she added, "And remember, no drinks!"

Jean made her way to Berkeley, taking a taxi to avoid the prying eyes of the subway. Once there, she checked in at her studio, and headed for college ahead of time. She smiled. She knew she had done the right thing, even if she didn't quite know 'why'.

A shiver went down her spine. Her memories of the last visit were shadows in the darkness. "Why did I do that?" she asked herself. She felt there were two parts to her: one physical entity, and two different people: elements of both darkness and light inside her. Occasionally, her darker side reared its head, and tried to take control of her; the warning was the monkey brain chattering, with the dark side of her waiting to pounce when will power was low, and self-confidence diminished. The booze made it easier for demons to prey on her.

Led by instinct and insight, Jean knew that the half-life she had escaped from was wrong. She felt pity for those trapped in a reality like that one, which, on the face of it, seemed paradise until it was too late. The truth was very far from paradise: it was a prison. She laughed and repeated her thought with a chuckle.

"Everything I had ever wanted was a prison - how funny!"

Nonetheless, Jean sought explanations. "Why here? Why now?" She was still confused about her new talents, her gross distrust of Richanti, and her connection with Murray. The balls were bouncing randomly round her brain. Instinctively, she felt they would link together in a pattern if she could only make the right connections.

On a practical level, how could she explain to Murray that she had travelled from the future to see him for no reason other than an instinct that he could help her understand her character clash with an oligarch from the 21st century? In business and political stakes, Richanti was a recognisable type so why the acute sense of dread and disaster in her mind?

Suddenly, two of the disconnected balls in her brain stopped bouncing and collided hard with each other. "Drugged!" she exclaimed, and repeated. "I was drugged. But that means someone knows!" A sword of fear rose through Jean's throat when it dawned on her that she was not alone in her quest. Someone else had a stake in the outcome. "Someone is watching me!"

Chapter Thirteen

Wednesday, 18th December, 2012
Manhattan Island, New York, New York, USA

If you want an extraordinary life then raise your standards.

The watcher was frustrated. He sensed the timeline had shifted against him once more, but how?

"She was mine!" he protested. "She always revealed herself to me, ignorant of the fact of course!"

He thought he had dealt with her, this meddlesome one.

"Can't be bought, eh? I thought everyone could be bought. Maybe not." He strode across the room. "If things won't buy you, maybe we'll trade something else, something less tangible."

He made a phone call, and it was done. "Was it really that easy?" he wondered.

Chapter Fourteen

Tuesday, 18th September, 1990
Berkeley Campus, Berkeley California, USA

Confusion is the first step in learning.

Though ostensibly it was the same place it was before - there were as many students milling around, and professors bustling about –it was a very different experience for Jean, this time around. She was not intimidated, and pretentious new kids failed to rile her the way they had before.

Berkeley contained a mix of America's finest. There were plenty of excellent, ordinary individuals, the mass of students who had been coached and cajoled into courses that might - eventually – give them a profession. This kind of profession was, of course, based on a society that insisted you needed a piece of paper endorsed by academia to get anywhere in life.

Jean knew that was not always true. Many individuals made it on their own in business and their professional life, starting from the bottom up. All the same, she was seeing a fair representation of life in America in the late 90s. There were preppy girls and boys, replete with their button-down collars and pastel coloured clothes; there was a core of Middle American right-wingers; and there were some *very* straight folk, some of whom were tainted with a twist of religious fanaticism.

Also, against all odds, many bright, black kids had made it into Berkeley; and they felt comfortable amidst the new wave of international students. These were mainly European, although a significant proportion of them had come from Japan and, more recently, China.

It was hard to imagine that, over a quarter of a century ago, the Far East was in pieces. Now it was an economic miracle. Jean was impressed by the sheer magnanimity of the American dream!

Finally, there were kids whose parents had been too liberal in the 60s. A reaction to permissiveness had rubbed off on the next generation; and they had become significantly more sensible and sorted than their chilled-out parents.

And there he was. Murray was making his way across the room, just as before. Jean waited to see what she could glean from the melee of personalities jostling for position. As she watched, Jean observed that he was a shy type, anchored to his mates like a comfort blanket. He stood alone slightly awkwardly when he was not with his geeky friends.

With a highly prized scholarship, Murray had become one of America's A-grade students; and it showed, even if he did look a little sheepish about his surroundings. He had a brain the size of a tree, but had no facile airs or graces to speak of.

Right now, he was deep in discussion about science. She remembered him talking to her last time about 'reality' or was it 'relativity'? She couldn't remember, but the conversation made her brain hurt at the time.

Caroline and Julie began sidling over to Murray, and Jean swiftly made her own entrance before they engaged the boys.

Murray was in full flow with, "Hi my name..." when Jean interjected.

"Hello, I'm Jean. A little bird told me you're particularly interested in 'human reality'. It's a fascinating subject."

Jean had a funny way of falling on her feet. Murray found the question enchanting, while her forwardness coupled with familiarity was strangely comforting. In fact, there was a powerful sense of déjà vu between them. Although dating had never been Murray's forte, he sensed something in Jean that transcended the familiar kind of friendship he was used to having with women. And she held herself in a mature way; which he liked very much.

"Some people get stuck in a reality of their own making; we seem to be designed that way. I was once... errr..." Jean corrected the mistake she was about to make and moved on quickly to avoid a complicated explanation.

"I mean, my mother always thought she was destined to be the spouse of a famous football player - my father - which would take them into new social circles. In reality though, they both sabotaged their future by believing that they weren't capable of going further. It was their belief and their reality which limited them, nothing more."

Murray thought her wise and sophisticated.

Jean sipped, rather than gulped a glass of champagne that arrived on a platter; and made everything up as she went along, finding that she was actually quite good at manipulating *her* new 'reality'. Then she decided to engage Murray seriously about his work.

"Tell me Ethan, why are you here? What do you hope to get out of your time at Berkeley?"

He looked startled at such a probing question, one he hadn't entirely answered for himself yet.

"Well, I'm interested in Quantum Mechanics, so your question about the nature of reality is an interesting one. I think there's a lot in the world that isn't quite the way it seems to be at first sight." He was off, and she was ready for him.

"In the West, we spend most of our time involved only in what we can prove scientifically; and that's a very narrow spectrum of experience. We ignore phenomena for which we have no explanation. This includes experiential ways of approaching religion, psychic ability, and déjà vu moments, as well as having a sixth sense, instinct, and intuition. Ghosts could be considered in this light, too.

He checked Jean out to see if she had fallen asleep yet. She smiled encouragingly at him.

"You know, this may sound like madness, but I admire those patient scientists who never discard anything from their research. They remain committed to their study, regardless of what they want the outcome to be.

"And the others?" Jean asked. "The ones who are locked in little boxes?"

"Yep, a great shame. They dismiss all kinds of amazing possibilities out of hand. It's not just them, either. It's easy for all of us to end up in a prison of our own making.

Imagine what kind of world we'd live in if all these things were true; and we could explain them. It's not that a combined culture hasn't existed before now - the Mayans achieved a natural balance in their culture, which lasted three millenia. Their currency was cacao beans.

"Imagine what level of trust was required in a society surrounded by beans...!

"Cacao beans make perfect sense if you work on the basis that everyone can be trusted. Imagine what kind of society we'd have if we all trusted each other, and gave a little more. And you can drink it together as well, huh. They call it 'kukuh'. Gold might look kind of pretty, but it's not really very useful."

Murray checked Jean out again from under his long dark eyelashes.

"I'm intrigued; aren't you?"

"I like the idea of kukuh!" said Jean a little flirtatiously, partly to throw him off the trail. Her instincts were in conflict. She looked at Murray carefully. Where did her instincts come from? She didn't know. Perhaps a lonely childhood encouraged adaptation in order to survive. At any rate, she was acutely aware that her instincts were rapidly *sharpening*; and what about the time travel? If only Murray knew. Should she tell him? No, he'd never believe her, and she didn't want to risk being hounded out of college for a second time.

"Yes, the whole thing's incredible," she responded. "I'm majoring in social science, but I'm not there yet. So don't go too fast, or you'll lose me."

Murray ignored her advice... or he sensed that she could understand ideas she hadn't come across before. "Think of the world as you might consider a video game. You start at the beginning and have many potential outcomes in life. Everyone comes here with different kinds of energy and abilities; and lots of them have been taught to jostle into a position to win and dominate the game."

"Amongst other things, our sixth sense, instinct and intuition can be used to plot different outcomes; to discover *all* possible futures. The ghosts are crossovers, 'game bugs,' like errors in the game. The impossible is *always* possible... in the game, at any rate.

"Most of the time, though, we only see one possible outcome. We hone in on the outcome we're used to seeing; the one that encourages us to believe the world is the world we already know. We ignore other possibilities simply because of our limiting beliefs. Just occasionally, though, miraculous events sneak in. The miraculous is what interests me."

"I want to wedge open the door to the impossible, even the improbable, and make every day extraordinary for all of us. It's like the Ruby slippers of Oz. I believe we have the ability within us to have whatever we want. It is simply that nobody has ever told us 'how'."

"That was a serious rant," Jean told herself. And she understood what he had said: Murray was both poetic and persuasive.

"Thanks for enlightening me," Jean told Murray. "I really mean it." He beamed.

Meanwhile it all went much as before. Caroline and Julie dug their claws into the geeks, and someone suggested they head downtown to see what the bright lights of San Francisco had to offer. Jean and Murray paired off with the others, talking as though they were newly reunited best friends.

The sky was singing for Jean, which was an unprecedented feeling for her. She *thought* she had felt it before, but it was a fake interlude; this time it was real. Jean was in love.

They came out of the BART terminal on downtown Market Street, the same as before.

"So far, so good," Jean told herself. History was repeating itself. It was almost as though the timeline had a basic flow and plot; and certain patterns would always emerge.

Of course, she hadn't tried to change much yet, or interfere with the timeline, but she was destined to exit from the lecture theatre tomorrow morning. What would happen if she tried to upset the flow and change it completely? She was worried that she'd just be snapped back, like the tide in a river, and her journey would be wasted.

When Jean saw Dinah Cancer and Charity Case a little further ahead, she remembered her feeling of being watched in the bar; and - with a shudder - the drunken revelry that followed. Noticing the boys looked twitchy, she decided to dodge the two drag queens; her first small test of a change in destiny. This encouraged her to try something new. It was just for fun, of course; or was it for something more significant?

"Hey guys, this is a little intense for me," Jean said lightly. "You're used to prudish preacher men rather than nuns on roller skates, so why don't we head out to Fisherman's Wharf? I've heard there's plenty to do and see, there. We can have some fun. Let's take a tramcar; it should take us all the way!"

The guys nodded in relief as a rather large guy in a leather collar started hitting on the boys, pretending to ask for a light, but with intentions of supersizing his opportunity.

They 'about turned' and moved towards the tramcar stop. Jean ushered them onto the cable car, where they hung on for dear life as the conductor rang the bell, and the driver released the brake. The cable car made its descent slowly. Jean was feeling smug about beating the timeline when something very odd happened. The tramcar lurched forward and the boys, who were holding onto the side rails, were shaken off. The girls were right in the centre and it was two or three stops before they had a chance to get off. The tramcar fell away, it swallowed up centrifugal force and tarmac like a python would its prey.

Now she'd lost her charges; and they were in the middle of the city. Although they scrambled back up the hill, the boys had gone. Well, after all, who would wait if they had only just met?

Caroline and Julie were glum over losing their dates and began to kick their heels restlessly. Jean voiced a half-thought.

"I wonder...?" She acted swiftly, sticking out her hand and flagging down a yellow cab.

"Haight Ashbury," she said with conviction to the driver. Caroline and Julie might have wondered what was going on, but tumbled in sheep-like fashion into the back of the cab.

They took in the sights as they were driven down Haight Street. There in front of them were the staggering and the stoned, all concentrated into one place: hippies who never got away in the sixties, still stuck in their own psychedelic haven, and new wave punks, rockers and preppies experimenting to find out what they could get away with.

"Stop, this is it!" Jean exclaimed. She had a vague recollection of the bar. The three hopeful revellers tumbled out of the cab and into the street. Jean entered the bar.

"I thought so," Jean congratulated herself. "I'm getting the hang of this."

Lined up at the bar in full view were the geeks, who had been intercepted by Dinah Cancer and Charity Case. And of course Murray was with them. Jean was slightly alarmed; everything had corrected itself and was back the way it should be, but how was she going to avoid being drugged? Murray had his back turned to the girls. The groovy tunes in the bar kick-started Jean's dancing feet, and she dived for Murray, turned him round and pulled him to the dance floor. He was slightly confused, but didn't give the re-engagement a second thought.

The two started to party. A slow dance came on. Murray grabbed Jean and pulled her close. For a split second, Jean thought about the consequences of dating a guy almost three times younger than her, but only for a split second; then they were locked in a loving, sensual embrace, connected now physically as well as mentally.

Murray braked suddenly, wanting to unravel the events of the last hour.

"How did you find us?" Jean wasn't ready to say. Not yet.

Thinking on her feet she said, "Well, we saw you fall off the tram, and followed you here."

"Ahh," said Murray. "A case of 'follow that cab!' Funny, we thought you'd left us when you didn't get off the cable car at the next stop, and flagged a cab driver ourselves. He brought us here. I'm glad you found us."

His words comforted Jean. There's something quite wonderful about another human being caring; being there just for you. Jean shed a tear. She wasn't used to being loved; her life had been hard.

Jean was looking across Murray's shoulder when her warning bells sounded. Squinting a little, she made out a familiar image; and clocked him. Someone was watching from the shadows. She had been frustrated again by a timeline that insisted on repeating itself far too precisely: their 'accidental' exit from the cable car and the guys' choice of bar; and she was just under half a day from being removed by the police from the Class of Nineteen Ninety. She could bear her own humiliation, but she couldn't bear the idea of betraying Murray's trust, again.

"It's time to flee," she responded grimly to fate.

"Murray, I can't explain right now, but will you help? I'm going to powder my nose at the back. Watch me go, and then leave by the front. I'll meet you outside and explain everything, then. Don't say goodbye to the others; just slip out."

He knew by her tone that she was serious. Both fear and purpose showed in her eyes.

Jean slipped by the stranger. He tracked her with his eyes, sipping his drink as she went to the back of the bar, and shuffled out of sight. She found a fire exit and made her escape. Then she walked around the block to Murray, who was waiting for her, but puzzled and confused.

"There. Now follow me." Jean flagged a cab, and they stepped inside.

"So?" asked Murray.

"It's all very 007," Jean replied.

"Well, funny you should say that," he quipped.

"There was a guy in the bar who freaked me out; he's been following me."

Paranoia, Murray thought. Jean saw that he didn't believe her. Nothing else for it, she realised; she would have to show him.

"Look in the mirror, Murray; watch that green station wagon behind us." Murray watched for a few minutes. It was making all the moves: dropping back, not coming too close, and as they turned left, the station wagon turned left and tailed them again. There was a solitary man at the wheel.

Jean was telling the truth, Murray realised. "Okay, I'm convinced. But why?"

"Beats me," she said. "The only crime I've ever committed is against fashion. But I have a bad feeling about this. Why would they follow me, a student? I'm no threat to anyone."

Murray looked at her. He didn't entirely believe her story; something was missing. True, she was surely no threat to anyone but, all the same, he knew she was hiding something.

Jean was tense. She knew what was coming. It seemed that she was locked in time and space into just one outcome. She tried to calm herself with the idea 'don't fight it' and remembered her first visit. She came up with a plan.

"Take us to Golden Gate Park," she told the cab driver, remembering their last walk together. The stranger in the green station wagon backed off. It seemed that the driver sensed her capitulation, and the car disappeared mysteriously from sight.

There was something calming about Murray, and she resolved to enjoy every moment with him for it could be her last chance. They walked towards the bridge, and took in the twinkling lights of distant Sausalito and the prison island in the Bay. They walked hand-in-hand, and contemplated their luck in finding each other. They were both misfits trying to conform enough to get a promising relationship off the ground. They made plans, and shared their tales of each other's lives and hopes for themselves and humanity. After hours of walking on air, they returned to the parking lot and Jean became anxious again.

The green station wagon burst out of nowhere, heading straight towards them. She clocked it first, and then Murray did. He thrust his body in front of Jean, pushing her back, but she summoned all her strength she never knew she had, and pushed Murray to the ground. She had to save him! He was crucial to the future. Jean knew this was *her* time; her last chance. She understood the rules because she had tested them, and there was only one thing that she hadn't tried. "Sometimes the place you fear most is the place you have to go", she said to herself. For a second she felt sad then the adrenalin kicked back in.

The station wagon just missed them, hitting a van parked beside them. Jean spotted a Harley inches away. Its rider was standing by his bike, transfixed by the impact of the car and van, and the rending of metal on metal. She turned to Murray, and looked him deeply in the eyes. She put out her plea.

Jean was sad; she saw the end, but understood how change could be for good. She said just this to him: "2012 the planetary alignment, Precession. It's important! You'll save the world one day." The words came from nowhere.

Then she seized her opportunity, pushed the bike's rider to one side, leapt on the beautiful machine and hit the throttle. The Harley roared. She knew what needed to be done. It was time to go out with a bang. She headed for the bridge.

Puzzled, Murray watched her snake down to the highway. Then he saw blue lights and sirens come out of nowhere like rats out of hell. They headed towards her as she hit the 101 freeway. Jean turned the final curve towards the Golden Gate: a portal to the land of opportunity.

Once again, she had been denied happiness; and yet she was crying *and* laughing.

"This is it!" The wind whipped her shout into the air, back towards those following her progress.

She sped up. The Harley reached the middle of the Gate and hit the curb. Both the Harley and Jean somersaulted in slow motion over the centre of the suspension bridge. Jean had gone, swallowed up by the cold water in The Bay. Peace came to her world at last.

At first, Murray was in a state of disbelief. He sank into a deep silence as he sought a reason for the accident. Returning to Berkeley, he spent hour after hour running through the last day of Jean's life in his mind. She had thrown him a puzzle. He ran over the word in his mind: "Precession..." And who was the strange, suited man in the station wagon?

Jean didn't lie, but she had certainly been hiding something from him; but why? He felt surprisingly unperturbed by the loss of his soul mate: the evidence simply didn't fit the crime.

"I'll see you again, I know I will," he said, the image of her going into the harbour imprinted on his brain. "I know I will..."

Chapter Fifteen

Saturday, 15th December, 2012
Bramptons Bar, Bearwood, Birmingham, England

Your conscious mind will trick you. Be guided by your instincts.

The machine diffused a burst of white light as Jean translocated back to her original time line. The machine's inventor smiled. He was content with his achievement.

"I've been waiting a long time for this moment," he mused. "Many 'Ages', in fact."

Jean awoke with a sudden jolt. She was back in the bar, prostrate, with a smile still on her face. A couple of very angry looking bouncers, a collection of bar staff, and what looked to be a rugby team surrounded her, peering down as Jean looked up, trying to work out where she was.

Paula, who was looking unsteady on her feet, stared down at her. When she saw that Jean had stirred, relief followed anger; and then sarcasm broke the ice.

"You gave us all such a shock, my dear!" Paula said crossly. "We thought you'd passed over. I'd look dreary in black so it was nice of you to make it back."

'Make it back'? With difficulty, Jean held her tongue. If only they knew! Paula was often on the money with her observations, but this time she was too damned close for comfort. Meanwhile, she began to piece together her surroundings. I'm in a bar, of course, but in what dimension, time, and space? That was the confusing question; she had been tricked before.

A heart beat ago she was falling in love with young Murray in San Francisco's slightly risqué environment. Correction, that was two decades ago! Now she was back; and alone. It appeared to be 2012, and Birmingham's best were leaning over her. The floor was hard...

She recalled falling into 'The Bay' from the Golden Gate Bridge. She even saw the outline of the great rollers from the Pacific sticking out their tongues on the bridge supports. She saw the underbelly of the suspension bridge; and the Harley had fallen on top of her. She had managed to disconnect herself from 1990 just before hypothermia set in and she became the latest victim to be swallowed up by the icy waters of The Bay.

A powerful sense of déjà vu hit Jean as she thought back to her office yesterday; and the dream of an accident, and of her falling. How was that possible? Had she just lived out her vision or was it a fantasy? She had heard of people hearing voices, of course, but not of living a completely separate existence from their normal environment. What's more she had been much younger, too.

Jean stood up and straightened her dress.

Paula's emotions got the better of her as she looked at Jean dusting herself down.

"Well!" she screamed, "That's the last time I come out with you!" Tapping her foot to accentuate what she was saying, Paul added, "You're always getting me into trouble."

Jean had heard that one before and remained silent. It was tedious. What's more it was rather unreflective of Paula, who quite easily created her own troubles.

"I'm never drinking again!" Paula pouted, still tapping her foot. Jean had heard that before, too. She gave Paula a long, thoughtful look. At that point, Paula looked at Jean properly, and saw something had changed. Jean had a sort of 'loved and lost' look about her.

In fact, she was remembering her walk in the park with Murray only minutes before.

Before the 'Terrible Two' had time to evaluate their present situation properly, the bouncers realised they were no longer dealing with a potential fatality. They simply needed to deal with two loud, middle-aged women who had caused a ruckus.

One of the bouncers took a stand. "Look, are you two going to leave quietly or do I have to get you removed for being drunk and disorderly?"

"I'm not disorderly!" Paula piped up.

"No, but you are drunk," the bouncer replied.

Paula stood, muted.

Jean composed herself and started to make her exit. Paula tagged onto her coat-tail for balance: a steadfast guide in all things. The rugby team started to cheer, and Paula gave a little kick of her foot in acknowledgment.

Outside Brampton's, Jean said goodnight to Paula, pointed her in the right direction, and started her own, short walk home. It was late, but the moon was bright in a clear sky. She looked at the empty street ahead of her. She was mulling over the events of the last few days - or minutes, depending on your perspective. Incredibly, she felt content with the ending. She was happy with her sacrifice; it had taught her a lot about herself. She had avoided temptation, and sacrificed herself and her own happiness for Murray; although she really wasn't sure why.

She was just thinking that it was all too fantastical to possibly be real when she pushed her hand into her pocket and produced a piece of paper. It was her Lotto slip; her winning Lotto slip! Jean giggled aloud, "Well that's tangible enough for me." Keen to get home and enjoy the rest of the weekend, she rejoiced, "No work on Monday for me. They can stick their job!"

But then her thoughts turned to Professor Murray. She recalled teasing him yesterday about giving her the lottery numbers. And it appeared she knew him intimately in another temporal existence. That changed things. She felt decidedly unnerved.

Her head exploded as she remembered certain moments in California; and she felt both embarrassed and worried about her foray into his lab. She might be a millionaire but she could spend the rest of life behind bars if they found out what she had done.

"But hang on, Jean," she argued with herself. "What have you done? You only asked Murray. And he didn't give them to you... did he? The idea of Murray giving her the numbers was too much for her mind, it plodded on obsessively with other minutia.

And what about Richanti, the green station wagon, whoever drugged me, and the chap who tailed me? Not to mention, presumably, a very angry motorcyclist who had lost his precious Harley! She hoped it was insured. Then there was the mystery of her lottery win, what if they found out she was a fraud? She could hardly turn herself in as the first time travelling fraudster, she'd be sectioned for sure.

Weariness caught up with Jean at that point, and she decided to put everything out of her mind until she got some sleep. As she turned the corner, her front door was just metres away.

She put her key in the latch, twisted it, pushed the door, and was safely at home.

"There's nothing that a cup of tea won't fix," she yawned. She was almost catatonic as she entered the kitchen and flicked the kettle on. She disappeared upstairs and made herself comfortable, changing into a matching pair of pink Paul Frank pyjamas with a paw print pattern and her freshly laundered fluffy white bathrobe bottomed off with a pair of bunny slippers. Preparing a pot of tea, she put it on a teak tray with her favourite mug, a silver jug and matching sugar bowl full of sugar cubes, and carried it all into her sitting room.

She had just sat down when there was a knock at the door.

"Oh no, it's Paula," she groaned. "She's probably locked herself out again. Sometimes it's like babysitting a four year old." Jean looked in the mirror, and was surprised, fleetingly, at how normal she looked; well, aside from the bags under her eyes. She strode to the door, took a deep breath, and flung it open all paw prints and bunny feet.

"Forgotten your key again...?" There was a stunned silence as Jean saw who was there in front of her. It wasn't Paula at the door. She froze; was mute.

After a long silence, she fumbled for some adequate words, her eyebrows performing arcs in the half-dark. "It's you! I thought..."

Chapter Sixteen

Wednesday, 18th December, 2012
Much later, Manhattan Island, New York, New York, USA

Fear can be your friend or your foe.

The Watcher felt a sudden shift in the course of events. All was lost, it seemed. He wasn't used to losing.

"I'm not going to start getting used to loosing," he said savagely.

He looked down at the file he had requested earlier and opened it up. There were twenty candidates, Professors with US origins living in the UK. He flicked through the photos. Murray's photo stuck out from all the rest, and he read the location. Murray Institute, Birmingham University, West Midlands, UK. He had won a Laureate for his contribution to science in Psychokinetics.

"That's the one."

He picked up the phone and barked "Get me our contact in the UK and do it quickly. I need a mercenary! Get their best man on the line." He put the phone down. Then he focused, watched and waited.

"She'll reveal herself to me once more, she always does."

Chapter Seventeen

Early hours of Sunday, 16th December, 2012
172 Marion Road, Smethwick, England

Have faith and focus.
When you least expect it, angels will appear from nowhere to aid your quest.

"Who did you think I was?" Professor Murray was standing in front of her, smiling. "Well, no matter."

Jean looked down shyly and rather embarrassingly at the pair of bunnies looking up at her. She was more than puzzled, and most definitely on the back foot.

"Oh, please come in," she hastened feeling slightly underdressed and grabbed a silk kimono that was hanging on the coat rack beside her.

Jean thought about the laboratory the day before. And did he remember her from 1990? Gosh, the etiquette involved in trans-dimensional travel could really add complexity to a new relationship. She let him in, but poked her head into the street, looking left and right, before following him through the door. She half expected secret service officers to pounce on her. Murray appeared to be alone, though.

Reverting to type, she said, "I was just making a cup of tea. Would you like one?"

Murray said, "Yes, that would be good. We might be a while. Actually," he confessed, "I could really do with a coffee." Jean didn't hear him. She was too busy pondering "... a while." Was that before or after she was busted? Oh Lord! She really was in deep with this one; he was bound to be working for the government. It was only a matter of time before she was in the bottom of the canal for knowing state secrets.

Jean pinched herself. Yes, this was real. It was difficult to be sure, these days. It might not *all* be bad. Murray didn't seem the type to murder her, although she *had just* thrown a massive spanner into his early educational development. He might even be grateful, she thought, still ruminating on her last trip back in time.

Jean picked up a china mug from the tray. While she completed the tea ritual, they reclined comfortably. She considered the strangeness of the situation as they sat together in the two, beautifully-restored, Victorian period armchairs that graced her living room.

Silence could be powerful. It allowed things on one's mind to surface. Jean knew this trick, kept mute, and called Murray's bluff.

"I suppose my visit demands an explanation," he said at last.

Jean couldn't hold her guilt down any longer; and nor could she toy with him. She interrupted him, blurting out, "The door was open, Professor. I had no idea what was inside. I'm afraid I'm the inquisitive type; and if it's about the lottery win, then I'd be happy to give all the money back."

"Hey, calm down, Jean. Nobody's going to put you in a body bag. Please relax!"

"Oh!" She gave him a sidelong glance, but felt a little calmer; and a little stupid, too. She blushed. He seemed so genuine.

"Jean, you've got nothing to worry about. I engineered the whole thing," Murray declared nonchalantly.

"You're joking! You must be." She paused in shock, and then demanded. "What do you mean?

"I left the door open in the laboratory. It was deliberate. I knew you'd go inside, and I left the machine set so that it would connect with you. It was all predicted; predictable, in fact."

"How did you know?"

"Because it was the only way you could possibly have visited me in 1990."

"So let me get this straight. You arranged for me to go back in time to meet you in 1990?"

"No, not quite. I built the time machine that sent you back to 1990, and you decided where to go and what to do with your time talents. I must say, the lottery win wasn't what I had in mind, but I can't blame you for that. Killing yourself, though... I hadn't thought of that." A tone of admiration came into his voice. "Very clever."

"Clever?" Jean gulped. "Clever? It didn't feel clever at the time."

Her mind returned to the moment she launched the Harley off the bridge. She was in free fall and, just seconds before she hit the water below, she had seen a large wave break against the bridge support. Then she was gone. She definitely couldn't go back to that life again. Clever! She hadn't thought of it that way.

"You'd be surprised. You're much cleverer than you think. I've been trying to work out how to defeat the Demagodran for decades, and you managed to work it out in a few hours. The Demagodran. Yes, Jean, those were the people who were following you. Richanti's men."

Another piece of the jigsaw slotted into place. Jean thought, "So that's how Richanti fits into all of this." She was beginning to understand.

Just when Jean had thought her day couldn't get more complicated, it had taken yet another twist. Her mind hurt. It felt completely overloaded.

"More tea?" She didn't wait for a reply, but took Murray's cup and began to pour until it overflowed onto the floor.

"Jean!" Murray objected, dodging the tea spilling onto the carpet. He pulled her back from deep space.

The last few days' experiences were flashing through Jean's head. She could remember sleeping on her office desk and then, yes, she woke up; and the door to the lab *had* been left open. It was such an unlikely event, it simply had to be staged; and she was the main character. She remembered the lab, and sensing that someone was nearby; that was why she left. She realised that he was telling the truth! How funny that she could only fit the pieces together after the event.

Jean steadied the teapot, arresting the flow of tea, and put the pot down. She handed Murray the cup. "Help yourself to sugar and milk," she said.

"Do you have any coffee?" he pleaded. She failed to hear him. Her thoughts had turned to Richanti and her instinct about him. She reflected on his image on the news; and the travesty of Ocean's wedding. How manipulative he was. And how did she get drugged on her first visit? Whose was in the green station wagon? She couldn't understand. Why her? What had she done? How much did Murray know?

She looked at Murray, and asked, "Why me?"

Murray looked at her, and replied, "Funny, I asked myself the same question. You have a gift, Jean. It took me a couple of decades of research to work it out, but you have a gift - as do many others - part of it's genetic, and part of it's social conditioning.

"What kind of gift?" Jean sensed something about herself that she couldn't quite put her finger on.

"Your instinct."

Murray leaned forward, thoughtfully. "You probably honed it in your childhood, which, I would guess, was a lonely and isolated one. You're a dreamer, in the sense that you see more than most people can; and you don't put stringent limits on the situations you find yourself in. It's in all of us, but most of us suppress it; many of us have it beaten out of us as we grow up. You never really grew up, though.

Jean was enraptured. She'd always had a gut feeling she wasn't like everyone else. She never really fitted a mould; and she never wanted to. She was an original - authentic - and this conversation with Murray was 'proof of the pudding', as her Nan used to say.

"Psychics have it; people who hear God speaking to them have it; those who see ghosts have it. So do people who hear voices or visions, and think themselves a little mad. Parents rely on it to tune-in to their children; and siblings - especially twins - use it to communicate with each other. In short, there are many different kinds and levels of communication."

Jean raised her eyebrows.

"I've spent my whole life researching this and it's real," Murray asserted. "It's all real."

Jean couldn't take anymore surprises today. She drifted off into her thoughts, again, and absent-mindedly reached for the pot, which was now stone cold. "More t...?"

Murray interrupted. "No thanks. I'd prefer coffee. But look, you've had a crazy day. Why don't you get some rest? I have more to tell - much more - but it can wait until the morning. You'll be better off with a fresh head. You get off to bed and, if I may, I'll sleep on your couch and clear up down here."

More? Jean wondered. 'Much more,' he said...

Jean looked at him; her instinct coming in again, and this time it was a very different feeling: both loving and companionable.

"I agree. Just one thing, Ethan, remembering his first name. When you've cleaned up, will you come up and sleep in my bedroom? I need a friend, tonight. It's been a very, very long day."

Murray nodded. Jean hugged him and retired.

Chapter Eighteen

Sunrise, Sunday, 16th December, 2012
172 Marion Road. Smethwick, England

If your successes outweigh your problems, you are growing.

Jean woke to the sound of a coffee grinder and bright rays of sunlight streaming through her window. Murray was making a brew with fresh beans in her kitchen and she could hear bacon sizzling on the stove. She sank back against her pillows; the smells made her pleasantly drowsy. It was a cosy Sunday feeling combined with the natural high from having someone new in her life who loved her deeply.

Murray apparently had impeccable hearing. He responded to her half-hearted attempt to get up by putting his head around the bedroom door and saying brightly, "I'm an early riser. I took the liberty of going to the deli to pick up a few things. Stay where you are. I'll bring you breakfast in bed."

This was too good to be true: a handsome, intelligent, accomplished man; and he can cook, too. She wasn't used to things going right for her. "Don't think I'm complaining, though," she murmured.

Murray soon brought in a tray and a selection of newspapers. He had strategically opened the papers. Some articles had been circled and then marked by folding the papers back on themselves. "Read those," he said. "I'll explain later."

Jean tucked into her food, speed-reading the various pieces he had selected. "Okay, Prof, you have earthquakes; you have war in the Middle East; and bankers are capitalising on the whole deal with construction contracts for a new city. Nothing new there, so your point is?"

"The point, Jean, is that each of these articles misrepresents what actually happened; and in each case there's a link to the Demran Corporation. Could you contemplate a world without conflict and greed? Does it really have to be this hard all the time? It is almost as if the whole damned catastrophe was planned."

"Planned... catastrophe?" Jean dwelt on this. She had never thought that such events were planned but supposed that, if you could plan a bar room brawl, you could plan a war. But what was the catastrophe he mentioned?

"Earthquakes in Japan and New Zealand: unpredictable, you would think. In fact, one group of scientists had actually predicted them. See this abstract on earthquake prediction with a correlation to earthquake frequency and solar activity."

Murray walked around behind her and put his hand on her shoulder. "By the way, Jean, call me Ethan will you? That darned 'Prof' stuff does my head in.

He brought up a paper that he had written on his iPhone. The essay described a phenomenon called Precession. *Precession*? That word again,

Jean thought. Its meaning puzzled her, but for some reason she felt that it was significant.

"Demran Corporation controls all the patents on earthquake detection and has been sitting on them for decades; they never see the light of day. As a result, the whole field of research is stunted. There's even a government department: the National Earthquake Prevention Programme (NEPP), to siphon off earthquake predications and release misinformation presented as fact. Let's just say the predictions that NEPP have come up with in the past decade are worse than if you'd tossed a coin for the results."

"And what about wars?" Jean could hardly speak from shock at what Ethan was telling her. It was overwhelming in an almost sublime way. "Surely they can't engineer them?" But wait. She was thinking just moments ago that if a bar room brawl could be engineered so could a war.

Ethan had another answer.

"Take wars in the Middle East. Demran Corporation has the most significant oil lobby in the USA, advising the presidency directly on oil markets. Oil supplies are plentiful; and renewable energy will easily meet demand before the oil runs out. Somehow, though, we're made to believe that we need control over the Middle East to secure our energy demands in the West.

"The Middle East has been a battleground for years; and the West has ruined it for the people who live there. Consider the parallel to the colonies, where we were thrown out for funding preferred presidencies. It's all a ruse for something more sinister. War is never justifiable, but these conflicts barely even stand up to gentle scrutiny! Anyone with their head screwed on should sense foul play!"

"See the name they have given to the city?" Murray - Ethan, Jean reminded herself - pointed at one particular article.

"The Oasis," Jean responded obediently. She'd heard the name before; yesterday, in fact. The name triggered a flashback to her dream again: that terrible vision of those poor people, and an elevator to hell.

"Interfering with nations doesn't work. In the end, people realise what is going on. A nation sometimes has to fight its own battles. Military aid can lead to dependency, and backing the wrong president only distorts public feeling. It's a powder keg; and unstable by design. Of course, this is a complicated issue, and it always is, but something is seriously afoot here."

Jean nodded again. She had believed this for years, and it was well documented too, so, presumably, it was very close to the truth. "Well, I can't disagree with you there," she concurred. "But where did Richanti come from?"

She was to going to regret asking that. Theories about 'proof of conspiracy' were enough for one Sunday morning, she mused.

"Alien genes."

Confusion overcame Jean, and words escaped her.

Ethan barrelled on. "Original earth-born humanity makes up the core for most of us, and the rest are alien genes. Some people have more than others do, but we all have some of them. There are two hundred and twenty three genes to be exact, and they mainly affect our psychological functioning."

"Richanti's family almost has a full set of alien genes. You too, Jean. I've checked. You asked why, and now you know. You won the lottery when you were born, but you didn't realise it; at least, not until now."

Jean sat in stunned silence as she tried to take it all in. She looked down at her hands. They weren't green, slimy or scaly but well preserved. He couldn't be talking about her. She was just Jean, a cleaning supervisor from Smethwick.

"Richanti never banked on the random creation of an extraordinary individual through your mother and father meeting, rather than his own bloodline. And of course he's custodian of that. He has managed carefully it for years: brothers, sisters, sons, daughters, cousins are all carefully interbred; and some of the world's most eminent banking families are based on his arcane craftsmanship. The alien genes bring great insight: you have the resources of the whole universe in your head. Knowledge is power, as they say."

Jean tried to interrupt. She was restless now, and wanted to talk, but Ethan was in full flow. He didn't know that Joe wasn't her biological father: very few would. Her mother took her secret to the grave, as far as she knew. The moment was lost, Ethan was off again.

"So-called 'Dr' Richanti is also the chairman of the Demran Corporation. His family history goes back aeons; and, over the ages, it covers everything from the Nazis to the Knights Templar."

"Richanti?" Jean was agog. So many questions ran through her mind, she could barely process them, but she knew she had to focus on Ethan.

"Do you remember what you said to me before your disappearing act over the Golden Gate?"

"No. I said nothing. I simply knew I had to get away. The only way I could think of was to make it look as though I killed myself in an accident - to disrupt the timeline. That seemed to be the only thing I had control over."

"You said something. Can you remember what it was?"

"No," Jean insisted. I said nothing." Nevertheless, she did think back. Hmmm. She had said one word: *Precession*. "Well, yes, Precession. You mentioned it earlier. Why would I say that? What is it?"

Jean reflected further on this. She did think it odd that a word that she had never heard of before popped into her head as if someone had spoken it; like some sort of cosmic alarm bell pushed out through her brain.

"It's your instinct again," Ethan said, picking up the thread. "We're all connected to a collective consciousness, Jean. It comes through another dimension and is accessed by the addition of alien genes into our genetic profile. All that exists in the world in that dimension is energy and thought. At the next level of consciousness, there's no time and no space, just energy and the flow of knowledge, although we perceive these as time and space, ideas or insights.

"That's how time travel is possible. Time doesn't really exist in the next dimension; and that's why you were given the word Precession to pass on to me. So yeah, that's why I'm here today: you gave me a clue, and a riddle to solve; and I've spent my whole life solving it. Not one life, in fact, but several.

"There is only one thing I haven't been able to solve, and that's how to defeat Richanti." Ethan paused for a breath to Jean's surprise. The next moment, she needed one herself.

"You seem to be the key to it all: you're the common thread running through the whole course of events. Our future will be determined by an exchange between you and him. I'm part of the story, but I have a feeling that, in the end, it will come down to the decisions you make."

"No pressure there, then," Jean said softly, a tad ironically. "So let me get this straight. I'm somehow connected to a higher power that gives me information, which I then use to defeat this evil axis called the Demran Corporation; and this comes from an alien bloodline of which I also seem to be a part."

"Yes that's right, but there's something else I haven't told you."

"Stop! Sorry, I can't take any more. I'm just a simple lass from Smethwick, and I'm not cut out to be a superhero. I don't have the wardrobe."

Overloaded, she reverted to ritual. "A cup of tea, please, to steady my nerves. Can't I just go on being me, just Jean, is that too much to ask?"

Ethan switched on the kettle and turned back to Jean. "This is all about you. In general, we're all destined to live lives that we have chosen before we're born into this dimension. What our lives are about is really a test; and through those tests, our souls grow or die. Also, through individual tests, the collective consciousness grows or dies.

"Energy is universal information, depicting the infinite struggle between dark and light, and the flow of both creation and destruction. It's been this way ever since our universe was first created: since the beginning of time, as we know it."

"So why me? What's my test?"

Ethan paused. He stirred the tea gently. There was silence between them as the teaspoon clinked around the pot, like a timer, counting down to Jeans quest.

"Just to be the person you were born to be, that's all. Do that and everything else will come out right. All our paths through life are linked and, yes, your actions will affect your peers, your community and your nation; even having a global impact but, in the end, all you can influence is yourself. Sort yourself out and be the best you can be; and for God sake don't worry about saving the world."

Jean looked down, more-or-less contemplating her navel. She instinctively knew what Ethan was describing, but couldn't give it a name: it related to an elusive part of her. Although she was greatly comforted by the idea that she only needed to sort herself out, what on earth did he mean by talking about tests, light and dark, energy and knowledge?

Then she looked at him and understood that he really did believe in her, even if he seemed to have trouble giving her the *right* explanation. Nodding at Ethan, she remarked with a wry grin, "Okay, so I sort myself out, and pass my test; and that sorts Richanti out. How hard can that be?" Jean, as ever, had taken the positive end of the stick. She had agreed to the challenge.

"Well, that's not all. Remember what I said, there's more." He paused. "Polar reversal and earthquakes!"

"Polar reversal and earthquakes?" Jean copied him in parrot fashion; she failed to understand the significance of Ethan's remark.

"Yes, another one today. Just look at the news breaking on the BBC: an earthquake in Spain; and it's much larger than normal."

Jean topped up her tea, seeking comfort from the ritual, which calmed and warmed her at the same time. Soothed by the process, she had time to compose herself, and took a sip, waiting for more information.

"Remember, earthquake predictions are being suppressed. So is real information about the Middle East, family bloodlines, wealth and power; and the fact that Richanti is controlling the state of play everywhere in the world."

"I have no idea what you mean," Jean said. "Enlighten me." Jean had capitulated to the improbable, which seemed to be unravelling hour by hour, as fantasy became reality. "I really am all ears. Do tell!"

Ethan exclaimed, "Precession! Your insight, remember. It's the end of the world as we know it on 21st December 2012."

Jean said incredulously, "But that's next Friday, less than a week away! I thought that we had another six billion years before everything went bang."

Ethan corrected her. "I said the end of life as we know it, not the end of life."

"Okay, so we'll soon be taken over by aliens and forced into slave labour and servitude."

"How did you guess?" Ethan replied.

Jean went white.

"I was jo...."

"I know that you were joking, but it's your instinct again; the truth is coming out in your dry humour, surfacing from within you. Remember your gift: you're tapped into everything that ever was, is, or will be."

"Take Precession," he continued. "The solar year begins over again every 26,000 years or so. And from the world's perspective, we drift back into another zodiac sign at that point. We are due to move from Pisces into Aquarius with the next one. However, because of other things going on, this time, like the solar wind, and a whole lot of other cycles honing in on Precession, things are going to be changing in a big way.

"They've been predicated - if not in detail - by the Mayans, by Nostradamus; and touched on in a variety of religious texts and schools of thought from the Hindus to the Jews, and from Steiner to the Masons, not to mention the Rosicrucians and mystery schools; focused on by Plato and myth down through the ages.

"Picture a massive earthquake on a global scale shifting the earth's rotational axis. Where do you think the legend of Atlantis came from? Why were the Pyramids set up, if not as experimental astrological stations to view certain kinds of events, including Precession, with crucial information written into their mathematics as a warning for future generations? "

"The earth's crust is so fragile, sitting as it does on top of molten lava, that everything going on during Precession will cause a rapid rotation of Earth's core of around 180 degrees, initiated by a polar reversal. In turn, that will affect the earth's crust, if to a lesser degree, but still a massive 30 degrees of latitude. And it is all totally predictable, already predicated."

"Richanti knows this and seeks to control events in his favour. He controls most of the infrastructure in the Middle East and is just waiting in the wings for the big event. Then he'll mop up. The earth's population will reduce to one per cent of what it is now, but with some big contrasts. In the Middle East, the survival rate will be almost sixty per cent, that's why he has built a new city there. In the UK, however, it will be almost nil; only a few thousand, mainly due to extreme weather changes. In effect, the UK will move to the Arctic Circle and its coastline will also be susceptible to tsunamis."

"Genocide," Jean affirmed bluntly.

"Almost: holocaust followed by genocide. My point is, it's *not* the fact the world will change that's inevitable and unavoidable, it's the betrayal of humanity that is so appalling.

Jean had paled and Ethan paused, pouring her a cup of tea before he went on.

It's too late now to change things. Given a few decades of preparation, we might have adapted to save ourselves, but that opportunity has been denied us. Richanti has put himself above everyone else. He plans to save his own skin, and some of his followers; followers who will dictate terms to weakened governments and individuals who can afford it. Predicated on such a foundation, life really will be hell on earth."

Jean's face puckered up. "What I don't understand is if I'm like Richanti, why aren't I evil, too?

Ethan explained, "We all have a part of the alien genes, it's just a question of choice as how we want to live our lives: two choices - dark or light - that's it."

"You must be extremely resilient to have resisted all this time," Ethan said firmly. "Your high standards have saved you. Look at how Richanti tempted you by giving you everything you wanted: a family, the home of your dreams, and your husband."

Jean thought about her celebrity lifestyle, which she had rejected with good reason. She would rather be ordinary and happy than have all of the objects, and the false friendships that came with the part Richanti offered her.

"Can I keep the lottery money," she asked with a mischievous smile.

"Yes, of course, for what good it will do you. Money is really of no use to you any longer," Ethan replied. "It might be nice, comforting even, for me to say that there's a god who will come and save you; and that you can sin and then be forgiven, but it's not true, Jean. There's just you and a set of alien genes bringing constant conflict about what's good and what's evil. It is so simple, but it's so hard. It is easy to lower a standard, but much harder to raise it; and in some cases, I know you had to make some very difficult decisions to hold on to your ethics. For instance, you had to leave the Ted you'd always dreamed of."

Jean looked drawn. There was so much information, and so many questions bouncing around her head.

Ethan was apologetic. "I'm sorry. I've been waiting ages to tell you and I just had to get it all out."

She reverted to type again, an inevitable result of the constant stream of tea. "I need to pee!"

Chapter Nineteen

Early morning, Sunday, 16ᵗʰ December, 2012
The Murray Institute, Birmingham University, England

If you don't control your life, life events will control you.

"Is it done?" the Watcher barked down the phone. Omnipotent as ever, he sensed fear in the subordinate on the other end of the phone.

"Just finishing up, now. Ten minutes and you'll know," his subordinate replied. You won't be able to miss this one!

His new boss wasn't the easiest to work with, he ruminated. There seemed a lack of rationale behind the job. Primarily a mercenary, he was used to taking out oligarchs for the government, or even the occasional politician. What he was doing now was just vandalism. He attached explosive charges to the eight, base supports for the building. It was easy. He didn't even need to gain access to the lab.

"Just one more set, that's it." The remote detonator started to flash intermittently with a slow red pulse. "Now the fun bit!"

Retreating to the safety of his car, he started the engine and got quickly out of the University campus. There weren't many people around at this time of day; just the odd jogger. He felt glad; the early hour meant no loss of life. Was he going soft in his middle years? In case there was any come-back, his last job at the Institute was to change the CCTV tapes.

Once clear of the gates, he stopped and pulled over. There was the familiar redbrick clock tower and, directly in front of it, the modern, new Murray Institute. The three storey annexe was covered in triangular panels of blue Perspex, and connected to the main building by a small, glass air bridge. It looked pretty. "But not for much longer," he quipped.

He pulled a remote out of his pocket and switched it on. The LEDs went from red to green as it picked up the signal from the detonators on each of the supports. He pressed the charge button. He saw white smoke and then heard a sonic boom as the eight charges exploded in the car park he'd been in only moments before.

He loved his job. Who else would they get to do this? It made him feel significant. Even if the feeling was only short lived, he craved it more than anything else.

-

The Watcher smiled as he saw Jean and devised a fresh plan. This one was stubborn.

Looking appraisingly at his face in the mirror, he remarked, "It's too soon for the human race to experience time travel. What would they do with it? They'd rewrite history for their own ends with no plan, and no vision."

At least with *his* plan, they had a future. He concentrated his focus until he saw Jean, and sensed her panic. Then he flicked the remote to a BBC news channel. They had picked it up quickly.

"Breaking News: Murray Institute explosion." As he read the supertitles, he rued, "Shame that Murray wasn't in it. But never mind, I've flushed her out. That's good enough."

The channel showed footage of the smoking building, and then a newsreader filled the screen.

"Nobel Laureate Professor, Ethan Murray, opened The Murray Institute at Birmingham University last summer. It was a research laboratory looking at the nature of reality. Some people believed he had altered our view of time. Murray received the Nobel Laureate award for proving that telekinesis exists; and that communication across vast distances is possible.

"Murray is unavailable for comment. His whereabouts are unknown."

The Watcher smiled. I know where he is. He picked up the phone.

"You're looking for a two-up, two-down terrace with a pub at the end of the road called Brampton's. Sweep the street looking for a man and a woman in their fifties. One of them is Professor Ethan Murray. I hope he has a trace on him, and that the inspector has been awake enough to follow it. Bring them in, and bring them to me. I want them alive."

Chapter Twenty

Sunday, 16th December, 2012
172 Marion Road, Smethwick, England

Faith, a journey of certainty down an unknown path.

Jean felt the sound strike her body: a powerful blast that shook the whole building. The windows vibrated, and came close to shattering. There was a moment of complete silence...

Then police sirens wailed as the city's emergency services responded to the alert, eager to be part of the action. Judging from the direction of the sound, it was a few miles away. Her intuition honed, Jean knew it was The Murray Institute.

She felt sick to the bottom of her stomach. This was all too real. She was on the run again, but the stakes had never been as high before. Her temporal excursions - like the somersault off The Golden Gate - were games, in comparison. The blood thudding through her veins was born of fear: fear of failure, fear of the unknown. Close on their tail came panic and the impulse to run followed swiftly as adrenalin pulsed around her body.

Ethan also knew the blast was from his lab. He'd planned for this moment, but not so soon! Who tipped them off? It was only hours since he'd interrupted the timeline. Murray was puzzled. Who were the moles? They must have a burrow full of them.

"Jean! We need to leave now!" He calmed himself, controlling the urge to shout orders up the stairwell to her in the bedroom. "Get dressed," he said. "I'll explain later."

Frozen with fear, Jean snapped out of her catatonic state when she heard what Murray was saying.

"But what about the machine?"

"Oh, you mean that experiment in the lab?"

"Yes, the machine that allowed me to time-travel."

"Partly true," he said in an unconcerned voice. The part of Jean that wasn't on the edge of a nervous breakdown thought his calmness was odd.

Murray reiterated his concern, and this time he did shout. "Jean we really must leave! Now!"

Jean, ever practical, replied, "I can't go and save the world in a pair of pink Paul Frank pyjamas." The humour helped her to deal with the situation. She pulled on jeans, a sweater, and a leather jacket. "Too late for the face," she grumbled. It'll have to be done on the fly. She dropped on a serious pair of shades, perfect for her new role as superhero.

Her role practice was disturbed by voices below, outside her front door. She went to the bedroom window and looked outside. To her horror, her humble abode was surrounded by a dozen men in flak-jackets. They had come for her and Ethan; she knew it. "The neighbours will have a field day," she said stoically, regaining her courage.

There was an almighty crash, and the front door burst open. She ran for the landing and looked over the banister. An armed man, head-to-toe in black, was pointing an assault rifle at her. The green laser occasionally flicked menacingly. They're pointing that thing at my head, she thought grimly.

Then she saw Murray pinned to the wall with an arm behind his back. That wasn't the worst of it. After nearly two decades, there, standing in the doorway shouting orders, was Ted, her ex-husband.

"Oh dear," Jean said quietly. "If you're back on the scene, this really is turning into a terrible day." Ted was aware the comment was addressed to him, and looked directly at her. He had a poker face, but scanned Jean's face for a little longer than he should.

"We're taking you both in for questioning."

"Ted, you weasel!" Jean screamed. "I see nothing has changed."

He ignored her cries. "It's a matter of national security."

Murray asked quietly, "What about cautioning us?"

"We don't follow government protocols. Make it easy for us, why don't you? No heroics, it's pointless."

The sight of Ted again after all these years flooded Jean's mind with dark memories: the drinks, the drugs, and the mental abuse. A whole lifetime of snapshots flashed before her in stills, each one bringing an emotional wave of helplessness. She fell backwards into her former life as if she had never left it; but the dark place didn't last for long. Not when she took a closer look at Ted.

He was drawn; old and tired. Seeing what sort of person he had become, she knew instantly that persuasion would fail. The die was cast. One of Richanti's henchmen now, she assumed; the perfect recruit.

The other men forced Jean and the professor into handcuffs. As they were manhandled into the back of the van, Ethan whispered into Jean's ear. "Have faith," he said.

Jean was annoyed. Did nothing faze this man? He never reached the end of the road, even when he was looking down the barrel of a gun. Her brain squawked, "This is insanity. I've reached my limit." Before Ethan came along, she seemed to be in control of her destiny. Okay, her goals were not *that* ambitious, but they were hers; and life was alright, thanks.

"Damn my curiosity," she groaned aloud. "Have faith!" her inner diatribe continued. "What a ridiculous thing for Ethan to say." She was forced down on the floor by another guard. "I'm not quite sure what threat a cuffed, middle-aged woman on the floor might be to National Security. They must credit me as an escapologist, a modern day Houdini."

The doors slammed behind them and Jean could hear the engine begin to chug. They were moving. Through the bars, Jean asked Ethan, "Well, how do we get out of this one?"

"Well, I know it looks like a tight spot," he said quickly, his voice fading as he tried to stifle his fear. "But sometimes you just have to go with the flow."

Jean prized open the chink in his armour. "Tight spot!" she exclaimed, her voice climbing higher as she repeated herself. "Tight spot...? You must be bloody joking. I've been arrested - no, not arrested, kidnapped by a gang of paramilitary thugs, one of whom is my ex-husband - presumably for interfering with your time machine." She took a shuddering breath and ploughed on.

"And through a strange coincidence, the machine has been blown to pieces in the biggest explosion in Birmingham since the blitz. And you say 'We're in a tight spot!' I'm not cut out for these heroics."

She took another breath, and saw that Ethan had crouched down on the floor of the van with his hands against the side of his head. It was obviously hurting. An element of practicality crept back into her voice, "So what is your plan?"

For all his calmness, for all the solemnity and caution, Ethan was at a loss. He didn't have a plan. To answer Jean's question negatively wasn't an option, though, so he changed the subject entirely; that became his plan. He always was a skilled improviser.

"Of course, I remember the Golden Gate. It was years ago. But in your mind, it was less than a day ago." Ethan began. "That was the moment everything changed for me. The whole event felt like an action movie, and I wasn't convinced you were telling the truth. You were hiding something, your actions were premeditated, and I could tell that.

"You helped in many ways though, and you gave me the answer. Precession led me to Armageddon in the 21st century; and that led me to Richanti and the Demagodran. Then you led me to time travel. I found you living in Smethwick with this shell of a man - I remember him, the same person who is, presumably, driving this van.

"All I had to do was fill in the gaps. It's easy to climb a mountain when you trust your mountaineer. It's even easier if your spirit is that mountaineer! But the challenge of conquering a mountain that nobody has climbed takes faith and a massive amount of self-belief. *You* gave me that, Jeanie. So please have faith now."

She *had* calmed down. In fact, Jean was touched. Sliding down onto the floor of the van like him, she moved her hands closer to his, and their fingers touched. The energy and closeness calmed her even more.

-

The roads were short, at first. Then they reached what they deduced was a motorway. Jean, disorientated, tried to guess where she was. Without a reference point, she felt lost and claustrophobic. Neither of them knew whether their direction was north or south, but, after a couple of hours, the van hit heavy traffic and slowed down.

She speculated, "What's two hours from Birmingham? Manchester, maybe, or London. Even Bristol?"

They went bumper to bumper for a good half an hour. The more she listened, the more acute Jean's hearing became as she tuned-in to sirens, articulated lorries, motorbikes and buses just the other side of the thin, steel wall of the van. She tried to develop a picture of where they might be. The van's engine turned over more slowly, and other vehicles were much closer than before. They must have arrived in a fair-sized metropolis. Finally, the van stopped. From the sound of the voices outside, there must be a crowd out there. She was more puzzled than ever.

She looked into Ethan's eyes. She could see that he wasn't concerned. She wondered why not. Clearly, he feared nothing. He gazed back at her steadily; and that made her feel at ease. When he gave out a smile, she smiled back.

The sound of a key turning in the latch broke the beauty of the moment. The van's double doors flung open to reveal Ted standing there, triumphant, proud, and despicable. He had a gun and was pointing it right at them. She could see him squeezing the trigger. Her heart pounded. "This is it!"

She heard a thud, and winced as a dart hit the guard beside her in the arm. He slumped forward and fell to the floor.

"Not dead, just dozing." Ethan and Jean looked at each other speechlessly as Ted, all smiles, removed their cuffs and gags. "Let's just say we're even Jean. Forgive me. Now go! You don't have much time. They'll see the van has stopped, so you have just minutes to save yourselves. I picked a crowd so that you'd have a chance to escape.

"Trust no one," Ted continued. "Richanti has a lot of followers; and they're everywhere. Fear keeps them together and under his control." Jean was touched and emotional. There were tears in her eyes, and she felt deeply sad. "What about you, Ted?"

"Don't worry about me, I'll be okay. You've done me a favour." Jean hugged him hard and tight. He didn't sound very convincing. He never was a good liar.

Jean looked around. She recognised where they were instantly: Piccadilly Circus, London. She could see a bank of tourists; and a tour group was taking pictures of Eros. Wedged between them and the tour group blocking their escape was a fountain of bronze horses and the open road to freedom. She hugged Ted tightly again. She knew it would be the only hug for a very long time. Then she launched herself into the fountain, banging her head on the belly of one of the bronze horses galloping above them. She looked back briefly, mouthing, "Thank you," and smiled once more at Ted.

Ethan took Jean by the shoulders and guided her in the direction of Trafalgar Square. There was some event on - not unusual for London - and they followed the chaotic flow of people.

"What next?" Jean asked. Ethan would have a plan; he was always a step ahead. "South Coast, Brighton," he replied.

"So it's Victoria, then?"

"Yes, we'll cut through the park - less CCTV - and take the back entrance onto an Express."

"Then what?" she asked curiously.

"You'll see."

"It's always important to have the ending in mind with everything you do. That's the nature of faith: a belief that everything will turn out just fine. No technology, this time around; just a hunch.

"Don't you see what is happening, Jean? It is not just about us. We have a collective consciousness to tap into, and it's responding with aid. Ted arriving was no accident."

"You mean I just conjured him up?"

"Something like that. Life has a way of balancing itself out. Ted owed you one. He responded to your call because it was 'pay back time'. He took a lot from you and he needed to pay back his debt. Until now, he'd had no peace."

They heard a volley of shots and the crowd surged forward behind them. They were caught up in the crush and could hardly move. Ethan pulled them up a set of stairs. She looked back, and could see Ted laid out, face down, the blood jettisoning out of his head across the floor, leaving only a wasted life in its wake. The crowd had cleared. He was motionless; he was finally at peace. Her hero, if only for a few moments.

Ethan consoled her. "We all have a part to play in life, Jean. Working out what it is, and why we're here, is the hardest part of life."

"If only I could turn back time," she said.

"You can," Ethan smiled. He bundled Jean into a rickshaw and gave a command to the young driver. "Twenty quid to Victoria station. There's a big tip if you can make it in fifteen minutes for the next Brighton Express."

"How big a tip," the driver asked?

"Fifty quid okay?"

"Fifty?" The rickshaw driver pedalled like crazy into the oncoming crowd.

Chapter Twenty One

Wednesday, 18th December, 2012
Much, much later, Manhattan Island, New York, New York, USA

Opportunity is elusive, take it when you see it, or the moment will be lost forever.

The Watcher lost his concentration for a moment. They were calling, and they were afraid to tell him something. The phone rang. The controller blurted out, "One of our agents helped them to escape. We took him out, but they're somewhere in London. We lost them in the crowd."

There was silence. He repeated, "We took the agent out. He won't trouble you again."

He thought the act of murder might have saved his own skin. The Watcher put down the receiver without bothering to respond or find out the details. He focused his mind, but saw nothing. They had vanished. All he saw was failure. The timeline had shifted against him again.

All he could was watch and wait. His impotence made him feel angry and tense; his temper was rising, like a small child who wanted his own way.

Picking up the phone, he snapped, "Take out the controller who's responsible for losing Jean and Murray Make an example of him. You know what to do."

That'll teach them, the thought. After lashing out at his underlings, he felt much better. "It keeps them on their toes," he murmured complacently, and reminisced - as he did quite often - about his childhood teacher, Mr Burns. He was cleverer now, and had more options.

Being buried alive would be too good for the controller who had crossed him. It'll teach the others a valuable lesson, though. He chuckled to himself, and got back to the business of locating his adversaries.

Chapter Twenty Two

Sunday, 16th December, 2012
Somewhere in Westminster, London, England

It's not what you are, but what you want to be that matters.

Jean was still in shock, and lost in thought, as she watched the cyclist's thighs zipping up and down in front of her. Always manic on the road, the promise of a large tip had tipped the rickshaw driver into a frenzy. He screamed at oncoming pedestrians, "Attention! Attention!"

One of the many workers from out of town who had flooded to the city and found work driving the revellers of Soho around on the three-wheeled bikes, his particular rickshaw was covered in cowhide with twinkly lights wrapped around the hood, and club anthems blasting out of a beat box.

It wasn't exactly a low-profile exit, Jean mused. Ethan pulled the rain cover back to help avoid detection. This also helped with Jean's nerves, and obscured the overwhelming view of a large, well-rounded, Eastern European backside swaying crazily in the saddle, highly motivated by he thought of a large cash tip.

Jean and Ethan got to the Brighton Line in record time. Rather shakily, they got off the rickshaw, paid up, and sped into Victoria Station from Buckingham Palace Road. Ethan bought first class tickets to give them a greater chance of evading people who might not be friendly.

They slipped from the ticket office straight into a busy bar, of which there are three on the Brighton Express route. Each bar was crammed with punters. They were either on their way into London to enjoy last minute Christmas shopping or heading the other way for a day at the seaside. They walked through each bar, towards the first class carriage waiting on Platform 16.

As soon as the train left the station, Jean ordered a couple of mini bottles of wine to settle her nerves. Old habits die hard. She felt herself relax as she sipped a warm Chardonnay from a plastic glass. Idly, she began to focus once more on her new role as superhero.

"Dare I ask what next?" she joked with Ethan.

"Well funny you should say that," he replied with a grin. "And how are you with water?"

"Water, well I'll drink it if I have to," Jean replied in droll tones.

"What I mean," Ethan said seriously, "is whether you're good at sailing?"

"Eccch. I can't swim and I get seasick. Move onto the next idea because I'm not getting in a boat."

"Well you'd better find some courage in that Chardonnay," Ethan suggested. "It's our only means of escape." Jean ordered another drink.

- / -

Oblivious to the danger, funnily enough, Jean was looking forward to visiting Brighton. She had a small life: work, the pub and soaps. For that matter, when did she last go on a day trip? Being a superhero did have its perks; and she really must remember to scoop up her lottery winnings at some point, too. The Chardonnay had started to kick in.

The train only stopped at a few places en route: Clapham Junction, East Croydon for South London customers, and then Hayward's Heath to let off the stockbrokers. It took fifty-five minutes to Brighton, but the journey gave Jean a chance to reflect on what was happening.

"Tell me about the machine, Ethan. I'm intrigued." Thinking back to her first contact with 'it', she asked, "Why stereos?"

"Stereos help you disengage conscious thought and activate the frontal lobe. The frontal lobe - or your third eye - is nature's interface with the field that allows us to communicate telepathically. I needed you to be perfectly still and focused."

"Why?"

"So I could target you with a small dose of radiation."

"Radiation?" She looked at him in horror.

"Yes. Surgery on your forehead to open up your third eye. I killed off a small amount of tissue at the front of your forehead." Jean frowned at him, rather aptly; and considered the operation.

"Third eye?"

"Yes. Everyone has one, but most people either fail to use it; or have never read the manual on how to use it, so its lost to them. The machine doesn't make you travel in time, it just tags you, and acts as a beacon to make sure you can get back! You're the time traveller; you always have been; but you never knew how you did it. What do you think your dreams are? All you're doing is learning to dream in a conscious state."

She pondered that briefly. "Crazy man..."

"Not so crazy. Think about it. My work on telekinesis proved that instantaneous communication was possible at a speed faster than light, and I was awarded the highest honour in science for that insight. The mechanism was first discovered thousands of years ago by ancestors of today's Mayans; they knew more about psychology than we do!"

"Distance is an illusion, Jean. Time is also an illusion. There's nothing in life other than thought and energy. Remember that. There's nothing more to life. It's like having a video with one million versions of your life on it. At any moment, you can view any version and yet, in a sense, they're all the same.

"In some lives, you'll die young; in some you'll live a long time; in others, you'll have great wealth or great power, and sometimes you'll be Just Jean. Our lives are played out this way - beginning, middle and end; and the whole universe in which we live is played out in the same way: beginning, middle and end.

"All you can influence is your path through life. If you offer a better option to the collective consciousness that you connect with, it will support you. That's how it works. When you do good things, people come from nowhere to help; concoct evil, and people will support you in the same way, but for their own ends. These two ends of the spectrum are constantly in a battle over what we know as eternity: jostling for position; fundamentally flawed by design."

"And the third eye?"

"The third eye switches you between these two points: from your own consciousness to a collective consciousness, and the part of you that exists in other dimensions. We're talking about a creative place where there are infinite possibilities and resources. There's an answer to every question. Sometimes, there's more than one answer."

She thought about this for a while. The chardonnay was connecting unlikely combinations of brain cells in her mind.

"It's powerful stuff," she said. "A genetic evolution of the mind not in terms of selection of superior DNA but expansion of the mind each generation building on the knowledge and insight of the one before. It appears the collective consciousness rewards us for good intent and creativity. The world would be a very different place if people knew that the more good you did for the world, the more extraordinary life would be."

"Or the opposite," Ethan observed. "I'd like to think good will win, but sometimes I'm not so sure." He produced a USB stick. "It's all here: my experiments, proofs, independent verifications and, most importantly, the key to a second machine."

"A second machine. Where?"

"In a New York vault. I had planned to go to the United Nations with you tomorrow, where we'd present the case against Richanti, but unfortunately our plans have to change. I'm thinking of just leaving it to chance

"What do you mean?"

"When I've been here before it usually means there is a lesson to learn but, on this occasion, I'm not sure. It is like a game, Jean. The pot of gold at the end is only available to you when you perform the correct set of actions, usually something within yourself. Get it right, and the collective will help with your quest. Alternatively, it denies your goal. Believe me, I've had decades to get used to this."

"So that's why you're always so chilled?" Not always, Ethan demurred privately. But best not tell that to Jean until she's ready for it.

She reflected on this. 'Faith' - that's what Ethan was saying after the lab went bang. That's why, even at the end of the road, he believes there's a way out; and he's right. She frowned. But how do I know that? She wondered what her part was in all this, and what her life lesson might be. The train was nearly at Brighton. It trundled past Preston Park, and reduced speed to pull slowly into Brighton station.

Jean saw people getting ready for a rapid exit as the train pulled in and slowed to a stop. Outside the station, the taxi queue was full, so Ethan flagged down alternative transport: a Tuk Tuk; it looked more fun. It was definitely a day for unexpected rides.

"I'm not getting in that," she said half-seriously, "not after the rickshaw!"

"Practice being brave," Ethan said. He told the driver confidently, "Brighton Marina, please"

Jean stepped inside warily. It looked just as dangerous as the rickshaw; and it felt even stranger to be on a large, three-wheeled motorcycle with a flimsy cover and rather dubious brakes. There were two speeds: stop and surge forward.

They tootled down Queens Road in the Tuk Tuk. Heads turned as the noisy machine made its way down the street towards the seafront and passed the Palace Pier with all its attractions and lights. The beach was packed with day-trippers from London.

"It's 'London by the Sea', really," she smiled happily at Ethan.

They took in the fish and chip shops, the karaoke bars, and kids' attractions that littered the sea front as they turned towards the east. The Marina was east of the city, and stretched out about two thirds of a mile along the coast road. Its man-made harbour protruded half a mile into the sea.

They entered the Marina from the beach road, and were confronted with a large number of uninspiring apartments built in the 80s and 90s. The Marina had two pontoons: East and West, both of them littered with all manner of craft. The Tuk Tuk driver was given final instructions by Ethan.

"Set us down at the entrance to the East pontoon, please." He paid him, and helped Jean out onto the pontoon.

Jean felt herself wobbling. "I'm unbalanced already and I'm not even on the boat," she complained.

Ethan replied "Don't worry. It's not you, it's the pontoon moving. It's afloat."

He headed swiftly towards a wrought iron gate, punching in a code that released the lock.

"Come inside. You're very lucky. Your first experience of cruising will be in luxury, and you can feel sick in a white leather-clad en-suite." Jean was not best comforted by Ethan's laconic description of her first night's cruising. She looked pale and nervous.

They made their way further down the pontoon, took a left turn, and followed the walkway to the very end where an extremely large Sunseeker sat on its moorings. Over 70 feet in length, it was sleek and streamlined in blue and white.

Ethan jumped aboard and wondered where the key might be. He tried under the mat, but maybe that was a little too obvious. He then put his hand into the bottom of an instrument panel, fished around, and produced a set of keys.

He turned the key in the galley door and undid the latch. They stepped inside. The interior of the cruiser took luxury to another level with its lush leather seating, a bar, well-equipped kitchen and, more importantly, a well-stocked fridge. Jean popped the cork on another bottle of wine; old habits do die hard.

They were both exhausted after their ordeal and decided to get a few hours kip before slipping out under the radar, literally, in the early hours of the morning. The bed in the master bedroom was already made up.

They climbed into bed and switched on the news. "A man was shot dead in Piccadilly, today. He has been identified as Edward Sotherby. The police have issued a statement saying they believe there were no suspicious circumstances, and that the killing was drug related. A young man aged 21 has been apprehended for the crime."

Jean felt sad. Things could have been so different for her and Ted. She asked Ethan, "And what about that poor boy who had been wrongfully arrested?"

"Don't worry," Ethan reassured her, the kid will be fine." He looked quickly at Jean, adding, "And we'll come back for Ted later, if we can."

He set the alarm for an hour before sunrise and looked at the TV again.

"Well, would you believe it? How did they manage to find a fall guy so quickly?"

Jean didn't understand, but she didn't question him, either.

"Tomorrow, France," Ethan said, pulling the snug-fitting covers up over them both.

"France?" Overloaded, Jean began to sober up and feel anxious, but drifted off before she could think overmuch about their plans. Although she was tired and troubled, with Ethan's arms around her, she fell into a deep, dreamless sleep.

Chapter Twenty Three

Monday, 17th December, 2012
East Pontoon, Brighton Marina, Brighton, England

If fear is what you focus on. your focus becomes the fear.

Ethan's alarm went off an hour before dawn, but Jean didn't hear it. The lack of sleep, adrenalin, and booze had left her deeply asleep, almost as if she was afraid to wake-up.

He popped his head up above the hatch as dawn began to break, and saw an orange light glowing on the horizon. He looked down at Jean, who had become restless at the sound of the hatch when it was ratcheted up, above the galley. He turned the key on the control panel and the diesel engine roared into life. Smoke billowed from the rear of *Princess*, the cruiser's name embossed in gold leaf on her gleaming white hull.

As they slipped their mooring, he switched on the ship-to-shore radio, and slowly eased forward on the throttle. The vessel moved forward gracefully in the water; and Ethan maintained a steady pace until he was in the open sea, outside the Marina entrance. Then he opened up the throttle properly. The vessel surged forward, up and over a bow wave, swiftly reaching its maximum cruising speed as it cut through the green blue water ahead.

As the yacht leapt forward, it woke Jean. At first, she thought she was at home but became disoriented by the movement of the boat; and then she panicked, and wondered where she was. Finally, she remembered the previous day's events and felt butterflies in her stomach. Sick paranoia followed. She was deeply afraid.

Ethan sensed Jean was stirring and called down to her, "It's a beautiful day. Come on up, you'll feel better if you can focus on the horizon." He was right. She could sense the gentle to-and-fro movement of the hull as it glided through the water, and made her way out of the galley to join him on the deck above.

The Watcher stirred.
The machine gave off a flash of white light, which rippled across the channel in front of him.

Richanti stood on the eastern arm of the Marina wall, this was too good to miss, he thought. He took his mobile phone from his pocket.

Richanti focused on the eastern arm of the Marina wall, and took his mobile phone from his pocket. The escapees were in clear sight, heading through the exit into the Channel. Good! He smiled. This time, there was no escape for them. The yacht's name, *Princess*, was embossed on the boat in gold leaf. He checked the sea to the left towards the Seven Sisters and tip of

Beachy Head just visible and right to the pier, where the lights were still visible. Dawn was just on the verge of breaking.

This should be easy, Richanti thought. He rapped orders: "Do we know anyone on coastguard patrol? I want a ten mile radius up to Beachy Head cleared of shipping, except for Murray and his mate. And I want them alive. You're looking for a yacht called Princess."

-

As Ethan took in the beauty of the sunrise at sea and deep bellyfuls of sea air, there was a crackling on the radio. "Mayday, Mayday," a squeaky voice chirruped over the radio. "*Vessel Sun Clipper, Sun Clipper*, one mile west of Brighton Marina, seeks immediate assistance. Mayday." The crackle of the radio split whatever communication might have been possible between them and *The Princess*. Silence followed.

After a few moments of consternation on Ethan's part, another voice broke through the airwaves.

"This is the Sussex coastguard, Sussex coastguard. We're imposing an exclusion zone on all ships, that's *all* ships within a 10 mile radius of Brighton Marina."

"That's odd," Ethan muttered suspiciously. "How could they have found us so soon?" He guessed what was coming next. They were heading for the French coast at a speed of twenty-five knots, and it would take a couple of hours to complete the journey.

"Damn!" he muttered. "They'll easily find and intercept us."

Jean looked a little sheepish as her head popped out of the galley.

"Are we on the run again?" she asked.

"Looks like it."

"How did they find us?"

"I've no idea."

"I'm frightened, Ethan." Jean was still feeling rough after her drinks on the way to Brighton and the top up from the boat's stock, which she had sipped secretly from a coffee mug. Her worst fears were coming to the fore. Mornings never were her strong point.

Ethan looked at her and suddenly recognised the expression on her face. The 'tail' at the Golden Gate, the raid after the University explosion; and now fake Mayday calls to clear the sea of any potential help or witnesses. He'd got it! He understood exactly how Richanti's mob kept finding them.

"Given congruency, and true intent, others are attracted to help you in your quest," he said out loud. "Perhaps the opposite could be said for evil? Take negative emotions. Can an emotion like fear feed an evil purpose? "Of course!" he murmured. Then he turned to Jean and challenged her.

"I thought you were fearless, Jean."

"Well," she reflected, "we all have fears, don't we? We all have moments of doubt."

"Fear's the mind killer," he responded, "and maybe more."

She was puzzled. Ethan was talking in riddles again.

"I'm sorry," Ethan said contritely. It must be really hard for you. Anyway, we can't take chances."

He began to rummage through the bar. Jean was mystified. Wasn't it a little early for cocktails? Ethan produced a tumbler of Jack Daniels on ice and thrust it towards her.

"Drink up!"

"I knew being on the run could be pressured," she protested weakly, "but it's barely 9am!"

"Ethan, are you having one too?"

"Fear Jean, it's fear."

"What do you mean?"

"He sees your fear. That's how Richanti finds us," Ethan explained.

"It's reciprocal. Do good things and people come to help; do bad things and people help you, as well. Think good thoughts, and others pick up on it; think negative thoughts, be fearful, and he picks up on that too; and it feeds his purpose, his plan."

Jean looked a little guilty; she was beginning to understand.

"It's not your fault, you're simply being human. I can teach you to eliminate fear, Jean. It's an easy process. Most of the human race is 'running scared', but you actually have nothing to fear. Thought and energy are partners, try and remember that."

Jean's eyes had rolled back a little. Ethan gave it another shot.

"Life looks tangible, but life is a dream; our dreams or visions are the reality. So it's much simpler to just regard life as a game. Death is really the winning position. People view death the wrong way, and fear it.

"Right now, I have to give you something to help. The Jack Daniels will mask your fear. You see, we were fine until you sobered up. It's not ideal, I know, but it *is* necessary for you to get merry again."

This time, Jean didn't argue. She took a big gulp and, in a remarkably short time, she felt courageous again. "Hic." Her stomach protested: she had drunk too fast.

Jean reflected on what Ethan had said. It made sense. Every time she started to feel vulnerable and frightened, their luck had changed. She flashed back through her life and thought of how many times fear had the same effect: in her childhood, with Ted, her career, and her dreams. All taken away from her, all lost because of fear clouding her mind and denying her happiness. What had fear cost her? What would fear cost her in the future?

Then she thought back to what Ethan said recently, "You seem to be the key to it all; you're the common thread running through the whole course of events. Our future is determined by an exchange between you and him. I'm part of the story, but I have a feeling that, in the end, it comes down to the decisions you make."

That's it, she exulted. That's what I am here to learn - to combat my fear and save the world, or fail and lose. Just as she had control over the timeline lottery, win or lose, there was a particular decision in the future was hers alone to make. She was beginning to understand how important it was to take control of her own life and become an individual with her feet firmly on the ground.

Ethan put his head back above the hatch and saw a formation of three helicopters coming towards them. "Oh dear, this isn't good," he remarked quietly. "More! Drink some more, Jean!"

She forced another gulp. "Hic..." He nearly laughed.

"Ethan" she asked inquisitively. "You said you could help me deal with my fear." The desperation in Jean's voice was palpable. Fear had been the only fertile crop on her farm of life for too long. She had to sow better oats.

"Yes I can," he replied.

"How?" said Jean, struggling to keep up with him.

"Just think of something different. You've always had the power. Most people simply don't realise this. *You* control your thoughts. All of us do. So just think of something different; it's that simple. Everyone likes to make excuses, but you control your own mind, nobody else does. Make a decision *not* to be frightened, Jean; basically, it is that easy."

Ethan was distracted by the humming sound of helicopter rotors. It was too late; they'd been sighted. A formation of helicopters was flying on a direct course for them, like black bees buzzing on the skyline.

Thinking on his feet, Ethan grabbed a flare gun and pointed it just ahead of the formation. He pulled the trigger. The flare gun fired and left a trail of white smoke. It exploded in the sky like a firework and created a cloud of white powder ahead of the Hawk 'copters.

"That should make you think twice before coming any closer," Ethan said grimly. He had plenty more where that came from. He ran below deck. The ship's Mac was already booted up and displaying navigation information for their voyage. He pulled a memory stick out of his pocket and pushed it into the USB port of the computer. Then he opened up the ship's Mac's email, hit 'compose message' and typed in the address funkypunkfish@gmail.com. He attached the zipped documents to the message from his USB stick, and hit 'send'.

-

"Remember lads, take them alive." That was their order, the commander of the Hawk squad reflected as the white powder exploded in front of them and. They flew through it, blinded for a second by the smoke. Disoriented, he didn't panic. Instead, he used the adrenaline to sharpen his reflexes. The best form of defence was always attack. He could see the two targets on the bridge. Without giving it another thought, he armed a short range missile, aimed for the bow, and pulled the trigger... The missile released and tailed forward. Seconds later, it clipped the target.

Too late, Ethan saw a flash through the galley window as the missile was released from one of the Hawks. It exploded on the bow, and a blaze of light and sound struck the seas, taking the front of the vessel's hull out. With the yacht moving at speed, the stern rose up as the vessel ploughed down into the water and stopped dead.

Drink in hand, and shaken by the explosion, Jean had a flash of insight. In a final symbolic gesture, she pushed the drink away and exclaimed, "I don't need this shit!" The profanity made her feel empowered, despite the overwhelming stress of the situation. She knew who she was, and she knew what she deserved. It was not this, she thought. She felt strong and clear-headed, even as the cruiser broke in half. She had purpose, she had power; and she was no longer afraid.

Jean was thrown from the deck and flew through the air like a rag doll. Everything went black.

The helicopter formation split up and winch lines were dropped down to the wreckage. The hull was floating upside down, and Jean was clinging to it, seriously disorientated. Ethan was nowhere to be seen. The commander radioed in, "We have one of the two targets: the woman. Murray's missing or lost."

The Watcher listened to the rattle of radio communications and intervened. "Bring her back to base and don't lose her. I want to talk to her."

The commander passed on the command. "Murray's lost. Take the woman to the heliport at Heathrow and drop her on the company jet for JFK. We'll need a security detail to get her through to Manhattan. Clear her for diplomatic transfer. Do it now. Richanti wants to see her."

Chapter Twenty Four

Wednesday, 18th December, 2012
Nearly midnight, Manhattan Island, New York, New York, USA

Foster your individuality by accepting others' values and beliefs.

The watcher sensed a change in his fortunes, again. She had gained courage. All the same, he was a risk taker, and he liked to know his opposition; he was also inquisitive, and inclined to experimentation.

He might learn something from this one; she had been so much more difficult than the others. Problems and challenges weren't unknown to him, but she was an adversary of a special kind. He would find out where she cracked.

He cast back his mind over history to world wars, colonisation, and religious strife - all of them, his family's creations; all designed to disrupt and divide; all so effective.

And he thought about his own, forthcoming contribution to world history. It was only days away, now: the last and boldest manipulation of them all.

Chapter Twenty Five

Monday, 17th December, 2012
The English Channel, Sussex Coast, England

Failure is a major part of success.

Murray surfaced and gasped for air. He inhaled deeply, and filled his lungs with oxygen. Before going down again, though, he turned quickly and saw the sinking wreck of the Princess a few hundred metres away. The Hawks were still hovering above it, and had started to circle outwards. They were looking for survivors, of course.

As he swam down deep into the darkness, images of the different lives he had led passed through his mind. The time he had taken out on a beach in Thailand to learn skin diving had just proved to be invaluable.

He surfaced once more, his lungs bursting for air, but his demeanour calm to preserve valuable oxygen. He was much further away from the cruiser now. He couldn't risk being seen and bobbed down quickly with barely a lungful of air. He knew he had to swim as deep as possible to avoid detection from an infrared sweep.

When he next surfaced, he saw them winching Jean into the black body of the helicopter and was pleased they had found her. She was alive. Jean was alive! He went swiftly from elation to panic, though, as he pondered her fate. Richanti would either kill her, or want to see her; and since he ran his empire from an office on the 74th floor of a Manhattan skyscraper, that was probably the best place to head for. The Hawk turned and headed for the shoreline.

Then he looked north and saw the coast. They were only a few miles off. Shedding any unnecessary clothing, Ethan started swimming. The water was icy cold so he only had minutes, maybe ten or more, to complete his trip. Almost lost in the energy of the exercise, he smiled.

He trusted what he had learned through the many lives he had lived. Call it faith if you will, but it was really quite logical. The collective consciousness responded to the call of a better outcome. However, it was too little and too late to influence the Hawks. This no longer mattered as the timeline had reversed in their favour, again; he knew it and so, probably, did Richanti.

Jean was the key. It was all about fear. How stupid of him not to realise it, before. That was her test; and passing it had left the way open for infinite possibilities. She could now reap the rewards of whatever came next. Ethan had no idea what the next few hours would bring, but he was sure they would be interesting.

He ploughed on through the surf, exhilarated by the vitality that surged through him. The pain in his aching muscles was of little concern; his strength came from the positivity he felt within him. His belief that all would be well was the right fuel for his purpose, and nurtured his soul long enough to ensure survival in his sprint to safety.

As he swam, Ethan mulled over his life and the important shift in fate that had ended with a swim in the deep, dark, cold sea of the English Channel. After Jean left him stranded in Golden Gate Park, and their brief encounter, he had become driven; and he was driven at the cost of everything else. That had become his blueprint.

He poured hours, days, and years into his research. And yes, he made discoveries, but the truly amazing breakthroughs never began until the day he met a tramp in another park. Sometimes angels appeared in the strangest of places - if you could recognise them. Edwin was one of those angels. He could certainly do with an angel now. Edwin's words comforted Ethan now, like a mantra: 'Enjoy the journey.'

A homeless guy was trawling through rubbish bins for food, one day, and Ethan gave him his bento box. The man was not grateful. Rather, he was puzzled as to why Ethan would want to give up a perfectly good meal.

"You don't want it?" he asked, all matted hair, unshaven face, and dark, dirty hands.

Ethan replied, "I think it's better that you have it." The guy said nothing. Ethan was intrigued. If anything, he might have expected him to be grateful, but why would he be *puzzled*?

He sat down next to the street guy when he sat down on a bench to eat.

"What's your name?"

"Edwin," the tramp replied happily.

"Where do you live, Edwin?"

"In that bin over there; that's home." It was the Victoria Embankment, to be fair, not such a bad place to hang out: a prime piece of real estate, but Ethan was still puzzled. This guy seemed happy, *really* happy. How could that be?

"So what's your story?"

"What do you mean?"

"How did you end up on the street?"

The two men looked at each other and Edwin replied slowly, "You know, the usual thing. My parents weren't really supportive or loving. Although I went to a decent boarding school, I was pushed about and my home life was no fun. At one point, I was taken in by a guy who I thought was my friend, but he really just wanted a trophy. I wasn't happy, but I believed it was all I deserved and consoled myself with drugs."

"You take drugs, now?"

"No. Kicked them a few years back."

"So, why are you on the street?"

"I like it, I like the people."

Ethan found it hard to believe him. One more question he thought, choosing it carefully. "How did you kick the drugs?"

"I wasn't enjoying them any longer. I thought I did, in the early stages. Who wouldn't? Then I stopped enjoying them. I suddenly realised what I was becoming. I ripped a guy off for some money and, when I took his wallet, realised that I knew him; we'd been at school together. It was just too close to home for me. I'd stopped enjoying the journey, so I stopped the drugs."

Ethan pressed on. "So, why are you still on the street?"

"I'm enjoying the journey, and I'm writing a book. Look." Edwin pulled out a chain from around his neck with a memory stick attached to it.

"Everything you want to know about life, it's all on here. It's a bible within a book." Ethan made a grab for the stick, and Edwin added, "Ah. That's interesting. You want it. What's missing in *your* life?"

"I'm not happy," Ethan confessed. He had no idea why he suddenly confided in this man, but there was something calm, honest and trustworthy about him.

"Then lower your expectations," Edwin smiled. "Expect the worst and hope for the best. Happiness is the difference between what you expect and what you are. If something good happens, it's a bonus. I'm not saying lower your standards or goals, just your expectations."

"Look at me. I didn't think I was going to eat today but then you came along! You have to enjoy the journey or there's no point to life. Drive, ambition, and the things they give you, are completely unimportant unless you feel fulfilled. 'To be a miserable millionaire or a happy hobo?' That was my choice."

As he had done many times before, Ethan reflected again on the encounter with Edwin.

"That's it!" he exclaimed aloud, startling a seagull as he emerged jubilantly from the deep. This time, he understood what Edwin had meant when he said, 'Enjoy the journey'.

He remained lost in thought for a while longer... until he felt the current change. He was near the shore. He had made it. His feet touched down on sand, which quickly turned into pebbles.

"It's all about the journey," he smiled.

-

Ethan found himself in a current, which pulled him into an estuary. He speeded up his own efforts as the force of the tide, constrained by the narrowing mouth, dragged him forward at ever-increasing speed on a flood tide. The water deepened, and as he threw in a sideways burst of energy, his muscles came dangerously close to failing him in the cold water.

Done! He was on the riverbank with more stones and gravel underfoot. The warmth of the cool, crisp, sunny December morning felt like a cosy blanket and an open fire to him.

He clambered up the bank and lay flat on his back, exhausted from his challenge. While the sunshine dried him, he dived back into his own mind. He always had his best ideas when he was relaxed. So now, he had to get to

Manhattan, New York, but all he was wearing was a T-shirt and boxers. He had precious little but cunning to get to his destination.

He chuckled to himself. Yes, of course, the answer was there all the time. He had been too caught up in the drama.

"I wonder," he thought as he narrowed his eyes and focused: Piccadilly Circus, yesterday afternoon. *The machine issued a blast of blue light, and a kaleidoscope of colour filled his mind.*

Ethan had gone.

Chapter Twenty Six

Monday, 17th December, 2012
Above, The English Channel, Sussex Coast, England

No fear.

A savage rip tide buffeted the remains of the Princess. Jean's grip was failing, and she struggled to keep her grip on the broken hull.

"Back in the soup," she spluttered indignantly. "Just as I got my nerve back!"

The helicopter buzzed overhead like a demented bluebottle. A waiting winchman dropped a few metres ahead of Jean. He swam back to the boat, quickly clipping a harness around her before she slipped away. He gave the signal to pull them up.

As they rose, the water drained away from her body and clothes. She spotted Beachy Head in the distance: a notorious suicide spot. Still sunny, the cliffs reflected a pearlescent white shoreline that stretched for miles in either direction, down the south coast of England.

Jean's reflections on mortality led to panic. Where was her companion?

"Ethan," she screamed. "Where's Ethan?"

She bobbed around on the harness, and frantically tried to see if she could make him out in the wreckage of the Princess. Alarmed, the winchman restrained and steadied her while his partner, a guy in a helmet and heavy waterproofed suit, grabbed them and pulled them both inside the helicopter. The sound of the Hawk's blades was deafening.

Jean was given a jumpsuit to wear; then placed with her back against the wall and handcuffed. The winchman took off his dry suit to reveal combats. He stayed close by to watch over her.

Ethan's gone, she grieved silently. She had known him so briefly, yet it felt like a lifetime. She couldn't believe he had gone.

"Ethan!" she cried again. Then she gathered her wits, and spoke more calmly. "Aren't you going to search for the professor?"

"Too late, Miss. I'm afraid the sea's taken him. We've checked the infrared. There's nothing on the surface for miles."

"Taken by the sea..." she murmured. But then again, he had almost a thousand years under his belt from various lifetimes. Why did he have to give up, now, in this one? Her grief turned to anger; anger that she had to sort the mess out alone.

Then she remembered: she *was* strong now. Her last thought on the boat before the explosion was about a life without fear. No fear. She had finally decided to kick the crutch of a lifetime - to combat her fear and ditch the drink. It was, however, one thing to think differently, and know what she should do; it was quite another thing to act on it As Ethan predicted, before she could save the world, she had to save herself. That meant being congruent and authentic; and what did that mean for her, now?

She comforted herself with the thought that she'd managed to cheat death once, so maybe Ethan had done the same. Maybe the lesson she had learnt meant he was no longer part of the fate that she had seemed locked into. She tried to think positively about her predicament; that's what Ethan had taught her.

With her newfound strength, Jean turned her focus on her journey. Where were they taking her? Ethan had said she still had her time travelling power and insight. Jean thought about this. Richanti? She looked for Richanti in her mind and closed her eyes.

There was a flash of white coloured light.

Jean's forehead tingled. She could just make Richanti out, but saw him more clearly when she refocused on his intent. He was in his office on the 74th floor of the Demran Corporation skyscraper, so that meant New York City. She could see Manhattan Island in one direction and the Statue of Liberty in the other.

She observed him more closely. He looked concerned, anxious. She laughed. Him anxious? Now she really had found her power and it came in an instant.

"It was there all along. I just had to know how to look," she whispered to the man she had lost.

She had to think quickly if they were taking her to Richanti.

"I can't imagine it's going to end well," she told herself, but she was factual, not fearful. "It is what it is," she shrugged. A megalomaniac with a worldwide army of bully boys had decided that a single parent mum from the Midlands was his biggest threat. Jean eyed the winch man, who might be regarded as eye candy. He was muscular, fit, well built, and looked serious. She had a plan.

"So where are you taking me?" Jean asked.

"Let's keep this professional, please, Missus. You know I can't disclose that." The man looked away from her gaze, but she could see his thoughts.

Jean decided on another approach. It had to be personal.

"Does your wife know you play when you're away?" He blushed.

"How do..." the man remembered his brief. All the same, it appeared that Jean's hunch was true. He looked the type; neither insight nor time travel were required to work that out.

"You know how it is, being away a lot..." he remarked and looked sheepish.

"No, I don't know how it is. Since we're probably going to be in here together for a while, why not enlighten me."

The winchman saw no harm in that and started to talk, taken in by Jean's ruse.

"Well, we've been together since we were kids, really. She was my childhood sweetheart. She was crazy and fun at school, but seems to have lost it over the years."

"Kids, I guess," said Jean. "They may have ground her down until she ceased to feel crazy and ready for fun anymore. Then you lost your passion; and lost the reason you fell in love in the first place."

"Yes, that's about it," said the winchman.

There was a silence. Jean thought carefully of her next move. If I help this man, he'll help me back. He might not like the approach, but I'll try it anyway.

"Do you want a bit of advice?"

Jean enjoyed having an alpha male to deal with, and relationships were her strong point. She'd analysed her own for years. It was time to throw in another volley to see if she could make a friend of this man.

"If you cheat, you'll lose her; and you'll pay for that. Do you really want to end up with another man bringing up your kids?" That should do it, she thought. It was truthful enough. Hopefully, he'll make the association and may even change as a result.

The winchman laughed wryly at her directness, and reflected on what she had said. A surprising sadness washed over him. She was right, of course. He did love his wife. It was just that he'd forgotten. He spoke after a couple of moments.

"What are you going to New York for, anyway? He'd given away what Jean already knew. "Oh! Guess I've blown it... "

"Yes, you have." Jean smiled. "But don't let it bother you." Tactically, she didn't want him to feel on the left foot over his indiscretion. She added, "I knew anyway. They're taking me to see Richant."

She looked wistful. "What's he really like?"

"Only met him in few times, and he gave me the creeps. He's pleasant on the surface, a really bright chap; and very friendly. There's another side to him, though, and you don't see it coming until it's too late. He'll invite you out, wine and dine you, and then, when you least expect it, he'll stab you in the back. He's capable of murder. I've seen him do it quite coldly. He'll have someone in his way removed: no emotion, none at all."

"So how did you get involved?" Jean asked.

"In too deep. He educated my kids, employed us all, and put a roof over our head. In short, he looked after us: the works. I used to be in the Army and it wasn't that different. He operated in the same way: you work and live together in your own little world." He paused and scratched his head.

"It's just that you're batting for the other side. I'm a mercenary. I do the work, whatever it is, and then I get paid."

Jean had no answer for this. It was only natural to try to justify your life, she thought. It saved you dealing with the reality of the situation; and of course, she'd just had first hand experience of this. "One more thing," she said slowly.

"No I've said more than I should have".

Jean knew he had, and it showed her how much more powerful she could be when she used her brain in unison with her feelings.

"Maybe," she acknowledged. But if I could get you, your kids and wife away from the Demagodran, would you leave?"

"Of course I would." He looked curiously at Jean.

"Then that's my answer. Free will and a world without fear. Isn't that worth fighting for?"

The winchman dwelt on her words for a brief moment but dismissed the opportunity, fearful of the approach. Better to stay exactly where I am, he concluded.

The helicopter was making its descent. She felt it bank and dive and looked out the window. It was Heathrow Airport, London.

The winchman looked at her and said, "Terminal Six."

"Terminal Six? I thought Heathrow only had five terminals?"

"It's the private jet terminal. Lucky you."

"Hmm, New York," Jean remarked factually.

"Yes, correct." A sense of comradeship had crept into their relationship.

"Are you coming with me?"

"No. My job's done."

The winchman hesitated. Jean knew that what came next would be important. Ethan had taught her well. 'The collective responds to good intent with aid,' he would say.

"There's one thing you need to know about the Demagodran," the winchman added carefully. "Take Richanti and his family out, and you take out the Demagodran." Jean stayed silent.

"They say he's not human. In fact, a lot of people think he's an alien or at least has alien blood, which might account for him being so cold-blooded. It's a myth amongst us all. Make of it what you will, but my bet is he's part of a bloodline that spans generations, with him at the top.

"Trust nobody," the winchman urged, "Richanti has henchmen everywhere in the world! There's nowhere you can hide; and nobody you can trust. That's his weakness, though, the love of power - power coupled with greed. Offer him that and you can control him."

Jean knew some of this from Murray, of course - she still thought of Ethan as 'Murray' half the time.

She also saw that her thinking was much clearer than ever before. She dwelt on his words and a plan emerged. She concentrated by focusing and directing her thoughts to her third eye, as Ethan called it.

She experienced an illuminating flash of white light in her mind.

"This is where you get off," the winchman interrupted. He looked closely at her face. She looked serene and pensive when she opened her eyes; and met his with a steady gaze. He returned the look, cautiously. This particular woman was no walkover.

"Thanks for the ride," she replied with a sunny smile. She felt a spring and confidence in her step. The winchman was slightly confused, and would like to have talked with her some more, but events intervened.

The door opened directly onto tarmac, with a just a few steps to the gangway of a gleaming, private jet. There were five small windows in its side. A rather officious-looking man stood in the entrance. The jet engines were running. In different circumstances, she'd have been excited about visiting New York.

Jean was transferred without handcuffs to the jet, which had a narrow cabin. Inside, there were four large, cream, leather chairs with walnut tables sitting in between them. There was nobody else but her guard and the pilot on board. He insisted on handcuffing her to her seat as soon as they were inside the cabin. Why? Where could she go?

They sat face-to-face, if not eyeball-to-eyeball, and she wondered if he'd insist on accompanying her to the toilet. Fortunately, the need didn't arise. The co-pilot came in from the cockpit to close the door, greeted them with a nod, and returned to fire up the engines.

They taxied forward almost immediately. There was a brief pause until the control tower gave the okay. Then, they turned left onto the Small Plane Runway, and the jet increased its thrust. Minutes later, they hurtled forward: a quick lift, climb and bank, and they were tracking north on a direct course to JFK and New York City.

Jean had plenty of time to reflect. Indeed, all this travelling had given her more time than she was used to for pondering life and its different pathways. Today, however, she was in completely uncharted waters. Okay, they were uncomfortable but not life-threatening.

She wasn't used to being on top, ahead of the pack, top of her game. She'd become used to life as an underdog. This new perspective on life - looking from the top down - was slightly unnerving. Something had changed for her on the Princess. It was a small insight, but a massive revelation. It was almost as if she was a different person. In her new life, fear was not part of the equation. She could feel herself growing as she reconsidered everyone and everything in her life from a different perspective.

Other images came to mind. She wasn't a rider anymore, trying to control and manipulate her environment or those with control over her. It was more like actually being a horse; one free to charge ahead at full speed. She was running with the herd; first among the herd.

She understood, now, how it was that Ethan could remain calm all the time, why nothing appeared to faze him. He was not alone; that was the whole point. He had the resources of the universe at his disposal, and the collective consciousness as his aid.

Provided that he focused on a common good, it would indeed come to his aid. It occurred to her that he probably had an alternative up his sleeve when he disappeared. It was logical. 'Have faith,' he would say. She missed him sorely. But after all, how could he have disappeared without trace? Jean's instinct told her that he *was* alive.

-

The flight to JFK took seven hours and soon passed. At some point, the guard got her some sandwiches and a bottle of water. Jean spent most of the time drifting in and out of thought, taking a walk through her life. She began with her earliest memories; pondering on how she had arrived at this point in her life, 'Just Jean, superhero.'

The jet began to descend. She could see the island of Manhattan in all its glory: silver towers punching high above the horizon; and somewhere in the middle of it all was Richanti, the master puppeteer, orchestrating his plan.

The jet touched down and taxied to the terminal building. Jean spied a slick black limousine with a small lady on its bonnet heading over the tarmac towards them. The door of the jet opened soundlessly. Fresh air and sun filled the cabin. The guard motioned her to the door, and Jean walked towards the exit. He released her cuffs before she stepped through the door, and walked down the gangway. The driver of the limousine got out to open the door for her. The car was a Rolls Royce Phantom, she noticed with a small smile. She knew who was meeting her.

Stooping, she stepped into the limo and sank gratefully into the inviting, soft black leather. The door closed behind her and she gazed with interest at the individual already in the limousine. It was Richanti, of course. They locked onto each other's gaze for a few second.

"At last. Pleased to meet you, Jean."

It was just as the winchman had described. Richanti was supremely pleasant and amiable. This should be fun, the new Jean decided. Fearless, and calmly in control, she delivered the first serve.

"How can I help you, Doctor, or should I call you Stuart?"

She had met him before, of course, albeit in another lifetime; she was prepared.

Chapter Twenty Seven

Monday, 17th December, 2012
Cuckmere Haven, Sussex Coast, England

Direct your future or others will direct it for you.

He looked down the valley and out to sea from his vantage point on the headland. As predicted, the whole incident unfolded like an action movie. There was the motor cruiser leaving Brighton; presumably, with the Marina in the distance until the cruiser was a few miles off shore; and then the intercept from the Hawks, followed by an explosion that disabled and sank the vessel.

A single body was lifted from the wreckage: Jean, he supposed. There was a short wait until a swimmer emerged from the flood tide at the junction of the Cuckmere River and Cuckmere Haven's estuary. All as predicted, but how could Murray have engineered this; and why? It didn't make sense to host such an elaborate event just for his amusement. There was only one way to find out. The mufti-uniformed man made his way carefully down the chalky headland to the estuary to meet his host.

Murray clambered up the bank and lay flat on his back, exhausted from a swim that would have challenged younger and fitter men. His eyes were closed, and he was glad, although not entirely surprised, to hear footsteps pounding across the pebbled beach. The steps came closer and closer until the stranger stood directly over Murray.

"Took your time, Ted," Murray said. He opened his eyes to see Ted standing above him.

"What was all that about?"

"The future unfolding," Murray explained calmly. Ted was none the wiser, but wisely kept his mouth shut.

"We don't have a moment to waste. Did you sort out the travel arrangements I asked about?"

"Yes, if we leave now, we'll just make London Heathrow for our flight."

"Our flight?" Murray asked.

"Yes. If you think I'm going to miss the action you're mistaken. I got counterfeit paperwork for both of us. We should be able to slip out before they have time to trace us. Jean was *my* wife, after all. I still owe her. Just tell me one thing."

"What's that?"

"How did you know I was going to get gunned down so fast?"

"Call it a hunch."

At this point, Murray has no time and even less desire to explain himself fully. Ted would find it difficult to understand that he had travelled back in time to reverse his fate. Anyway, to his mind, some things needed to be kept secret; the 21st century was definitely not ready for them yet.

Meanwhile, Ted thought back to yesterday afternoon. He had just released Murray and Jean in Piccadilly Circus when Murray came back, out of the crowd, and tackled him to the ground. The shots missed him by inches, hitting a tourist behind him, and taking him out. It made front-page news: odd for a murder in London.

"I'm simply glad you did or I would have been toast."

Murray put out his hand and Ted helped him up. Two unlikely companions, but with one common goal; and that was to help their friend: the ex-wife of one and lover of the other, Murray mused, although he wasn't sure that Ted was entirely aware of the intricacies of their relationship.

As they had a date with a 747 bound for JFK, they made haste, and returned back down the valley to the car park on the edge of the A259.

Chapter Twenty Eight

Monday, 17th December, 2012
Demagodran HQ, Manhattan Island, New York, New York, USA

Best friends make you better.

It was late Monday afternoon in Manhattan. The rush hour was in full flow and it was an easy task to sneak into the HQ of the Demran Corporation. Access to the 74th floor would, however, be different - it was restricted. This was Richanti's executive level and boardroom, one floor short of the penthouse, which comprised an additional two levels. The penthouse was Richanti's private residence when he was in New York.

The lift went as far as level forty-two. Security was tight: nigh on impossible beyond that point. Ted had thought ahead, and planned to take the stairwell to the roof, and then force entry via the roof conduit into a mezzanine, which overlooked the three floors.

"One of the advantages of being one of the trusted is that it's pretty easy to hack the security from inside, "he said with a wicked grin.

Nevertheless, if Ted could get them in, he was honest about saying he had no idea how to get them out again, once the alarms were tripped. Richanti had a small army resident in the building. Any alert would see the whole building locked down and searched. In a skyscraper, it was easy to cover the exits, all of which were on the ground floor and in the basement.

Ted beckoned to Ethan. They entered the stairwell on the parking level, where they waited outside the door for someone to exit. As a steady stream of employees left the building, they quickly seized an opportunity to enter and take the lift to the 72nd floor.

From the lift exit, they took the 'escape exit' signs and headed for the stairwell. Beyond that point, all the doors were locked. With Ted's access codes, they tapped into the key pads, and eventually came out onto the roof. This consisted of an array of air conditioning units, communications equipment, and a helipad.

The view from the top was stunning. There's not much competition in Manhattan from the roof in a building with 77 floors. Lower down, smaller skyscrapers jostled for attention as they rose into the atmosphere from the street below. The Statue of Liberty looked tiny across the Hudson River, although the green belt of Central Park was clearly visible at the upper part of Manhattan Island.

"God exists up here," Ted exclaimed.

"Just up here?" Ethan quizzed. "Doesn't he spend much time at street level, then?"

"You know what I mean. You're the scientist." Ted didn't prolong that conversation. He wanted to explore a different matter.

"Do you mind telling me how you and Jean met?" Ted asked, while he unbolted an access panel to the air-conditioning unit he had located and recognised from the building's blueprints.

"Well, that's not altogether straightforward," Ethan parried.

"Let's just say that she found me first, when we were both students."

Ted's brow wrinkled and he looked confused. Sometimes Ethan amazed him, other times he made no sense at all. To Ted's knowledge, Jean had an aversion to studies. She rarely attended school when she was young. "She must have changed a lot then!" Ted said incredulously. I always thought she was just a dumb broad.

Ethan shrugged. The idea of someone in your future coming back to influence and alter your past was not easy for anyone to get a handle on; even for him before he found his own place in the universe.

Basically, he saw it like a major alteration to a building. When you added the penthouse, it needed a lift from ground level. The future was the top of the building and the past was the foundation. Time was not fluid but played out in between the two points. You can see its beginning, middle and end, and can tinker with it, but you cannot fundamentally change the infrastructure.

It was not until Ethan saw it all as 'present time' that things started to make sense to him. Past, present and future all merged into one.

As an afterthought, Ethan observed, "Ted really does pick his moments: no wonder Jean ditched him."

"Uh huh, that's it," said Ted. The question about Jean no longer required an answer because the task before them had forced a change of subject. The panel was released. He positioned the panel so that it leant against the unit and was not *obviously* dislodged. Then they both crawled into the space inside the air conditioning pipes and shuffled along on their knees a few feet until they hit an access panel. Ted lifted it to reveal, below them, a landing that ran around the top of a large atrium. The atrium extended across three levels of the building. They could hear voices below them.

Cautiously, they lowered themselves onto the floor where they could hear voices. To avoid detection, they stretched out fully so the drop to the floor was less than a foot. The mezzanine had a low balustrade and its purpose seemed more ornamental than functional. The two rescuers placed their backs against it so they couldn't be seen from the levels below them. They were all ears.

The man's voice was articulate and well spoken; amiable, even.

"Can't you see that wealth is power? In the old days we used to fight, but we've learnt it is much easier to control the economics. The World Wars were so horrific that people wanted to avoid such a situation again at all costs; and it did cost. I use public fear to my advantage, that's all.

"We're a global corporation, shared between family members, and we control approximately seventy-five percent of the world's wealth, and ninety percent of the power, influencing all of the major G8 countries in one way or another.

The newspapers are toys in comparison to the network operating within governments on a worldwide basis. It's so much more effective if we're invisible. Become visible, and you become a target; your days are numbered."

"So what of this alien bloodline?"

Ethan and Ted looked at each other, recognising the voice instantly. In tandem, they mouthed, "Jean."

"It existed alright; but 'little green men' would be far-fetched. I know nothing more than you do, other than the fact that most of us have some alien content. We have found over the years that the more alien 'genes' - for lack of a better description - anyone has, the higher their ability to overcome psychological challenges and barriers in life in order to direct others. Aliens bring an extra dimension of intelligence, really."

"Moving on from there, using the latest technology, I've been able to turn this 'extra chromosome', and you might say it allegorically, into an exact science. I have almost a full set, but I was born naturally; my parents didn't have the luxury of the latest techniques that science could bring to my birth.

Of course, the number of babies required to get the right combination was significant. My parents ran a breeding programme using surrogates and kept the offspring with the higher percentages of genes."

"What happened to the other babies?"

"Oh don't concern yourself with that; they all found good homes."

Ethan didn't like the sound of that.

"So I have a role for you, my dear. With your talent..." Richanti switched topic.

"Murray's machine?"

Ethan was concerned; it was supposed to be secret.

"Ethan..." Jean replied. "But he's dead, isn't he. Did you find him?"

"No, afraid not." Richanti made no attempt to qualify his statement.

"I have it, but I have no idea how to use it - the machine, that is."

"But you bombed the institute; the machine's in pieces."

"Now, come on. A man like Murray, with his resources, having only one working version? No. I don't think so. Anyway, I know where it is. It's in New York, in a vault in the basement of the United Nations."

Ethan nearly fell from his perch and Ted looked across in alarm. He objected roundly, if mutely. "His machine! How did he know about the copy? Only a handful of people knew, and they were all close to him. Oh dear, Richanti's network runs deeper than I had guessed."

"So, I'd like your help," Richanti continued smoothly. "If you wouldn't mind, of course. I know you've been time travelling. You're not really *Just Jean*, are you? As you'd like me to believe..."

There was a pause. Ethan sensed that Jean was uncomfortable. He was working on a pincer movement with her, he thought, and she was tougher than Richanti had imagined. She'll hold out, Ethan felt confident of that, but Richanti was slippery. He was up to something. For the first time, Ethan was *really* concerned. He didn't like surprises; he was only human, after all.

Strange. He hadn't felt like this for a while: concerned, he remembered the feeling. He realised Jean was the key. It wasn't he, himself that he was concerned about but Jean. Life was easy when he had only himself to worry about but to balance the needs of another; that was hard.

"I have no idea what you are talking about Mr Richanti," Jean said formally. "I was the cleaning supervisor," she said pointedly, "not the inventor."

"We'll see. Why not make yourself comfortable. Tea? I know you're fond of a brew."

"No thanks," she replied.

Richanti seemed to have switched on a monitor. There was a static crackle as the monitor sprang to life and Ethan heard a girl's voice talking in the background.

Jean gulped. "Ocean? I'd expect nothing less from you. Harm her and I'll haunt you until the end of time."

Ted gestured in Richanti's direction. Ethan clamped a hand over his mouth and held him back. "If you make the wrong move now, your daughter's as good as dead. Hold your anger back until later; you'll have your moment."

"Now, now, nobody is harming anyone," Richanti said, pausing significantly for a moment or two. "Well, not yet."

The guy was a monster, Ethan realised; aghast. He looked at Ted and whispered, "What's the plan?"

"It is over to you now, Murray. I got you here. You have to finish it; and it had better be fast. He's got my daughter, too, remember."

Ethan surveyed the mezzanine area. There were spiral staircases in opposing corners. He motioned to Ted to take one and he took the other, giving Ted further instructions before they split up.

"On my signal, distract Richanti. There's a small chance I can take him down before he can sound the alarm."

Richanti and Jean were talking again.

"Do you expect me be afraid of you, Richanti? If that's your game, you've picked the wrong woman."

"That's my girl!" Ethan and Ted mouth in unison, each of them nodding approvingly. They saw each other across the floor like mirror images; and realised, almost telepathically, that they were in thrall to the same woman.

"Okay, so you have my daughter," Jean said, keeping her cool. There was a considerable pause while each of them sussed the other's strengths and weaknesses out.

Ethan wondered what would come next. He needed to pick his moment carefully, but was slightly distracted by what Jean was saying.

"Shall I call you Stuart, or even better still, brother?"

Ethan was about to jump down the stairs and signal to Ted. What Jean was saying computed, but didn't quite fit. "Brother...?"

"Brother...?" Richanti repeated.

"Yes, Ocean's your niece. I've done a good job on her, don't you think?"

Richanti went an ashen colour, and his brain went into overdrive while he tried to work it out. Then anger set in. More than anything, he hated being crossed.

"You're lying!"

"Me lie? That's funny, coming from you. Of course, you'd never lie, would you? What happened to the babies in your parents' breeding programme, Richanti? Of course you know."

It was a guess on Jean's part, but apparently it was accurate. Richanti's face had flushed red with anger.

"Sister..."Ethan looked at her. He understood, now, how sheepish she had looked when he told her about her alien genes.

"It looks as if a bitch got over the wall when they made you!" Richanti gasped incredulously. "You can't be... they were all, all..." His voice sounded uncertain and confused.

"All murdered," Jean replied. "Well this bitch has a full set of alien genes. I'm no mongrel, like you, so answer to me now."

"No." Richanti reached for his desk.

Ted saw Richanti going for the desk drawer and made his move. He'd been trained for this, after all, and that was his wife out there.

Richanti pulled a gun, cocked it, pointed it at Jean, and pulled the trigger. As he did, Ted launched himself in front of Jean. The sound reverberated round the atrium: a gunshot blast, distinct and deadly.

Ted fell to the floor clutching his chest. He smiled back at Jean and said, "I usually wear a flak jacket." He was still smiling; smiling up at her. I guess we're even now. I love you, Jeannie. I always did. I just forgot for a decade or two. Forgive me." Ted's eyes closed shut. He was smiling as he went.

Chapter Twenty Nine

Monday, 17th December, 2012
Richanti's Penthouse, Manhattan Island, New York, New York, USA

Walking on water is easy if you know where the stumps are.

Richanti seized his opportunity and ran towards the lift. The lift door sensor opened just in time to avoid interrupting his hurried exit. He turned round, still brandishing the gun, and the lift doors closed.

Jean and Ethan turned to each other, and then back to Ted. He was motionless but serene.

"I thought Ted had died already," Jean wept. "Now I have to mourn him all over again." A tear rolled down her face. "He wasn't all bad, I guess, but he didn't *owe* me anything."

"Well Jean, technically, he simply died *again*, today. I managed to bring him back, but only for a while. Some things were meant to be, regardless of how attractive it might be to manipulate them."

Ethan had turned lecturer and philosopher with his audience of one. "Ted dying to save us was his destiny; his life purpose, if you will. And yours is unfolding day-by-day."

Jean looked at Ethan sternly. "You're so damned uncompassionate! "

"Death is just the beginning," he said gently, "not the end. You had no power to interfere with the outcome for Ted, Jean, and nor had I. All that I managed was to put his death off by a couple of days. If we try to bring him back and re-run the day, some other tragedy will befall him. Remember, everything is played out; everything has happened already. Time is circular... or a spiral, when you get it right."

Jean nodded, and began to realise how a professor works with his pupils.

"Come, I have a plan, but we must be quick."

Ethan led Jean up to the Mezzanine floor and, from there, into Richanti's private quarters. Jean was shocked. It was the epitome of bad taste. The decor was high-class trash, although the quality of the art works could hardly be faulted. There was an original Van Gogh, admittedly tiny, of a purple Iris; and what appeared to be the original canvas by Rubens, *A Massacre of the Innocents.*

"That's apt!" Jean grumbled, although she had nothing to pin the feeling on. Not yet. She continued to give a caustic, running commentary as they explored the penthouse.

Her rant was partly grief, Ethan supposed.

"There's strange ugliness about this place," she remarked in horrified tones. "I mean, even if it does contain some of the most beautiful art ever created. But essentially, it's simply a collection of the most *expensive* art ever created. Each piece probably reaches double figures, in the millions. There's enough wealth in one corridor to pay off the debt of a small, third world country for a whole year."

Jean paused to wonder why they were going further up when the exit was on the ground floor. She continued to examine the decor as they walked through another corridor. This, she guessed correctly, was designed to intimidate people. It led to a large lounge with several leather Chesterfields and a panoramic view of Manhattan through a crystalline picture window, running from floor to ceiling.

It was getting dark and the neon lights of 'the city that never sleeps' were beginning to twinkle. "Why are you giving me an art appreciation course when Richanti is probably sounding the alarm and sending his bully boys to kill us as we speak?" Jean grumbled. It seemed perverse reasoning to her.

"We have a few minutes yet. You learn a lot from the way people live, and what they choose to have around them," Ethan replied.

He paced round the room, checking everything out and then steadied himself, standing still for a moment just taking in the environment. His eyes fell on a rather unusual-looking bookcase at one end of the room. It looked misplaced. He walked over to and studied the shelves more closely. Jean followed him, wondering what he was looking for. She stood behind him.

"There, look there!" She pointed to a shelf at waist height.

"How do you know what I'm looking for?" Ethan asked.

"No idea," said Jean, continuing on, "but look at that shelf. It's more highly polished than the rest and completely free of dust. I don't know who Richanti hires in for cleaning, but they should be fired."

"Yes, you're right. Why didn't I see that?"

"Because you've never had to clean up after yourself, I suppose," Jean replied smugly.

Ethan pulled out some of the books and, right behind them, was a small panel with a red flashing light and a key pad. "I wonder what the access code is?" Ethan looked disheartened.

Jean sounded even more smug. "If I can win the lottery, I should be able to crack the code. Hold on a moment." She focused on the panel and, in her mind, saw Richanti punching in a code earlier that morning.

"Try 21122012."

"Interesting date," Ethan said drily, and tried the code. The bookcase started to revolve and revealed another office beyond. "We conceal what's important to us," he added.

As Jean and Ethan moved inside, they were confronted with the real face of Richanti's power: his control room. There was a bank of monitors and CCTV monitors for the apartment and boardroom - some of them more like bugging devices. On one side of the room, monitors displayed stock and commodity prices; elsewhere, breaking news was streaming in from nearly every country on the globe, East and West alike.

There was one screen, however, that was not quite in keeping with the others. It had a countdown button on it, reading '4 days', and a set of statistics that made no sense to either of them. There were also four titles, presumably related to operating levels: *Oasis readiness indicators, Food stocks, Arms inventory* and *Fuel levels*.

The decor was very different to the room they had come from. It was dark and gothic-looking with what appeared to be family portraits dotted around the room. They went back generations, most of them portraying creepy-looking folk. The panel closed behind them.

"What is this place?" Jean asked.

"It's his control room. The boardroom is just a circus. This is where the real decisions are made. I've known about his secret power hub for some time, but never had the opportunity to look at it before."

"And what's the Oasis?" It was that name which had conjured up her visions of Armageddon.

"It's preparation for the aftermath, when Precession occurs. There are big changes coming. Unfortunately, nobody can predict exactly when they will come, let alone *what* will happen. We should know in four days' time.

"The number of earthquakes, volcanoes and tsunamis in recent months is no coincidence, though. Nor are the outbreaks of human violence around the world, the famines; and the hysteria in financial institutions as whole countries slide into mountains of debt they can no longer repay.

Nor is it any accident that so many governments are bankrupt. Richanti began to execute his plan a decade ago; he's been reaping them of cash, siphoning it off into his personal project: the Oasis.

"Anyhow, the Precession of the Equinoxes occurs at the solstice point of 21-22 December. This is an astronomical line-up, which comes around once every 26,000 years. It links to long-term sunspot cycles and NASA projections[1] for 2012 corroborate this.

"The night of the winter solstice ends both the Mayan Long Count Calendar and the long period of Precession. The Sun will stand exactly at the southern 'star-gate' crossing point of the ecliptic, at the centre of the Galaxy.

"On this date, anyone looking at the Sun will also be looking directly towards the core of the Milky Way, the place where astronomers say there is a black hole.

"According to one well-known researcher in Mayan prophecy, the dominant message is that galactic synchronisation will bring humanity to a point of radical and threatening change, but with a positive potential."

Jean ignored the theory and came back like a terrier. "What aftermath?"

"The Middle East is where Richanti has his focus; has done for years. He's been building resources there and buying off dictators. It is predicted

---

[1] Gerald Benedict, The Mayan Prophecies for 2012, ISBN 978-1-907486-11-1: Acknowledgements - Px -NASA were kind enough to respond to my questions about sunspot activity and changes in the Earth's magnetic field during 2012.

that, after the impact of Precession, the Middle East will be relatively untouched by the holocaust; and its climate will become more temperate.

"Richanti plans to capitalise on Precession, and dominate the globe from the Middle East. That's why he's pouring a massive amount of money and resources into the region; actions that, on the face of it, make him look charitable. In fact, he's simply getting ready for his main assault on the planet.

"There will be forced emigration because of Precession; and slavery or citizenship, depending on your resources. Richanti intends to cream-off off the lion's share of the wealth. As the effects of Precession unravel, Richanti will sell ringside seats to his new world order. It will be extortion on a grand scale."

"Well, if his family killed their own children to further themselves, I guess he's capable of anything. But what does that make me?"

"Heh!" Ethan half-choked. "Look, you weren't born evil. Richanti was *made* that way. You might have a full set of alien genes but, in the end, it's what you're trying to be that counts. The crucial element is that you've chosen to use your abilities for good."

"So far. What if I start swallowing small rodents whole, and shedding my skin periodically?"

"Come on, Jean. There's very little chance of that happening. Richanti was born into - and brought up by - a family of psychopaths. You haven't had the same upbringing; in fact, you're his exact opposite."

"My father was an alcoholic."

"It doesn't make you a bad person, Jean... or your father, for that matter."

"So you're saying I could use my time talent for good? Being alien doesn't necessarily mean evil genes?"

"That's right. For all we know, most alien genes derive from good-mannered, peaceful aliens. This preconception with little green men and reptilian monsters is fantastical. Humanity has simply put them to bad use."

He put his hands on Jean's shoulders. "Human beings are fundamentally flawed, biologically tempted, and drugged by dopamine shots and adrenalin rushes. I'm surprised that we function at all. I think the alien genes contribute to the cerebral part of us; and have allowed us to evolve from the forest floor."

Jean looked up at Ethan, curiously. "Uh huh, that's it?" Ethan had spied a laptop lying on Richanti's desk.

"Right," he responded in a slightly distracted way. He added, "And now we must go. This is what I came here for."Ethan snatched up the laptop then turned back to Jean. They returned the way they had come.

As they went, he checked out the room beyond on CCTV. There were guards in the lounge outside and they obviously knew nothing about Richanti's secret study. That was no comfort, though: the two intruders were trapped.

"What do we do now?" Jean frowned.

"We watch and wait. They don't know that we're here and Richanti isn't with them."

As they watched the CCTV images flick through, Jean caught a shot of Ted being stretchered out of the boardroom. Ethan diplomatically distracted her.

"Let's see what we have here." He booted up the Mac Book and clicked on Outlook. The icon bounced as the programme loaded. "Richanti's address book might be entertaining."

There were around 1400 contacts and Ethan speed read through the list. "Quite impressive," he remarked, his eyebrows raised, but his face also registered concern. "Richanti's network runs deep and wide."

Jean looked over his shoulder, and said, "Just because they're on a list doesn't mean they're part of Richanti's tribe. The President of United States is there. Tell me he's not on Richanti's side or I'll give up."

"Not directly, I agree. Being on the list doesn't condemn you, but just look at this filter. There's a file reference, too. All my known contacts within the Demran 'bully boy network' are on that list. It's pretty compelling stuff. I think that links to the inner circle; he has a file on them all."

As he talked, Ethan exported the list and emailed it to funkypunkfish@gmail.com. He also did a scan for the file references and zipped up all of the documents, emailing them to the same address.

"Okay, what's it like in the outside world?" he asked Jean. The CCTV activity on the scan appeared to be focused purely on the boardroom. Everyone had gone from the external lounge.

"Time to go!" Ethan grinned and punched '21122012' into the key pad. The bookcase rotated back into its open position. Jean and Ethan walked through and he used the code again to close the door. They heard voices downstairs.

"If I'm not mistaken, this will take us to the roof. There's a spiral going up to a landing." Ethan grabbed Jean's hand and guided her up the spiral. They took the exit onto the rooftop. There was a light breeze and glorious sunshine.

"So, now where?"

Ethan gestured in the direction of the helicopter pad. There was a Hawk sitting on the pad. It was empty and there didn't seem to be anyone else on the roof.

"You want me to go in that with you?" Jeans asked in amazement. "Is there anything you can't do?" She added, "Maybe even walk on water?"

"Walking on water's easy if you know where the stumps are," Ethan smiled at her over his shoulder. "We're off to The White House."

"The White House!"Jean exclaimed, her voice rising. "Have you forgotten about Ocean? That monster's got my daughter."

"Your daughter's safe and sound, Jean. It was just a bluff on Richanti's part. You should give Ocean more credit; she'll be bigger than you are one day soon."

Jean looked puzzled. "Okay, I'll go with that. I trust you. I wonder what the tea's like at The White House."

Chapter Thirty

Tuesday, 18th December, 2012
Helipad, Demagodran HQ, Manhattan Island, New York, New York,
USA

Truth has a power of its own.

Ethan broadcast the Hawk's call sign and intent to the Manhattan Regional Airport air traffic controller. "Manhattan ATC, Hawk, Delta Echo Mike Romeo November, on Demran Corporation Tower. Request clearance for northbound departure Manhattan Island. Over."

"You are cleared for immediate take off, Delta Echo Mike Romeo November."

"Demran Corporation built the airport, so it's pretty easy to get clearance," Ethan explained.

"Are we just going to fly straight into The White House?" Jean asked incredulously. "And then tell the president that the most powerful family on the planet needs to be put behind bars."

"That's about it," Ethan confirmed.

"I think you're a little misguided, this time," Jean retorted. "They'll shoot us down before we get near the building."

"That's why you're going to phone ahead to let them know we're coming," Ethan said."The number's on the laptop." He had it open on a small seat between them. "See, here."

"A laptop?" Twenty-first century technology was not Jean's strong point, but she was becoming a fast learner. She opened up the Mac and it booted up instantly. Ethan guided her. "Click 'O' on the bottom row. It will start bouncing when it's loaded. Then click on 'Contacts' and search for 'President'."

"What happens if the President's in on Richanti's little game?" Jeans asked, concerned.

"I'll take a risk that he's on our side. He's too much in the public eye to be of real interest to Richanti. Besides, Richanti had no personnel file on him. That's good enough for me."

Jean entered 'President' and clicked the search button.

"Presidential Office, The White House. There's a number and PA contact. "There's a phone number, too, but we don't have a phone."

"You should have a network connection. Use Skype; we're not too high up."

"Sky Pe?" Jean asked. "What's that?"

"Click on the Blue 'S' symbol at the bottom and look for The President in those contacts."

Jean did as Ethan suggested. When she clicked on the S, it did bounce again; and before Jean had a chance to click on a contact, a message popped up on the screen.

"The computer's talking to me, Ethan.

The message read: "Have you got instructions on how to access the machine yet? Did she give in or did you have to take the girl?"

"I guess 'her' means me; not very polite, these computers."

Ethan interjected, "That's not good news. It's not the computer, it's someone on The White House staff. Hmmm. Okay, so be it. We'll have to change our plan."

"You're changing a plan that you haven't told me about," Jean observed wryly.

"Type this," he said, ignoring Jean's tone. He dictated, "Yes, got what we need. I'm bringing her in. Can you clear us with security for a landing on the lawn? We're coming in the Hawk, call sign DEMRN."

"Hang on", said Jean. "I can't type that fast."

"Got what we need. Bringing Jean in. Cleared for landing. Hawk, call sign DEMRN."

"You alright?"

"Yes perfect," Jean replied in a miffed tone.

"You're getting the hang of this. Fun, isn't it," Ethan said blandly, turning away to hide a grin.

"Can you order us some tea (and coffee for you), please" Jean asked politely. She fell back in her seat, startled, when the computer replied.

"Okay, will do." There was a pause. "Grumpy Mule for the pilot and Darjeeling for you, Madam, or Twinings Breakfast?"

Jean gulped. "Any Lipton's? And some cheese and tomato sandwiches would be nice, too" The computer replied in the affirmative.

It was a short flight to Washington DC: less than two hours, door-to-door. Jean had a chance to take in the twinkling lights of the cities sprawling below them all the way along the East Coast of America. As they flew, she thought about the progress that had been made in the last few centuries - just the blink of an eye for the planet.

Jean was not a scientist, of course, but she thought the maths was obvious. If the 'civilised world' had been around for twenty to thirty millennia, in one form or another, and the Cycle of Precession was twenty-six millennia, there was unlikely to be any evidence available.

She frowned. It all made her head hurt, but she was determined to push on with her struggle to comprehend the situation. Something flicked through her head about the Mayans.

"We've been so arrogant about our culture," she reflected while Ethan focused on flying. "We're lucky to have emerged from the forest. Then again, we might all be bonkers. There may have been civilisations that knew more than we do. Information that's been lost, or is 'invisible', save for a few old wives' tales and some obscure hints from prophets like Nostradamus, Edgar Cayce and those people who drink cacao.

"How many times has this potentially creative and destructive cycle happened? What were earlier civilisations like? Did they have burger bars or gas stations? Did they live longer by living more healthily than we do? Maybe they had sustainable energy and technology in perfect balance with nature."

She supposed it was all a question of priorities. Jean had never thought of people in the past as being equal - or possibly even more advanced - before. Her brain nearly fused at the notion.

The inner dialogue continued, "We're focused on living each day with no thought about how we fit into the scheme of things. We're no different, basically, from any other living creature reacting to its environment. Except that our environment has TV, air travel, fast food, pop music and bars where we can lose what minds we have, instead of lions, tigers and bears; and we have changing seasons to develop strategies for or to amuse us."

Ethan, intrigued by the expressions crossing her face, interrupted her ponderings. "What are you thinking about, Jean?"

"Just piecing together some of the things you've said. What will happen to us all?"

"Well, that's the big question, isn't it? It depends whether we work together or against each other. If we work against each other, we have no hope; but if we make sacrifices, and become less selfish, there's every hope of a bright future for us all.

"Change isn't necessarily bad, it's just different. Most people want tomorrow to be pretty much the same as today or yesterday - with a bit of fun and variety along the way. What we're talking about, though, is tomorrow being radically different from yesterday; and soon."

"So getting rid of Richanti just gets us an even playing field," Jean said with pursed lips. "There's still a lot to do after that?"

"Pretty good," Ethan replied. "You're catching on fast."

The White House was lit up like a Christmas tree as they approached from the sea, in marked contrast to the darkness of their approach over bays, inland coves, and the dense river meandering towards the bright lights of Washington State.

They reduced altitude, hovering for a while over the Whitehouse lawn, before dropping down to a welcome party that was made up of two security guards and, presumably, a member of The White House staff.

"This should be interesting. They were expecting Richanti, not me," Ethan said.

"So what's the plan?" Jean asked.

"I don't have one. Trust your instincts," Ethan replied. "But remember, we do have the element of surprise."

"Oh, just great," said Jean. She didn't let on that, funnily enough, she was looking forward to the random nature of the encounter; and she was learning to trust Ethan's judgement.

The Hawk landed gently and Ethan cut the power. The rotors were still spinning as they made their exit and Jean instinctively ducked. Then the two Ambassadors for the larger part of the human race walked smartly over the lawn of 1600 Pennsylvania to their welcoming party. As she walked, Jean examined the faces watching them. Nobody looked fazed by Richanti's absence.

"Hi. I'm Assistant to the Chief of Staff for the Presidential Office," a stocky, well-built man in his late twenties said in neutral tones. "Come quickly, please. We need you to brief the COS." Jean and Ethan looked at each other surprised, but took his suggestion on face value.

"Of course," Ethan responded politely.

"You're aware of the latest news? The world's in an uproar. Demran Corporation and its directors are under investigation."

Ethan smiled. "So she did it."

"*She* did what? Jean enquired, totally lost by his remark.

"I'll explain later. Looks like we have work to do."

Ethan and Jean followed the small party into the West Wing of The White House. Once inside, they were shown through a number of connecting corridors into an ante-room. The focal point was a fairly modern, oval table. An ornate fireplace graced the opposite wall, and there were a few pieces of period furniture. Select paintings of the good and the great from American history looked down from brocade-clad walls.

"Anything I can get you?" asked an assistant.

"There's the crucial matter of tea," Jean said in a firm voice. "Tea and sandwiches, as promised."

The assistant looked puzzled. "Well, of course. I'll get some sent right in."

Jean and Ethan sat down as the Assistant COS left. The two security men remained outside the door. Before long, an amiable man came in to greet them. He was eccentric-looking, with tufts of wiry untamed hair, and wore a distinctly moth-eaten grey suit in contrast to a new, very bright tie. Jean felt a spark of alarm about such an unkempt-looking man holding a position of authority.

"Well, you have caused a stir!" he reported, sitting mid-point in front of them. He added in a relaxed manner, "I'm the President's Chief of Staff. Pleased to meet you.

"The Demran Corporation's on the verge of collapse because of its links to the Demagodran Group. The news was released by WikiLeaks and the press are having a field day with it. Then it went viral on Facebook with students revolting in every city and demanding explanations. They're demonstrating in the streets and outside public buildings all over the world."

Ethan beamed: "Funkypunkfish."

"What are you talking about?" Jean asked. "Funky-what-fish?"

"Ocean, Jean. Ocean is 'funkypunkfish'. I sent her all Richanti's files and my papers on Precession and the Demagodran. She must have dropped it on the internet for the whole world to see. The truth has a power of its own and is gaining momentum. The world will be a different place tomorrow."

"Yes, quite!" the Chief of Staff said without enthusiasm. People are coming forward by the minute to give testimony. Well, we can hardly keep wraps on it."

"Why would you want to keep wraps on it, if it's the truth?" Jean asked, looking closely at him.

"It may be the truth, but there will be civil unrest on a grand scale if we don't control the release of this information."

He changed tack abruptly. "Now, tell me what you know before you meet the President. He wants to put you on the networks to help control the unrest. Will you help us, please?"

Ethan and Jean regaled him with their stories of the past few days. The report began with Jean activating the time machine, and her journey back in time to affect Ethan's future, then went on to the loss of the Murray Institute and the sinking of the 'Princess'. It covered Ted's help and two deaths; the discovery of Richanti's secret room; the laptop they had managed to secure and, finally, the flight from the UK to New York.

Tea and sandwiches arrived, along with coffee for Ethan, although they were cucumber and tuna, not the cheese and tomato kind that Jean had ordered while they flew on the Hawk. Maybe robot servants were not as good as humans were. She tucked in, though. She was starving. The arrival of the food created a natural break.

Eventually, The Chief of Staff spoke. "It's an incredible story; fantastical, even," he remarked. Are the public ready for it?"

"Maybe, maybe not, but to keep it from them would be wrong," Ethan said firmly. "We have a duty to be honest; even if it makes things rocky in the short term. It's our only chance. We need everyone to be focused if we are going to come out intact on the other side of Precession. We can't do that if one part of society is planning to capitalise on a potential disaster for most of the world."

"So when do we get to meet the President?" Jean demanded.

"Well I was thinking 'about now', actually." The Chief of Staff clicked on a panel at the side of the room and a door opened. The passage beyond was very different to the others they had been through. It was made of steel and concrete and had a lift at the end of the corridor.

"Follow me," he ordered, ushering them forward.

"What about the real Oval Office?" Jean asked in a disappointed voice.

"We haven't used that since 'nine-eleven' - well, except for press launches and the occasional State Visit. The President's Office, and all the real work in

The White House, is now done a couple of levels down below the old Oval Office. "

Jean and Ethan thought this a little odd but went along with it. What else could they do?

They entered the lift and the doors closed behind them. The Chief of Staff accessed the panel via a retina scan and pressed the button for Level Five. They descended five levels of a ten-level, underground complex. The doors opened into a cavernous, open plan office.

"We connected this up with the West Wing in 2011. It took almost a decade to build, with underground car parks and a railway extension thrown in for good measure." The President's man added laconically, "It was quite an undertaking."

He led them to the end of the office, where there was a set of double doors. The doors were clearly marked 'President of the United States' and displayed the familiar seal of office: the eagle, an olive branch... but there was a quiver of thirteen arrows.

Jean had never noticed the last symbol before. It seemed odd and she promptly had one of her insights. Her solar plexus bounced uneasily.

"Olive branches and arrows, that's odd," she murmured to Ethan. "What does it mean?"

The doors, guarded by security staff, opened as Jean and Ethan approached. There was another large room ahead of them. Sitting at the desk in front of them was a man with his back to them. The chair turned slowly to reveal Richanti, who was looking smug.

"Did you enjoy your tea and sandwiches?" he asked.

Chapter Thirty One

Tuesday, 18th December, 2012
Dean's Place, Alfriston, East Sussex, England

Individuals are the building blocks of family, communities and nations.

Ocean awoke to a bright sunny day. It was early in the morning and she was in recovery mode. Leaving London had been simple, but the trek across The Downs had been a real struggle. She had arrived at her haven - a YHA hostel for walkers and young visitors from all over Europe in the remote village of Alfriston - weighed down by a solid back pack, and with her heels and toes stinging from blisters.

It was late at night when she arrived at the hostel. A mostly young, adventure party of adult males was still up, celebrating their freedom. She found her bunk in a women's dorm for four, which, thankfully, was unoccupied by anyone else. After a quick shower to get the grime off, she stuck gel patches on the worst blisters and fell into bed. Clicking off the light, Ocean fell into a deep sleep.

Her eyes were sensitive and always opened at first light; too early, really. She opened the door to her dormitory and found a beautiful view over the hills and dales of the Downs right in front of her. It seemed a safe haven from a busy, dangerous world. She thought back over the last few days, with Ethan's emails at the forefront of her mind.

"Dear Ocean, although you don't know me, I am a good friend of your mother's. I am sending you this in the event that we might not make it through the day. The story is a long one, but once you read this file, you will understand that everything written here is for real.

"You are in danger, too, by association. Find a place to hide. Tell nobody your location and trust no-one. Release this information to the distribution list in the file if you have not heard from us by tomorrow morning. I know you are fearless. Keep faith with your gut feelings and you will find there is nothing you cannot do. I hope we meet soon, Ethan Murray."

Ocean thought about Ethan's words: 'I know you are fearless. Keep faith with your gut feelings... there is nothing you cannot do.'

"How does he know?" she wondered aloud, and continued to muse over the revelations from Ethan Murray. "It's obvious that he knows everything about me, presumably from observing me and my mother for years. But who is he, where does he come from, and why do I instinctively trust him?"

She had read the files. They were dynamite. Each file numbered and profiled a faceless member of the Demagodran. They held positions of influence in every major corporation and government institution around the world. They were saboteurs in a society struggling to do its best for everyone. Ocean, however, was not surprised that the world was apparently sliding into an abyss. The decline appeared to be engineered by one man.

Ocean had always refused pressure to merge into mainstream society; and it was clear that she had been justified in her stance. Her preference was to hang out with the creative crew of the Camden Kitchen, the last bastion of punk and rebellion. A funky, pink-haired punk, her in-your-face appearance hid an astute brain and other, singular talents. She was about to use them to ruffle the Demagodran s tail feathers.

Jean had always taught her to develop her own individuality. And, unlike some mothers, she had never limited her or put her down. She found it interesting that Ethan was evidently a like spirit. He echoed Jean's approach to life by saying that she 'could do anything'. She liked that.

'There is nothing you cannot do. I believe in you,' Jean would say. Ocean sighed a little wanly. It seems she now had the opportunity to prove it. She reached for her laptop and plugged in the dongle; her connection was working, if slow. Downloading the first of seven hundred and eighty eight emails took hours. She could not quite believe the influx. The email replies to Ethan's files and research on the Demagodran was causing an email storm. From WikiLeaks to the New York Times and Kindred Spirits, they were all asking more questions than she was qualified to answer. She couldn't possibly read and reply to them all. She left the laptop updating and lay on her bunk to think.

It really was a glorious day. She had picked her retreat well. There was a festival going on at Michelham Priory and a hedonistic ritual was bringing in an influx of revellers for a 72-hour party at Dean's Place and other, local watering holes. It would all end in the winter solstice, fuelled by rumours of the end of the world. This was not just any old winter solstice, but the one marking Precession and our world's entry into the Age of Aquarius. It would occur on the 21st December 2012.

Those tracking her down would work out where she was soon enough, but their chances of pinpointing her in the crowds that were forming were slim. She could hide here easily; and she would have the support of her tribe. She lay back in her bunk again, deep in thought. She realised she was over-loaded and got up again.

Looking around, Ocean found a straight-backed chair in a corner of the dorm. Sitting down, she carefully aligned her spine and head. After 20 minutes of meditation, the monkey din in her brain had quietened down and she felt calm and chilled, which was a relief after finding herself somehow implicated in the biggest exposé in the history of humanity.

She was aware of everyone around and her hearing was acutely sensitive; in the distance, seagulls squawked, and a light breeze played on her face. Thoughts played through her mind like pictures on a film screen, but she let them go and remained calm, detached.

Then she felt that familiar tingling in her forehead and a kaleidoscope of colours entered her head. When they cleared away, they revealed a strange paradise. She was with child, it seemed, and there was a man with her. He was collecting firewood. It was cold, very cold.

"This should see us through the next day or so. There's plenty more," said the man, making a statement without expecting a reply; he was focusing on being diligent in his work. Then he looked over to Ocean properly, and smiled. "The winter is closing in fast; it's hard to believe it's nearly a year."

This rugged, Italian-looking man was not her usual type. She then wondered what had happened to her hair. The bright pink Mohican had gone and been replaced with dreadlocks, in her natural colour. She looked closely at her body; she must be close to term, but whose was the child? Was it his? Where was she? The place looked like England, but not the England she knew with its snow and moonscape and the occasional remnant of a crumbling building.

The rainbow colours came again, and Ocean emerged from her dream. She wondered what the strange vision might mean for a few minutes, and then an idea came to her. I knew I'd find one, she complimented herself, and then grimaced slightly over ego jumping in so quickly.

"All the same," she remarked aloud, "I wonder if...? I wonder...?"

When she was meditating, it sometimes *felt* as though she had the resources of the whole universe at her disposal. All she needed to do was tap into it. Jean had always said, 'Think big. Don't limit what you think you're capable of.'

For a moment, Ocean mused that she now called her mother by her first name, and their relationship had become more one of friendship than mother and child. Then she remembered her focus. And lo, it appeared she has conceived a six-point plan for the future. She returned thoughtfully back to her laptop. There were now eight hundred and twelve emails.

She speed-read the emails and found another one from Ethan. She was glad his were marked with a rainbow hologram so they stood out. Just a moment, she thought, 'hologram'. Is that what I have when I get that feeling in my forehead? Hmmm, she might return to that.

His latest email contained a huge batch of personnel files. There was a brief message.

"These speak for themselves." The files covered high profile appointments in government bodies and corporations around the world. Each file had a second title within the Demagodran organisation.

She mailed out the information to Ethan's distribution list, then switched on her 'Out of Office' signature and pointed it to her Facebook profile. In hurried prose, she wrote her reply to an email she had singled out and fired it off.

"There, done," she said. "Throw out a pebble and watch an avalanche come back?"

The truth started to spread as headline information percolated across the globe. Messages asking all manner of questions rolled in from around the world. Students were rioting in all the major cities, beginning with Beijing, London and Paris. With the Demagodran exposed, the 'big reveal' spread virally. Truth always has a power of its own and people became increasingly angry over their betrayal. The full extent of this became clear as reports cited the documents Ocean had sent out.

Gradually, ordinary people around the world realised that a group of malevolent people in government and industry had been conspiring against the interests of humanity for decades, if not aeons.

By this time, Ocean was hungry enough to chew her fingernails. She put on a colourful pair of velvet trousers with various tops, threw a Tibetan blanket coat over the lot, and then walked half-a-mile down the road to Dean's Place. She had noticed it served food to the public when she passed the night before.

When she got there, everyone in the hotel was buzzing with the breaking news. Many were crowded round the TV in the bar and lounge areas as key public figures were identified, one-by-one. The anarchic nature of the exposure fed the festival mood; little did they know that Ocean was at the heart of it - a 'touch paper' for the world's press.

Ocean fixed her gaze on the monitor. Under the video footage, there was a message running:

"World searches for Ethan Murray and his accomplice."

Disturbed by seeing the banner, she listened closely to the spoken report.

"The wanted couple were last sighted at the weekend, fleeing the scene of a bomb blast at the Murray Institute. On Monday morning, they stole a boat from Brighton Marina. Police want them for questioning in relation to the Demran Corporation collapse and the Demagodran. They may be dangerous, and armed. Do not approach them at all costs."

"More lies," Ocean muttered, frowning. An eye caught hers across the room. She smiled blandly and turned towards the casual catering area set up under canvas outside, on the patio area of the hotel. She needed to keep her feelings under control when there were potential enemies around. She chose some simple food and scarcely noticed what she ate before heading back to the main reception area to check out the TV again. As she walked in, she wondered, "Is the truth so far removed from reality that it is impossible to report?"

It made sense that the Demagodran were using their news network to dampen down reporting on the Demagodran. To attack the two people who were trying to tell the truth was a smart decoy.

"Let's just hope my idea works!" she remarked under her breath.

On returning to the main festival bar, Ocean had begun to feel pensive and anxious; and it showed. If she held back from joining in with the growing revelry, her mood may have drawn attention from some members of the crowd. Additionally, the guy she had noticed before was staring at her from the corner of the room. She recognised him, but couldn't think where she had seen him before.

He smiled, seeing that she had noticed him watching her again. He innocently responded and started to walk towards her. As he stood in front of her, she had a strange feeling. He held out his hand. "Hi, my name's Fitz. Pleased to meet you," he said with a beaming smile.

She recognised him, now. She was certain... yes, she was quite certain. His voice was the same. It was the man from her dream.

Chapter Thirty Two

Tuesday, 18th December, 2012
Helipad, Demagodran HQ, Manhattan Island, Washington, USA

The greatest love of all is to love yourself

"Sandwiches?" Jean sniffed disparagingly. "There was no 'cheese and tomato', as ordered with your robot," Jean replied, squaring up to Richanti.

"Well... "Richanti said, disconcerted by Jean's punchy start."Well, that's a pity, but I *am* pleased to meet you again. Shame about Ted," he added, harking back to their last meeting, "but moles have to pay."

Jean picked up the glint of insanity in Richanti's eyes: the same, dark side of him that she had picked up during the newsreel in the pub only a few days ago; he really was mad. Now she was closer to him, though, she also sensed sadness in him, and felt a squeak of pity for this lonely creature.

Ethan looked around, noticing similar monitors to the ones in the secret, New York room. The counter had reduced and the 'Oasis readiness indicator' had switched to hours. It was past midnight in the early hours of the 18th December. The monitor was flashing an amber colour and read 76 hours.

The whole concept of the Oasis concerned Ethan deeply.

"Richanti you really are mad. You're acting out the end of the world, setting yourself up as God, creating an Ark, and controlling the Demagodran for your own, incredibly selfish ends. In fact, you're trying to capitalise on humanity's fears of Armageddon, as prophesised in the bible.

The Demagodran may be in the Middle East, but not just the middle-east the cradle of civilisation, history is repeating itself."

"How clever you are, Professor," Richanti said, addressing him by title, not out of respect but with a mocking tone. Richanti knew he had the upper hand.

"Less than seventy-six hours until the winter solstice. It should be a spectacular event, don't you think? I know you've done the research, but do you really know what will happen? How could you? Neither of us was around 26,000 years ago."

"What are you getting at Richanti? Stop playing games."

"Games, games," Richanti mimicked. "I'm not playing games, but inventing a machine to change the timeline is definitely a child's game. Well it's of no consequence. You have tried and failed." Richanti looked smug. He seemed to think it was 'game over' for Jean and Ethan.

Ethan recalled that he had revealed how to activate the time machine to the Chief of Staff. With Richanti's alien genetic profile, he should easily master the machine as he had a natural ability to time-shift.

"How stupid of me!" Ethan cried out, realising his mistake. He had given the Chief of Staff details of how to activate the time machine.

"What do you intend to do with it?" Ethan asked quietly.

"To start with, take out this funkypunkfish who's causing all the bother on Facebook. I know it's something to do with you. It's quite obvious that you stole my files from the office in New York. As for Precession, any idiot could have worked that one out.

"My family has been around for aeons: the signing of the Constitution of the United States of America, Dissolution of the Monasteries, Knights Templar, the Last Supper and Judas, of course. Oh yes, not to forget the most prized possession of all from the library of Giza: a written account of the planetary alignment and the death and destruction it caused last time discovered by my grandfather."

"How long have you been planning Armageddon?" Ethan asked.

"It's a lifetime's work. My parents started in the thirties, when they excavated the Giza Plateau, proving the myth of the library beneath the Sphinx to actually be true. They decided to keep the archive secret, though. I just exploited the idea. There was never going to be a way of saving everyone."

"Who said you could play God?" Ethan remarked.

"God-like, please. Don't elevate me above my station," Richanti said, almost smiling at the inadvertent compliment.

Jean interrupted, "He *is* mad."

"Not that it makes any difference with less than seventy-six hours to go," Richanti sneered. "What can you do? Students rioting everywhere and occupying public buildings was a distraction and the Demran Corporation had served its purpose. There will be no need for large corporations in a few days' time. People will be begging for food and shelter; and organisations like NASDAQ, FTSE and DOW will be impotent. Your revelations have come too late, I'm afraid. However, there are many other uses for that machine of yours.

"The one that will give me the greatest delight will be changing your life for the better, my dear," Richanti said, looking at Jean with hatred in his eyes. "We can't have you running around being meddlesome, can we? You've scrambled above your station, and need to be sent back to the place from whence you came - cleaning toilets in the lab."

That did it. All Jean had was her handbag, and she used it, swinging it as a missile around her head and propelling it at Richanti. He was caught unawares by the bag, but ducked just in time. It smashed into the mirror behind him. With an almighty crack, the mirror splintered. Richanti fell back on the mirror, to be hit by shards of glass raining down upon him.

"I feel better for that," Jean exclaimed. "I'm glad that I dropped a bottle of that posh sparkling water from the West Wing in there. A handbag can be a lethal weapon to unsuspecting villains and you're a villain, Richanti; one of the worst."

Security personnel ran into the room alerted by the furore. They restrained Jean and Ethan. Richanti slowly got up. Pieces of glass fell from his Saville Row suit as he steadied himself, still stunned.

"I should expect nothing less from you than a violent outburst. You're an absolute animal," he stormed. "No matter, Lady, you have an important schedule today. First, there's your photo call; and then we'll take you off to somewhere where you'll be safe from harm." His voice oozed with sarcasm.

Ethan interjected, "Photo call! What are you up to now, Richanti?"

"You're going to be portrayed as traitors for hiding all your work on Precession from the world for your own ends, to save your own skin. Then I intend to follow with my own rescue package, which involves salvation for everyone and come out as a hero. Won't that be fun? Now *I'm* playing games and I always win my games."

"Yes, save them... at a price," Jean said disdainfully.

"Of course. Every decent civilisation needs a class system. Unfortunately, food, water and the comforts in life will be in short supply so we're going to sell tickets for places."

"And what does a ticket cost, Richanti?" Ethan asked.

"They start at a million US dollars a person and go up to one billion, payable in precious metals."

"And what happens if you can't afford a ticket?"

"Well, I've thought of that. We have a second tier where you can work your ticket."

"You mean slavery?"

"Well someone has to do the menial work, as you know." The comment was clearly meant for Jean's consumption.

"We won't do it," Jean and Ethan said in tandem.

"You don't have to," Richanti smiled. "I have most of the video footage already. It's in the Demran Corporation Building and was prepared from the CCTV footage. A quick edit of you is all that is needed; a priceless picture, shall we say, of you both captured and in handcuffs. There's no need for an Oscar-winning performance."

"And then what?"

"I'll leave you here to make your last, heroic stand in the rubble. You and the bulk of this miserable civilisation will be wiped out in three days' time. But those who can pay will get a chance to renew the world."

"Yes, renew it your way," Ethan snapped. "That's not what I'd call 'democratic'."

"Well, democracy has failed hasn't it? What would you do?"

Jean was speechless for a second. He had a point. Then she launched into a rebuff: "Freedom, honesty, truth, integrity, self-sacrifice... I think you've missed these from your plan."

"Pfftt! Weaknesses like that have no place in my New World," Richanti retorted.

"I'm done here," he said abruptly and motioned to the guards, who restrained Jean and Ethan, cuffed them and began leading them out of the room.

Jean turned back to face Richanti. "You'll lose everything. This is the end for you *and* your family," she said as she looked at him. She was determined and sure of herself.

"How can you be so sure?" Sarcastically, Richanti added, "Are you going to clean us out of existence?"

"I have conquered my demons, Richanti. I know who I am. But do you know who *you* are? For all your wealth and power, you know nothing about yourself; that makes you weak and vulnerable."

"Uh huh, what's that, then?" Richanti said, not impressed.

"Love, Richanti. Love is all you ever needed; and that's what your parents stole from you. You've hidden your fear of being alone by becoming cold, through and through, but you had a love once, didn't you? And it was taken from you."

Jean's instinct had kicked in, "There was someone very special in your life once."

Richanti looked up. Jean had his attention and she looked deep into his eyes.

"A woman..." Jean guessed, pausing for effect. She could see that he was agitated. "Not just a woman, though, a child as well. Yes, a child. You had a child, a boy. I can see it in you. You loved him and they took him away from you. They took him away from you in the same way that I was taken away. They called him genetic dregs, like me, your sister."

"Get her out!" Richanti shouted. He picked up Jean's handbag and chucked it back at her, but the throw was weak.

"Thank you," she said, catching the handbag. "Thank you, that's all I wanted to know. You can't win, Richanti. You have to love yourself or there's no hope for you."

Jean knew that better than anyone did. She turned confidently and walked towards the door between the guards who were stunned and silent. Ethan followed with a wry smile creasing his face. Is it really that easy he wondered?

Chapter Thirty Three

Tuesday, 18th December, 2012
Deans Place, Alfriston, East Sussex, England

Coincidence doesn't exist, everything happens for a reason.

"Who are you?" Ocean asked.

"I could ask the same about you," Fitz grinned.

"You're the man in my dream," Ocean mused and then, realising what she had said, she corrected herself. "I know that doesn't sound right, but I had a dream and you were in it."

"That doesn't sound right, either. Why not relax, chill out and start from the beginning? My name's Fitz; and I'm a 27-year-old, prep school dropout. My life has been fairly well sorted since that. Fulfilled and fun is what I am," he grinned.

"Mother was a socialite and Father a high flyer, but only really interested in paying for my education and paying my mother off... if you know what I mean."

"That's funny," Ocean replied. "I'm the same: great mum, my dad was never around for me when I was younger. Mum kicked him out and brought me up herself. We had no money, but I did have lots of freedom to do and be what I wanted."

"So why are you here?"

"Same reason as everyone else, to enjoy the festival," she said sheepishly, her flight from London in the forefront of her thoughts as she did so.

"It's going to be a great one this year. Have you heard the rumours?" Fitz responded.

"What rumours?" Ocean knew what was coming.

"The end of the world on the solstice: what a show!"

"I'm not sure I'd call it a show. It sounds pretty real to me."

"Must be a hoax; another attempt to strike fear into the nation and sell a whole load of TV commercials on the back stories."

Ocean hadn't bought into his explanation. Fitz noticed her mood. "Why so serious?"

"No reason."

Fitz puts his head on one side, raising his eyebrows in a comical way, and changed tack. "Can I buy you a beer, snakebite? That's what punks drink don't they?" Fitz asked, looking at the Mohican with a cheeky grin.

"No I don't, and my mother told me never to take drinks from strangers."

Ocean cracked a smile and said "I'll buy *you* one. A bottle of wine, okay? Snakebite was an 80's concoction, and not a very nice one at that; designed to get you drunk rather than tickle your taste buds. Lager and cider, uuurggh."

They had found a cosy corner in which to swap stories at the back of a large bar and entertainment area, set up in a marquee on the terrace. It had been erected for the festival so management could keep the crowds under cover, but not too much underfoot in the main hotel. It was not quite lunchtime, but that scarcely mattered during Festival Week.

They say you know instantly when you meet your soul mate. This random meeting between Ocean and Fitz quickly led to deep conversation of the kind that friends and partners who have known each together for decades would easily recognise; there was serious chemistry at work. They felt relaxed and comfortable; basking in each other's every word.

"When did you get here?" Fitz quizzed Ocean. "I haven't seen you around, before."

"I arrived late last night and crashed. I've just woken up. Actually, you guys woke me up." Ocean was slightly caustic.

"Ditch the attitude," Fitz retaliated, sensing that he was being tested.

Ocean laughed and cheerfully back-tracked, "Actually, I had a great sleep and got up early this morning to nurse yesterday's blisters and take photos of the winter views on The Downs." She noticed that her mood changed in response to his directness. "The stark silhouettes of the trees against the grassed curves of the land lent themselves well to black and white shots."

She liked this guy. He 'got' her; and not many people got her. Jean had said 'special'. The problem with special people is there weren't many of them; and they were often confused with the odd and idiotic when, actually, they were the creative force on the edge of change in the world. That was certainly what Jean meant by special.

"Ok, I was a little tough on you," Ocean admitted, "but you deserved it. You'd walk all over me if I let you."

"I guess you're right," Fitz agreed. "We could change the world, the two of us."

Ocean looked at him closely. If only he knew. Should she tell him?

"Change the world..." she said slowly. "I'm not sure that it needs more change, right now. Anyway, you're bumming around; you said so yourself, moving from one party to another. Why should you want to change the world?"

Fitz realised that Ocean was a highly complex young woman. She was testing him again.

"Because it's not working, isn't that plain as day? Look at the two of us. You had a mum who could barely put the clothes on your back, and went to a mediocre college, whereas I had everything money could buy on the educational front but flunked."

"Look around at the rest of the people here. Most of them have opted out because what they have to opt into simply doesn't make sense. Why get involved in a world of work with no reward, a society built on which car you drive, your postcode, and which school you went too? It's nuts. Yeah, I'd definitely change the world, given half a chance. "

"Then tell me, what would you do? Put some of that prep school education to good use. I'm not going out with a festival flunky."

Fitz let loose a big grin. "Going out are we?" He leant across the table and kissed her lightly.

"I'd better think about what I say if it depends on keeping you." He repeated his own line and Ocean's question, thinking deeply. "So, if I could change the world, *what* would I do?"

"'Love, love is all we need', as the song goes. If we all gave just a little bit more, the world would be a better place."

Distracted by beeps on her iPhone, she picked it up and opened Facebook. There were 22,456 updates.

"Bloody hell," she exclaimed in shock and picked out one message at random.

It read, "Let's make the changes the world has been waiting for." She typed an update on her page, Love, love is all we need.

"Hey!" Fitz shouted out. "That's rude. I was being all deep and you're texting on your phone."

"Ok. Sorry. 'Love, love is all you need.' See I m listening, but what does it mean?"

Ocean tuned into Fitz but remained pensive about greater matters at work on Facebook.

"It means people need to start giving, creating and sustaining," Fitz said, and to stop taking, destroying and polluting. Most people wouldn't entertain the idea. We live a very selfish world. If I had the opportunity to prove that the more you give, the more you get back, the world would be a very different place."

"Well done! You pass," Ocean responded. She typed it into her phone. "People need to start giving, creating and sustaining, and stop taking, destroying and polluting. What you give out is what you get back." There was something fated about what she was doing, almost as if she was just a medium for the messages.

She looked into Fitz's eyes. "But what does it actually mean?"

"It means what it says. If your neighbour is hungry, give them a meal; get the old to care for and teach the young; care for your environment; be industrious and contribute whatever you can. It seems simple, but most of us get it wrong. The reward can only be real happiness, contentment and a balance our society has never experienced before."

Fitz liked the attention. Ocean was interested in him; and in what he had to say. In fact, he had majored in social politics and economics before dropping out. Right now, it seemed his degree was becoming useful after all.

"Well, it's simple really," he continued. "You create small communities, appoint a few local individuals as a council for your community; and get them all to work for everyone's interests. A close-knit community, that's the key."

"Wow, I didn't expect that. A little like where we are now - a hostel full of like minded people?"

"Yes I guess you're right."

"So why did you give up?"

"Give up?" He asked, not really understanding her question.

"Yes, you gave up. You had these great ideas and you gave up." She was typing rapidly into Facebook.

"It may sound crazy but it's an idea that's more honest than most ways of organising humanity. Put it this way, if everyone joined small communities, with a few chosen from within each community to manage that group's needs, with the same process for new levels of management, up a groups of a thousand people, it would be a lot fairer than the present system.

"It would be realistic for a few people to know a thousand people, personally, but at the moment it 's more like one for nearly a hundred thousand. How can one person manage the interests of a hundred thousand people effectively?

"Let them direct you, and direct your community to give, create and sustain. The time is coming to work together, not apart."

Ocean continued to type wildly on her phone.

They had been talking for hours, punctuated by Ocean linking to people around the globe. Minutes seemed to stretch into hours. Next time she looked at her phone, Ocean realised Facebook was overloaded: 123,488 updates! That was insane.

They realised it must be lunchtime from the smells wafting outside. The waiter had switched on the TV monitor and tuned-into MTV but it was being interrupted by breaking news. The newsreader had a Facebook icon behind her and the logo for the Demran Corporation.

"Funkypunkfish, the Facebook site that exposed the Demagodran linked to the Demran Corporation collapse, suddenly came to life a few hours ago. The posts are somewhat cryptic. They began with: 'Love, love is all we need,' followed by 'people need to start giving, creating and sustaining and stop taking, destroying and polluting.' The last message said that 'everyone should focus themselves into small communities, with a few to manage a thousand.'"

The newsreader took a breath. The funkypunkfish messages concluded, 'Let them direct you and your community to give, create and sustain; the time is coming to work together not apart.'

'These statements have caused a lot of controversy as people look for direction. A global search is being carried out to track down the sender of the messages, which seem to be originating from an iPhone somewhere in the UK."

Fitz was looking in astonishment at Ocean by this point, incredibly confused as to how his conversation with her moments ago has been plastered over the TV news. Ocean had gone distinctly red in the face.

"In contrast to the naming and shaming of the leaders of the Demagodran Group today, there has been the exposure of Professor Ethan Murray and his cleaner, who he is believed to be having an affair with. She's known as Just Jean."

"It is believed that Jean was responsible for the bombing of the Murray institute, and placing a bomb in a restricted area." They ran the videotape of Jean in Ethan's lab.

The newsreader continued. "She is also believed to have been at the heart of the Demagodran command." They then ran a video of Jean in the boardroom with Richanti carefully edited out and Ethan in the background.

Ocean went pale. She was speechless.

Fitz went into attack mode. "Who are you and what are you trying to do?" My father has had enough bad press. Can't you just leave him alone? You're a reporter I guess, or some kind of weirdo.

"Father? Richanti is your father? Well Jean's my mother."

Fitz exploded, "Mother! Is that supposed to make things better?"

The rest of the cafe looked round to see what had caused the sudden outburst.

The TV caught everyone's attention again. "An important message follows - direct from The White House - where the President of the United States has cancelled his schedule to address the nation. The message is being relayed across the globe."

They cut to the UK cabinet office which had assembled to watch the broadcast. A sub-text, 'Breaking News', flashed underneath the announcer's remarks.

"The President is to deliver an important statement of national and international importance."

There was a familiar scene of a podium with the seal behind it of the United State of America. The president entered.

"This is a solemn occasion; the most significant in the history of our Nation and, I venture to say, of the world to date. I stand before you to confirm rumours in the press from the dossiers published most recently regarding the effects of Precession on the planet - a cycle that occurs every 26,000 years - in three days time: 21st December 2012."

"I can confirm that the effects will be catastrophic. It has been calculated that fatalities in the North American region are likely to reach holocaust proportions. There is, however, hope. This office has determined that the safest location is in the Middle East, where the chances of survival range from fair to good."

"With the aid of our brothers in the Middle East, there is a possibility for life to go on almost normally for some people. I am hereby ordering a state of emergency and the immediate evacuation of essential staff to a safe haven. The Demran Corporation will act as agents in expediting a 'Noah's Ark' movement."

"The United States of America will soon be forced into an Ice Age, following a significant seismic upheaval, as yet unmeasured in recent earth history."

"This will be my first and last address as President. I will not be saving myself, but giving my place to another. I herewith transfer authority of The Office, with immediate effect, to The Committee - an emergency council set up to manage the transition of the United States' interests in the new world, in the Middle East."

"I shall spend the final hours with my family and staff in The White House. Nothing short of a miracle will save us; and my duty is to my country, in its final hours. God bless you all."

There was a profound silence throughout the hotel and precincts.

Fitz looked at Ocean. "Why are you here?" He was calm now: collected and in control.

"I could ask you the same question. All I can say is that I didn't engineer being here. You can trust me and the thing I can promise you about me is that I'm authentic."

"But what about Facebook and funkypunkfish?"

"Call it instinct. To add what you said to the chat did the trick. You have the world watching and listening. Be careful what you wish for." She took a breath. "Besides, I don't believe in coincidence."-

Fitz took Ocean's hand and suggested quietly, "Let's get out of here. I think it would be a good idea for you to go undercover at the hostel."

They crossed the road from Dean's Place to the pathway leading back to the hostel, much of it invisible to cars driving by. They brushed against each other in the dark, and Fitz pulled Ocean to him. He had that feeling again; the feeling that they were meant to be together. Quite why, he did not fully understand.

The kiss was long-lasting. She loved the way he smelt; and vice versa. Soporific with wine and endorphins, they became wobbly on their feet, and released after a while to continue the walk back to the hostel.

Ocean told him she had also checked out the back exit at the YHA earlier in the day, just in case... she picked up her iPhone, she selected her inbox and penned a rapid reply to Ethan.

"Richanti has a son. He's ok. I'm safe and sound. Say hi to Mum ;o)."

Chapter Thirty Four

Tuesday, 18th December, 2012
Deep below, The White House, Washington, USA

Evil is all in the mind.

The master dwelt on his triumph. He was happy again; he was back on top. He told himself, "I just need to tidy the loose ends."

He sat content in his penthouse: A Master of Manipulation, that's what he was. He laughed. Jean and Ethan were just like all the others before them. They always thought they had him beaten, right up until to the very last minute and, then, he took them out when they least expected it; a strategy he had used with consummate effect for years.

On reflection, of course, it had always been like this. Richanti reminisced on his childhood. Kicked around as a kid, he had developed strategies to survive. He thought about his parents. They had murdered their own offspring: his sisters and brothers. He had learned how to be ruthless from them over the years. (They always did it in a pleasant way, of course.)

One of his siblings would be there one day and gone the next. It was the worst kind of genetic and psychological cleansing and all in the name of what, he wondered for a moment. But the truth was too much to face. He told himself the answer lay in their power over other people. It was absolute power and, with it, came the kind of wealth that was unimaginable to most people. This is what gave them control over everything, and everyone, on the planet.

In the view of his parents, murder was justified to further the family line. After all, his family had controlled world history for millennia and nobody had even come close to noticing until now.

"Have I failed? Is the secret out?" he cried aloud in a moment of fear, comparing himself to 'the good and the great' before him.

He remembered the excitement when he first started to wield his own, personal power. To him, it had seemed an innocent affair. One of the teachers taking his class at school had upset him for one reason or another and attempted to discipline him, quite without success, in the days when violence was allowed. The teacher had lost it. He banged Richanti's head against the desk in full view of his fellow students.

The vengeful young Richanti had sorted him out by turning up early the next morning and loosening the fixings to a significant light fitting that was positioned just above the teacher's podium. He rigged it so the final bolt could be released connected by a piece of fishing wire, which he could remove with a single, light tug, at will.

He waited for his revenge until the whole class had assembled and was in full flow to ensure the maximum, most dramatic effect. Just as the teacher was recalling the French revolution - another historical event that his family had influenced - the heavy Gothic candelabra came crashing down. The effect, Richanti considered, had been quite poetic.

The teacher's hospitalisation for just two weeks after a brief term in intensive care was his only disappointment. Richanti had meant to finish him off. None of the teachers touched him after that. They could prove nothing, but they knew it was him. There was also no doubt that he had gained the respect of his fellow classmates. After that, their fear gave him complete control. This was the first occasion - of many - that he experienced the feeling of being untouchable.

All the same, something was troubling him. It was deep, very deep below the surface.

"Dammit." He breathed out slowly. It was Jean who troubled him. What had she said? He became agitated, trying to remember her exact words. "What was it?"

Did she say he could not win? He needed to know this for himself. What *was* she talking about? How dare she! But she seemed so sure, so certain. Then he remembered her saying, "Thank you. That's all I wanted to know. You can't win, Richanti. You have to love yourself or there is no hope for you."

"Love?" he thought about it. He had experienced love once for a brief moment, which unexpectedly led to unrevealed depths of pain over losing his son. And where might he be? His raw feelings leapt in his face; they were too painful to accept. He preferred to suppress the memory and turned his attention back to Jean.

Then he had an inspired thought. "I'll teach her about love!"

He made his way out of his office, down a corridor of White House staff, and headed to the lift. He caught one of the monitors running the news story on Jean and Ethan. Ha! A brilliant set-up. He was quite pleased with the result and must remember to thank the editor, personally.

"How easy is it is to distort the truth," he chuckled blackly. "Edit coverage the way you want it and throw it up on a billion TV screens: simple but effective. Then give the credit to someone who will become... hmmm, quite indispensable in a few days' time."

Richanti entered the lift and selected the button for Level Ten. The lift demanded a retina scan. "Access to that level is restricted," a bland, disembodied voice drawled. "Stand on the square and face the screen." The lift scanned him and processed his request. "Access confirmed." The lift rapidly moved downwards.

He made his exit at Level Ten, a warehouse and archive. Unlike the other levels, it was dark, but, as he walked forward, the lights clicked on. He knew what he was looking for and paced forward a few metres, then right, past a case displaying old manuscripts and another rack full of Old Masters' paintings, some marked Rembrandt. There were early Greek statues, and precious relics from civilisations that had long since passed.

This treasure trove was a collection built up over millennia, and passed down from generation to generation; he was now the custodian. At the end of the Old Masters' row lay a grey metallic box, his most recent acquisition.

"So that's it." He looked at the machine, eager to try out his new toy, having only recently been enlightened by clear instructions over its use. He was surprised they had revealed their secrets so readily, but people do that when they think they're on top and have the advantage.

He looked at the apparently featureless grey box and then realised it was made up of millions of pixels: stereos. He defocused a little and felt a tingling in his forehead. Then he saw the letter M framed by a circle. He smiled. His next thought was of Jean in another decade: the nineties seemed appropriate to him.

The machine gave out a pulse of energy and a dark shadow burst from its core like a tsunami, capable of crushing all hope before it.

-

Downtown San Francisco in the nineties suddenly appeared. To be precise, it was mid-afternoon on Saturday 15th September, 1990. Richanti was impressed. This really would be a useful addition to his collection.

He found himself driving a station wagon and tailing a taxi, having recognised the silhouettes of the passengers in front. When the taxi turned left, he turned left. He sensed Jean's power and confidence. This made him back off. There will be a better moment.

"I need to get this right," he told himself. He had a plan for her.

One of the advantages of being the head of the biggest secret society in history is that you can grab resources wherever you are, whatever time you come from; although it might sometimes take a little explaining. Richanti was going fishing and he was about to reel in those who could help. He pulled over and dialled the operator:

"Collect call for Demran Corporation's Head Office. Now!"

Richanti put out the call. "Is it done?" he snapped.

"Yes, it's done," the agent replied but, typically, the boss had gone. Winning friends was not Richanti's style.

Now, it was just a case of getting Jean off-track. If he could discredit her, he could get control of Ethan; and he would put Jean back where she belonged:

"Jean the janitor," he snarled. She had played her hand well, but she was dangerous and had to be stopped. It would be too late before she realised that she had been drugged and set-up for dealing and possession. He'd had the local police in his pocket for years; they were only too pleased to help.

"Sister!" How dare she even mention it; she wasn't his equal. She was a reject, a retard. But something was bothering him. She had said: 'a full set of genes'. Could that really be true? He felt troubled, deeply troubled, and yet another thought flew up in his face: a silly comment of hers that was grating on him: 'Love yourself'. What could that have anything to do with anything? Everyone adored him, feared him.

- / -

He left the temporary office arranged for him in the downtown, West Coast headquarters of the Demran Corporation, in San Francisco. A little shorter than the 21st century version, the skyscraper he had commissioned was twenty years ahead in the future and had over seventy floors. He hit the button on the elevator for the parking level. The doors opened and he entered the lift. Once again, he felt pensive.

"Time travel?"

He had figured it was possible but had never worked out how to achieve it. How had Ethan managed it? He had never really understood human nature. They achieved their best work when they were in the greatest of peril; the rest of their achievements were mediocre.

He had to be careful. He needed Jean out the way, but Ethan still had to deliver the time machine in *his* lifetime, so manipulating time would be tricky. The lift reached P1 parking level and he took the exit. His green station wagon was straight ahead of him. He turned the key in the lock and stepped inside.

"Now, where is she?" He smouldered, thinking about her; then he saw a park and a bridge: the Golden Gate Bridge. "Ahh, they're in Golden Gate Park." He realised that was only a couple of blocks away.

He called urgently for back-up. A few more police won't harm a drugs' bust; it makes it all the more authentic.

He got on his radio phone:

"I need some Plain Clothes Officers to pick up a couple in Golden Gate Park. Two students. I'll point them out to you. Hang back until I give you the order."

When Richanti reached the outskirts of the park, he headed straight towards the parking lot in the north. There, he would have a view of both the park and the Golden Gate. He saw Murray and Jean in the distance; he had only seconds before she sensed him.

"I'm in the North Parking Lot. There's a couple on the edge of the car park, walking shoulder-to-shoulder. The woman has auburn hair down to her waist. Bust her, now! And search her handbag."

The blue sirens started and Richanti aimed the green station wagon straight at his target, then realised he was going too fast. He veered off and hit a van.

"Death would be too good for you," Richanti said. Jean pushed Ethan to the ground.

Jean seemed about to say something to Ethan but, instead, turned abruptly and made for a Harley Davison parked nearby. It was too late, though. One of the plain clothes officers had her. The other was close behind and grabbed her bag. Ethan was watching, not quite sure what to think.

The cop rummaged through her bag and pulled out a packet full of white powder. It looked very much like cocaine, plus some wraps of LSD. Ethan was horrified and stepped back defensively. The cops bundled Jean into the back of their car to question her. She was looking down and seemed ashamed, but it was more that she knew when she was beaten.

Richanti had been waiting for this moment. He stepped out of the car and walked towards Ethan. "A close call, that" he said smoothly. I've been following her for a while and she's the worst kind. She tells you everything you want to hear, and projects the person you want her to be. It's a good job we got in when we did or it would be the first and last day of your esteemed career."

"Who are you?" At first Ethan was angry, then confused and now increasingly inquisitive. "What *esteemed* career?"

"You wouldn't believe me if I told you," Richanti replied.

"Try me." Jean seemed to think you were one of the bad guys.

"See what I mean. She already has you. The manipulation would have kept going until you didn't know what the truth was. So what did she say to you?"

"Oddly, she just said one word: 'Precession'."

"Precession." Richanti copied him and immediately understood that his plan was too green to be leaked two decades ahead of its fruition. He knew what he needed to do.

"Ok. I'm going soon, but we'll meet again."

He paused, because the next part would be difficult to understand.

"I'm from your future. You're going to invent a time machine and you're going to help me save the world in 2012. You don't need to know anymore than that right now. Just remember who kick-started your esteemed career when we meet again."

The silver machine pulsed again and a shadow rippled across the earth. Ethan felt a chill run down his spine. Time had shifted irrevocably as darkness descended on the world. Richanti the puppeteer and Ethan the puppet.

Richanti disappeared before his eyes. He was standing in the park alone and heard the sound of sirens racing towards him. He looked at the green station wagon. There was a man slumped over the wheel, blood streaming from his head. It was the stranger. Richanti was lifeless, or so it seemed.

Chapter Thirty Five

Wednesday, 19th December, 2012
172 Marion Road, Smethwick, England

Many worlds, many outcomes.

Somewhere in another time and space, Jean and Paula had embarked on their favourite pastime: TV. It was a special evening as Paula's recent lottery win had meant she had been able to buy Jean a brand new flat screen, a massive 52' HD that extended the full width of her tiny living room.

It had been a considerable lottery win - in the millions - and the money had gone to Paula's head. She knew how to live beyond her means, but was finding it a bit hard to live beyond them now. A night in with her best friend - an ordinary evening - was Jean's attempt to bring her back down to ground, although of course she was grateful for the TV.

Unfortunately, their soap schedule that evening was interrupted rudely by a special broadcast. It was the US president.

In general, Jean and Paula believed that political broadcasts really did not apply to them. They were for the movers and shakers; those people who made a difference and ran countries. Jean was the sort of person who turned up and voted once every few years. A floating voter, she was a perfect candidate for new campaigners; and her local councillors and MP were all too well aware of her swinging support.

Both Jean and Paula yawned at the official announcement and switched channels, only to find the broadcast was being repeated on all 300 channels. They had no choice but to watch.

"This is a solemn occasion. May I venture to say it is the most significant event in the history of our Nation and the recorded history of the world to date," the president said gravely. "I stand before you to confirm rumours in the press about the effects of *Precession* on our planet. The cycle occurs once every 26,000 years. It reaches its zenith in three days time; on 21st December 2012.

"I can confirm that the effects will be catastrophic. It has been calculated that fatalities in the North American region are likely to reach holocaust proportions. There is, however, some hope. This office has determined that the safest location is located in the Middle East. Here, the chances of survival range from fair to good."

"With the aid of our brothers in the Middle East, there is a possibility for life to go on almost normally for some people. I am hereby ordering a state of emergency and the immediate evacuation of essential staff to a safe haven. The Demran Corporation will act as agents in expediting a 'Noah's Ark' movement."

"The United States of America will soon be forced into an Ice Age, following what is believed to be a series of significant seismic upheavals and a magnetic polar shift.

"Alas, there is little more I can say," said the President, waving a hand helplessly in the air. "I assure you, we will continue to provide updates on the situation. When and where possible, broadcasts will be carried on all channels from this point forward. God bless you all.

"Please note down the number and website that will go live after this broadcast to facilitate applications for passes to the Demran Corporation's haven. This is known as the *Oasis*."

The President continued. "The lucky applicants will be transported to safety from around the world over the next few days. They will be taken to an airstrip in Iraq from whence they will be taken on to their final destination, the Oasis."

"The rest of us will have to fend for ourselves. I shall be amongst you. There will be meetings held in your local communities over the next two days to prepare us for the challenges ahead. I appeal to you all to remain calm.

"Finally, this message is being broadcast on behalf of the United Nations. I urge you to stay calm and go about your daily business as if nothing has changed, but note that a curfew will be imposed from the 21st December, 2012, until the danger has passed."

A UK phone number flashed in front of them, Jean missed it but got the website address: http://demagodran.org.uk

Paula and Jean looked at each other. "It looks serious," interjected Paula. "Just my luck to win the lottery and then the world ends the following week."

As Paula picked up the phone, Jean asked, "What are you doing?"

Paula dialled the number on the screen instantly. She was used to all manner of competitions and knew it was important to get to the head of the queue.

"Saving us, Jean," she said with an abstracted air.

Jean retorted, "What makes you think they want to save us?"

"Well, who's going to make the beds and pull the pints?" Paula replied.

She waved triumphantly. Paula's experience with travel competitions got her past the first, automated service and a series of Sudoku-style challenges with numbers and words. An upbeat, but singularly condescending female voice then relayed precise instructions to her.

"Welcome to the Oasis selection service. You can make one application. All applications are selected randomly and you will be notified immediately at the end of this call if you have been successful." Paula frowned.

The Oasis customer service spiel continued: "Please enter the number of applicants."

Paula entered number '2' on her phone.

"Please state clearly: name, date of birth and present address for applicant Number One."

Paula gave her name, but was reticent about her date of birth. Reluctantly, she eventually supplied the full details and gave Jean's address as the point of collection for them both. She then did the same with Jean's details.

"Thank you. Please wait while we check your records."

"Thank you. You have been pre-selected to complete your application. We require payment in full of 40lbs of gold, per applicant, at current market values. There was a pause.

A little confused, Paul muttered, "They want to charge us in gold."

Jean replied, "We'll that's me done for. I've only got my wedding ring and I can't imagine that's worth much."

The machine advised the total funds that would be required in a somewhat strained American voice. It read out the figures one by one: "Two million... (Pause) two hundred and fifty eight thousand... (Pause) and two hundred... (Pause) US dollars." It added crisply, "Please provide a valid credit or debit card number to complete your payment."

Paula had turned ashen. "It wants two million quid. What if it's a hoax?"

Jean gave her 'It is not a hoax!' look. She pulled back her net curtains to see an armoured car run past the door. "State of emergency," she replied.

The machine seemed impatient.

"Sorry. I don't seem to have received your payment. Please confirm that you want to proceed. Press '1' to confirm your booking or hang up to cancel."

Paula was convinced. She pressed the digit '1' on the telephone.

"Just calculating your payment, please hold." The machine turned over the information again and blurted out the figures one by one:

"Two million... (Pause) Three hundred and twenty five thousand... (Pause) and two hundred... (Pause) US dollars.

"Please provide a credit or debit card number to complete your payment."

"It's gone up nearly one hundred and fifty thousand dollars in less than 30 seconds," Paula gasped.

"Panic must be setting in," Jean remarked. "If you can afford it, just pay it!"

Paula pumped in her credit card number. Luckily her six million pound win was still sitting in her current account.

The machine chimed up again. Paula was nervous. For some reason, she always expected her card payments to bounce: a lifetime of no funds. Old habits die hard.

"Payment accepted, thank you. Your booking is confirmed. You will be collected at... " the machine was calculating again... "Ten am tomorrow morning. Please have your passports available for inspection. Your baggage allowance is thirty-three kilos. We look forward to welcoming you to the Oasis."

"Well..." Paula was still shocked over parting with nearly two million quid. "We're being picked up tomorrow at 10am."

"I should hope so at those prices," Jean remarked acerbically.

"It does sound more like a hotel."

"Can we really go? What about all those poor people left behind?" Jean then thought about Ocean and panicked. "Ocean, what about Ocean? She's at a festival this week."

"Ocean will be ok," Paula assured Jean with conviction. She's resourceful. Leave her a message. I'll buy her a ticket. Money, it seemed, would be of no use at the Oasis.

"Best take our jewellery boxes," she added as an afterthought.

Excitement and fear vied for dominance as the two friends prepared for the Oasis. They were excited that their lives were about to change, but riding alongside this was fear of the unknown. An ark for Armageddon was hardly a mundane choice!

When Paula popped home to pick up her things, the streets were buzzing. Mainly, this was with people loaded down by as many bags as they could carry. There had been a run on the shops to beat all Christmases but the takings would not help balance banking deficits, government coffers or retailers' books. The world was largely in shock, trying to work out what the next move might be.

At home, the friends emptied the fridge of wine; the usual crutch for Paula. Jean was more modest in her drinking, these days, but broke her rule on this occasion. It provided just the edge they needed to get through the next few hours.

Inbetween glasses of wine, leavened with random nibbles from Jean's cupboards and fridge, the two women busied themselves packing, unpacking, and packing again; sometimes with shrieks of frustration.,

Aside from that, they were glued to the news channels. The world was starting to fall apart. There had been a run on the pumps, travel was almost impossible, supermarkets were empty and, in some cases, had been ransacked and burned. Finally, they fell asleep exhausted in the early hours.

The alarm went off at 7am. Jean and Paula slept through it. The next thing they knew, there was a hammering at the door. It was 10am. There was an armoured vehicle outside with Demran emblazoned on the side. Jean and Paula panicked. Luckily, they had packed their suitcases and laid out their clothes.

Jean ran down in her pyjamas and opened the door. A lean, stocky military type, all sinew with the square jaw line beloved of war cartoons, greeted her at the door. He would have been great eye candy if she hadn't felt sick with nerves.

"Five minutes? Sorry, we overslept." She had a déjà vu moment and thought she had met him before. In my dreams, she supposed.

"We haven't got five minutes, Missus. Be quick. I have a schedule to keep and unrest is brewing. We'll be lucky to get to the airport if you don't get down here at a run."

Paula lurched down the stairs behind Jean, all bedraggled, her makeup running down her cheeks from the night before and her hair piled on top. She struggled with her suitcase but perked up when she saw the guard, and stopped struggling. He moved forward to help and she went all girly on him, reaching for her handbag to try and sort out her appearance.

"Come on Jean, we can change when we get to the Oasis." Paula stepped out and held the car door. They were not being transported alone; there were other passengers in the bright red, armoured vehicle. Jean followed her lead, and motioned to the guard to take her case, then pulled some clothes quickly, upstairs.

Downstairs again, she began fumbling for her keys.

The guard interjected, "You won't need those again, Missus. This place will be rubble in two days from now."

She couldn't take that in and still doubled-locked the front door. Then she stepped onto the pavement. There were youths and grown men looting the shop at the end of the road. She stepped inside their transport, and had another déjà vu moment. Everything seemed unreal, but she seemed to have relived some of it before.

Paula had settled herself in, as usual, ever capable of adapting to her environment. She was sitting next to a man Jean recognised, but couldn't quite place. She sat down opposite the others; and the man extended his hand to shake hers.

"Hi. My name's Ethan. I'm from the Murray Institute down the road. You may have heard of it."

As he bent forward to shake her hand, he winked at her. Of all things to be taking with him, he was carrying a verdant green and pink parrot in a cage.

"Pleased to see you again, Ma'am," it chuckled.

Chapter Thirty Six

Thursday, 20th December, 2012
The Oasis, Iraq, Middle East

All that is, was and will be is one experience.

The red jet, emblazoned with its distinctive logo, started to descend onto the Babylonian airstrip. It seemed that this was a trip back to where civilisation began; and a fitting place for civilization to end or be renewed depending, of course, on your point of view.

They were aboard an Airbus A380, one of the latest big craft in the sky. This one had just a single class of travel - first - suitable for all its wealthy occupants. Unlikely 'new friends' were acquainting themselves with each other in the bar or chatting across private doors.

Jean noticed that Ethan appeared nauseated by Paula's constant advances towards him. In contrast, Jean's innocence beside her larger-than-life friend didn't go unnoticed. She looked around, celebrity spotting notable TV stars and a smattering of politicians and entrepreneurs.

The passengers on the A380 knew they had been lucky to call 'The Lifeline', as it was now known. They had all managed to become part of a select migration by calling in response to the President's plea.

There were 500 passengers, each paying at least a million dollars for their ticket to salvation. That was half a billion dollars in receipts for this plane, alone. It was one of a number scheduled to fly around the clock that day.

The lifeline had closed within the first hour of operation, with tickets becoming increasingly more expensive as the gold price soared to unprecedented levels. It was rumoured that the last tickets went for 100 million each.

To Jean's way of thinking, it was odd to give a price tag to life. She wondered what kind of world it would be like with everyone a celebrity or moneyed in some way. Well, except her. She also realised that the others would not, necessarily, be encumbered with cerebral, cultured or creative minds; and integrity or the kind of standards she valued might not stand out where they were going.

As she continued to look around the plane, she could see a lot of what she would describe as 'new money', and, judging by the look of some of the passengers, it might be from ill-gotten gains. She was not impressed.

"There doesn't seem much of a future for the human race," she told herself a little wistfully.

"So Prof.," said Paula, already being 'uber' familiar, "Tell me what your Laureate was for." Of course, she was simply pretending to understand what she was asking about.

"I proved that telekinesis was a form of communication that was based on insights into other worlds - dimensions, if you will. These project from your current domain of existence into future events." Totally lost, Paula was agreeably silent.

With one eye on Jean, Ethan continued. "Humans have adapted to their environment and see the world as distinctly temporal, but time doesn't really exist at all. Everything is ordained and predictable, but with one further complication. There are many possible outcomes within almost parallel worlds.

"On the whole, these parallel worlds appear to be very similar but, for those of us who live in them, the experiences in each can be very different; and you can influence the outcome, a little like switching tracks on a record. That's the element of choice, of the individual.

"The defining moments in your life take you down many, potentially different tracks; the decision over which you choose is yours alone."

He concluded, smiling almost imperceptibly at Paula's lack of comprehension, in contrast to Jean's understanding, "Life is all about getting the best experience from a whole myriad of possibilities."

Ethan had indeed lost Paula, but Jean was listening avidly. Seeing an opportunity to get a word in, she said, "Makes sense to me, Professor. I sometimes get visions of things that don't make sense to me. I'm a little psychic, if you will."

"Interesting..." When Ethan smiled, it lit up his face; and he was looking past Paula to Jean. He knew it was mischievous of him, but he relished the opportunity to exclude Jean's over familiar side-kick from the conversation; at least for a minute or two.

Leaning over the aisle to gaze closely into Jean's remarkable, sapphire blue eyes, he mused, "Some people are genetically predisposed to be psychic. They can become adept at it with the right socialisation and some practice. I'm quite sure you are one of them."

He added after a moment's thought, "Sometimes I am, too."

"Really?" Jean looked at Ethan with growing confidence. He made her feel significant and she liked that about him.

The plane began the last few minutes of its descent and banked sharply. The seat belt signs went on and Jean looked out of the window at the desert below. In the distance, she could see a metropolis; it was like nothing she had ever seen before. It was a city of egg-shaped buildings perched on a nest of sand.

Ethan saw that Jean was interested in the architecture and anticipated her question. "The secret's in the shape. If you've ever squeezed an egg, you'll know that it's impossible to crush the egg under pressure but, if you punch the side, it falls apart."

"The Oasis uses the same principles. When the 'big quake' comes, we're predicting that the land mass in this area will sink considerably and a massive flood will follow. The whole city is designed to float and then, because it is anchored, it will be submerged under the sea to help protect against pollution, raging fires and radiation fallout."

There was a long silence. Jean broke it as she realised what Ethan had said. "Radiation fallout?"

"Yes, most of the nuclear reactors, on a global scale, will be damaged by the quakes. There's also volcanic activity to consider. This will turn day into night for many around the globe."

"We will be submerged for 12 months, just below the surface of the sea; at least until the atmosphere improves and water levels readjust. The defrosting and refreezing of the polar caps will contribute to the rapid rise of sea levels."

"Just like Noah's Ark!" Jean exclaimed.

Ethan paused and looked at her. "Funny you should say that, but our records suggest that Noah is a legend carried down from the distant past and, yes, quite possibly is from the last Precessional cycle or some other cataclysmic event connected with Precession."

"You see, this event has occurred before; many times before. That's why Richanti has had time to plan and build such an adventurous solution to the end of life, as we know it."

"Richanti?" Jean felt a shudder run down her spine.

"Yes. Do you know him?"

"No, I don't think so, but..."

"He's a great guy," Ethan enthused. "He inspired me when I was younger; as a student in Berkeley. I've delivered on a number of projects for him. Without his funding, I couldn't have done as much as I have."

Jean had one of her déjà vu moments. The Golden Gate Bridge flashed in front of her and she re-experienced a feeling of falling, of the New York skyline and a grand office... and with that, she saw...?

Yes, she saw Ethan with her. How could that be? She had been having strange feelings about him all day, akin to finding one's soul mate... but what was the vision all about? She shook her head and turned her attention to the Oasis city.

It was big and bold, now, like nothing she had ever seen. The Airbus touched down and hurtled along the airstrip. The huge jet switched into reverse thrust and Jean leaned forward to watch the landing. Taking off and landing always made her feel very alive. She noticed that Paula had nodded off. It must have been the free champagne and lack of sleep.

Jean and Ethan resumed their talk as the plane taxied into base. She tried to sum him up. He was single, it seemed; and he was very handsome, despite having quite large ears. But so did Prince Charles. More importantly, he seemed genuinely interested in her.

The plane pulled up at its nominated stand and shortly afterwards, the doors were opened. The hot desert air hit them in waves as they stepped onto the air bridge. It must have been about 39 Celsius outside although it was early evening.

The three new friends pledged to meet up once they had settled into their new home. Ethan had a welcome party waiting for him and was ushered off quickly.

The airport was odd in the extreme. There were no Customs or Immigration authorities; and consequently, there were no passports or baggage checks. Nor was there any currency to exchange; and everyone had a pre-allocated apartment.

Meet-and-greet people guided the passengers to a rapid transit system, which took them straight to their accommodation. They were told their baggage would follow. Jean and Paula had been allocated a concierge called Ty. He was a fit young man in his twenties. Jean and Paula were amazed. They were simply not used to the upper class lifestyle.

The last holiday they had was rather ordinary in comparison: a guest house in Bournemouth on Alum Chine. They knew the owners from previous visits to the town and were warmly welcomed.

Paula had a holiday romance there with a guy called Reg. Alas, it ended tragically when he had a coronary right in front of her. It took a while for her to snap out of her self-obsession and realise that the poor guy was in need of A&E and a 999 call.

Jean simply used to tag onto Paula's apron strings and mop up the pieces, although she would be the first to admit that she loved the drama; this was why they were the best of friends.

Their personal concierge slid the pass key into the door slot for their apartment, opened the door and stepped aside for Paula and Jean to enter. It was stunning. Ty showed them around the streamlined, contemporary apartment. It had two large double bedrooms with en-suite bathrooms, a kitchen that was more of a wet bar than a kitchen; and there was a lounge with an amazing view of the Oasis city. The apartment was shielded from outside intrusion by a huge piece of continuous glass stretching across the vista.

There was no greenery outside to speak of, but amazing fountains towered 100 feet into the sky, the water danced in the sunlight. Inside, there were exotic plants covered in vivid flowers. The smell of frangipani and orange blossom filtered through the air shafts.

Ty broke their awestruck silence.

"You can open the balcony windows by using this panel over here. They will close automatically in the event of a quake and you have a three minute warning before they seal. After that, nothing can open them, so please take the warning seriously! That's the safety briefing over with.

"If you look at this panel over here, there's a list of fridge and dry goods. The fridge and cupboards will be stocked daily. Just tap what you want onto the iPad shopping list. Likewise, drop your laundry in the baskets provided and, should you require any additional shopping or gifts, just order the items on the panel provided. I"ll bring your orders directly to your rooms."

He smiled agreeably, "And please call me at any time. I'm available 24/7 to attend to your needs. Well, that's it. Welcome to the Oasis."

Jean and Paula looked at each other. The view, the apartment and the extras had overwhelmed them.

Jean piped up. "How do we pay for all this?"

"Madame," Ty said slowly, "You've paid already. Everything comes on a complimentary basis with your ticket."

"What about you? Who pays you, Ty?"

"Nobody, Madame. Don't you think I'm lucky to be here?"

"Yes, I suppose so..." Jean felt a little unsure about Ty's situation. "So did you buy a ticket?"

"No, Madame, but I was selected. It was strange. I'm lucky. My friend was, too; we were both from the same modelling agency. It was as though someone had a database for all the agencies. We're all here. Dr Richanti addressed us all, personally, and said we're are all very important to the functioning of the 'whole machine', as he calls it."

He gave a little bow. "Someone needs to provide service for all of you and we're grateful that your money paid for us, too."

Jean and Paula looked at each other again. They could hardly believe what they were hearing. Before Paula could do any damage, Jean interjected, "Well, we're both very grateful, Ty, and look forward to spending more time with you."

He nodded and smiled as he closed the door.

Jean exclaimed, "So that's how they did it. Everyone was pre-selected. They knew how much you had in your bank account before you even dialled the number. They milked everyone, all of us, right down to the bell boy. It's a designer society and Richanti is the designer. Oh, Paula, what are we going to do?"

"What do you mean, what are we going to do? We're going to enjoy it, aren't we? And I bet the bell boy does more than stock the bar and change the sheets."

"Paula!"

"Well Jean, get real. The world has changed and we're very lucky we've changed with it."

Jean couldn't quite reconcile herself to Paula's reaction. She reflected that this kind of behaviour was, alas, probably to be expected. The self-obsessed would become ever more selfish as the 'designer society' made everyone feel good about their position in the world. And, of course, they would never let it go. They would defend selfishness to the hilt. It would be a nice bubble to live in for some.

All of a sudden, Jean felt sad and yearned for her simple two-up, two-down once again. This was not what she had planned for the rest of eternity.

She roused herself and said, "Paula, I'm going to take a look around and get some air while I can."

"Ok, lovely. I'll just help myself to the bar, have a power shower, and do some online shopping. Take your time."

Jean took a door pass and walked back to the transport. She took everything in, but from a different perspective this time. "The whole Oasis is superficial," she mused. "It's amplifies the worst traits of humankind."

She arrived at the halls for transport, entertainment and food; the mall swarmed with invitations to culture and cuisine. Then she saw Ty enter the transport next to her. As he swiped his card, she jumped in behind him.

"No!" He objected. You can't come with me, Madame. It was too late. The doors had closed. Ty looked downwards.

"What's the matter, my dear?"

"You have got me into trouble."

"How can I get you into trouble?"

"You're not supposed to have access to the servants' quarters."

"Servants' quarters?" she repeated in a baffled tone.

"Yes, servants' quarters. I'll probably be on washing-up duty tomorrow because of you," he said half angrily, half fearfully.

Jean was startled by his reaction. She knew it wasn't Ty's fault so what was he so scared of?

The doors to the transport opened and she couldn't believe her eyes. It was a barren kind of barracks area. There was a cavernous hall at one end with people swarming in, lined-up clutching their small belongings, unlike Jean and Paula, whose possessions had been taken off them, borne aloft and unpacked neatly. The incoming crowd was being split into a number of queues.

Ty was behind her.

"I'm sorry to have snapped at you, but it's terribly dangerous for me; and now for you, too."

He whispered to her that any queue was a good queue, apart from the one on the far left.

"What happens to those people?"

"Liquidation, plant food!"

Jean paled with horror.

"You wanted to know," Ty replied quietly.

"Now, I suggest you get out of here as fast as you can and forget about it." He opened up the transit for her.

Jean stepped back, still in shock. The doors closed and Ty walked away.

Chapter Thirty Seven

Thursday, 20th December, 2012
Jean and Paula's apartment. The Oasis, Iraq, Middle East

Never fear death, it's not the end.

Jean made her way back to the apartment. She was lost in thought about what she had just witnessed; and unsure what to do about it. She pushed her key card into the lock and the door opened. She saw Paula busy on an electronic panel in her lap.

"This is amazing!" Paula enthused. 'It's an iPad. I've already stocked the fridge, ordered breakfast and done some urgent shopping for the big party tomorrow night."

"Party?" squeaked Jean, incredulously.

"Yes. Would you believe it's called *Armageddon*? An invitation was delivered while you were gadding about the building. Apparently, the party has been organised to help us through the loss of the world we've known. It's more of a wake, I guess, and you know what fun they can be."

Paula burbled on, "I thought black the 'colour du jour', don't you? I've ordered a black Vivienne Westwood cocktail dress with a brand new pair of Jimmy Choo stilettos; and I've even got a jewellery loan. Do you think a tiara is over the top?"

Jean couldn't believe what she was hearing. An elite portion of the world was turning into the greatest natural disaster in history: a show with ringside seats while the rest of world perished and a small part of it was enslaved. It seemed they were the lucky ones, or so Jean had been told.

Paula could see the disapproval in Jean's eyes, but she was used to it and parried her mood with a quick riposte. Yes, it is a tragedy," she continued unconvincingly. But Richanti says we *all* need to be positive and move on."

Richanti!" Jean exclaimed. Before she could finish, the iPad popped up onscreen with 'email'.

Paula's eyebrows rose. "I wonder who that's from?"

Jean picked the machine up. "Dr Stuart Richanti requests the pleasure of your company for Armageddon, the end of the world as you know it." Jean couldn't believe her eyes. The invitation had been forwarded from Ethan and gave directions to Richanti's private dining room.

Slowly, she said, "So you're right, Paula. And Ethan is inviting us as his guests..."

Paula swooped on the iPad. "We've finally arrived! It couldn't be any better. Right at the top with the triple 'A' guest list. Aren't we lucky, Jean? She was falling over her words in amazement and delight. "I can't believe we've got an invite to Richanti's private dining room."

Jean thought to herself, quietly, "If you have good intentions, then the world rises before you to help you in your quest." She was dreaming again. She often dreamed. Where did that come from? But she knew what it meant and what she had to do.

Paula piped up as the screen popped up again. "What's this? You've got an email from Ocean."

"Ocean?" She had forgotten all about Ocean in the midst of life spinning by on high amps in recent days.

"Read it to me please, will you Paula?"

"Dear Mom, managed to get your message eventually. Great that you have a pass to the Oasis. Sounds like they need some real people there, by all accounts. All good here at a festival on The Downs. Met an amazing guy, Richanti's son, Fitz, can you believe it? A prep school dropout and a great guy. I'll be ok. Don't worry about me. You taught me well, Ocean xxx"

"Son?" Jean puzzled aloud. "Richanti has a son?" She was not sure about that, but she knew it was important, although she was certainly not sure why. Her mind moved to Ocean.

"But fancy that! Ocean contacting me here."

Well, she had done a great job on her daughter and, as a result, never had to worry about whether she would be ok. Ocean had an amazing ability to get into but also get out of the worst possible scrapes.

Jean, lost in thought, had given up any notion of trying to explain to Paula what she had seen: the dark side of the Oasis. If she couldn't explain it to her best friend, what chance did she have of explaining it to Ethan? All the same, she hatched a plan.

"Don't you think it's time for room service?" Paula asked, being someone who rarely turned down the opportunity for a drink.

"An excellent idea," Jean murmured in a distracted way.

Paula demanded, "What's your tipple, then?"

"Gin and tonic for me, thanks," Jean replied.

"I'll join you. Let's have a large one. It's going to be an interesting evening."

Jean tucked several images quietly away in her mind and said, "You don't know just how interesting."

Within a few minutes, there was a knock at the door. It was a waiter; but not Ty.

"Oh... Ty not working tonight?" Paula asked, aggrieved that her manservant was not in attendance.

"Ty has moved on, Ma'am. My name is Mario," the lad said. He looked sheepish.

Jean knew exactly where Ty had moved to. She would have to move fast because she had compromised him, albeit for the greater good.

Mario carefully placed a linen-lined tray down on a glass table in the middle of the room. It held a bottle of Bombay Sapphire and two crystal tumblers, and was accompanied by an ice bucket and two bottles of cold

Schweppes tonic. He was carrying an extra six-pack of tonic as well, and asked if he should put it in the fridge. Once he had done so, Jean sprang into action.

"Mario, please can you do us a favour?" she asked, and put a friendly arm around his shoulders to distract him. Swiftly, she slid her other hand into his pocket.

"Please will you take a picture of us for our Facebook profile?"

Jean had what she needed and handed him the iPad.

"Sure, I will," he responded.

"You've lightened up, Jean," Paula tittered, "but what do you know about Facebook?"

Mario took the snap as requested.

"If that's all, I'll leave you two ladies to it," he said with a quick nod and left Jean and Paula to their drinks. Jean waited for him to exit before she raised a question with Paula.

"Why not see if Ethan would like to come round this evening," she suggested.

"Great idea," Paula said, and tapped out a reply. "Thanks for the invite, Ethan. How kind to think of us. Most gracious of you. We would very much like to join you. Meanwhile, why not drop by this evening to catch up over a cocktail. Is around six ok? Jean and Paula."

"That should do it," chortled Paula.

Paula received an immediate reply. "Why wait. I'll drop round now."

They both leapt for their make-up kits to regenerate their faces. Shortly, there was a knock on the apartment door. Jean leapt up and answered it, almost as if she had been counting the minutes while Paula tucked into the bottle of gin she had ordered.

Jean jumped up and opened the door. "Great to see you again, Ethan," Jean said, and hugged him. He was surprised; it seemed like a desperate hug. He was not sure why, but he trusted Jean.

As he walked into the room, Paula eyed him up over the top of her G&T. He remembered the plane and was not at all sure he could manage an evening of Paula's advances. Jean sensed he was a little uncomfortable and interjected, "I explored the city earlier. Fancy a whirl on the transit? It's amazing."

Paula pulled a face, but was too languid to put a spoke in Jean's wheel.

"Sounds like fun," Ethan replied with enthusiasm. "I've been working non-stop since I got here. Richanti is a slave driver..."

If only you knew, Jean thought and asked, "You don't mind if we pop out for a moment, do you Paula?"

Paula hardly noticed. She was back on her iPad exploring a new, virtual world of entertainment. The two slipped out and left her to it. There was a transit at the end of the corridor and the two escapees made their way to it.

Jean pulled out the pass she had procured earlier. As she used it to open the transit doors, she saw that the options on the panel in the transit were markedly different to the ones she and Paula were offered. Only the lower levels were available to the working classes. It seemed there was no shopping or entertainment allowed for those in servitude.

She pressed a button marked 'embarkation' and the transit accelerated downwards. Ethan was completely unaware of where they were heading to.

As he looked out of the window of the transit, he exclaimed, "Isn't it beautiful, Jean. It's a modern Noah's Ark." The transit passed the waterfalls with a tall glass-faced building towering above them. They then began to sink down to the large conduit below the city.

"I had a hand in most of this, Jean," Ethan said proudly. "Richanti consulted me on the design elements; and we worked on Precession together to predict the safest haven with the hope of preserving the human race. This city has been built for a million souls and can withstand Tsunami, Earthquakes and a wide range of temperature changes, as well as toxicity from the environment outside."

Jean felt a little uncomfortable over his abduction but felt she had to intervene. "Well, Ethan, that's actually why I wanted to show you round. I'm not sure you know exactly what's going on around here."

"What do you mean?" Ethan frowned in perplexity.

The transit took another sharp turn downwards and, with perfect timing, slowed down as the decorative walls became breeze block and the natural light had all gone. The doors opened.

"I mean this," Jean remarked tersely.

"Seeing is believing!"

Ethan was speechless as he looked at the dungeon-level reception hall. Droves of people were entering below. It was very different from the lobby they had entered. People were being split into queues, according to ability; a simple but effective process with skills in service being the order of the day.

There were guards dressed in black uniforms and holding stun guns standing on either side of the lines. They split up the masses of people who were still entering through the entrance gates. Many looked exhausted. Some had travelled thousands of miles to get to the Oasis in the hope that they might be part of the safe haven. When the location was leaked, people who were not selected took the initiative and tracked the city down.

The guards were corralling superfluous people into a larger queue than the service one. This one led to the far end of the hall where a large lift the size of an articulated lorry was enveloping about fifty people at a time.

"The lucky ones get to stay," Jean said. Ethan looked at her inquisitively, not really understanding the comment.

"I want to get a closer look," Ethan said. He had absorbed the vista and his acutely inquisitive intellect had kicked in. They dropped down a stairwell to the floor below. The area was cordoned off from the survivors, who were clearly visible but inaccessible. It was as though they provided a visible warning for those who were lucky enough to be picked to serve.

There was a cage wall in front of them, guiding the larger queue of people to an unknown fate.

Ethan tapped into an access panel at the side of the door and swiped his card across the reader. 'Access denied' appeared on the panel. "Funny, I have access to all areas. Can I try yours, please Jean? Where did you get your pass from?"

"I procured it from our waiter," Jean replied in a tight voice.

Ethan swiped again. "That's better," he remarked, as he tapped into the site map. "They seem to be entering the recycling area."

"Plant food," Jean exclaimed in horror. "Worse than that, even. If this place is self-sustainable, it's because we're living off plants and animals sustained by human remains."

Ty had been correct, after all.

Ethan had gone both white and quiet. He was deep in thought.

"He tapped on the screen again and pulled up the CCTV, unable to look at the scene for more than a few seconds before killing the session. The same people he had seen just moments ago were being corralled into a fire pit in the incineration plant.

He groaned in protest to himself. "No, it can't be so." He was computing this new information and what it meant. As he had designed a lot of the Oasis systems, they were meant to preserve life. But he had seen only a cross section of the completed work...

In fact, he had been uncomfortable when he set foot in the lobby on their arrival, surprised that it was more like a seven star hotel than a biosphere of the most able people in the world. It was not a cross section of life in the way he had hoped it to be.

His life flashed before him as he reprocessed the meaning of every event in it and realised that Richanti had manipulated him from the very start. All Richanti had wanted was to get access to the technology he had produced.

Initially, this had simply been to gain insight into future events but it had culminated with his best kept secret, the time machine, which could shift realities at will. And now everything was a lie and he was the sorcerer's accomplice.

He looked at Jean. Why this woman? What had caused the complex feelings he had about her? And how had she become so important in all of this? Very little made sense to him but he knew how to find out.

Finally, he spoke. His mouth was almost too dry to get the words out. "Jean thanks for showing me this. It is abominable! I'm going to need your help. If we're going to do anything about it, we need to get close enough to Richanti to achieve an element of surprise.

"I need you to keep quiet until tomorrow evening at the Armageddon party."

More questions spilled out. "Can you act normally until then? Can you trust Paula? Do you trust me?"

"Yes I trust you," she said simply. "And of course I can trust Paula. She looks pretentious but, deep down, she has a heart of gold and would give her life for me. She and Ocean both look out for me."

"Ocean?"

"Ocean's my daughter. She's ok. I got an email from her and she's apparently with Richanti's son at some 'end of the world' festival."

"That's odd: Richanti's son," Ethan was puzzled. "Richanti doesn't have a son! Well, he's never mentioned one."

Ethan put his arms around Jean's shoulders and motioned for them to go up. She punched the panel once more and they rose swiftly to the world of plenty.

Chapter Thirty Eight

Thursday, 20th December, 2012
Ethans Apartment, The Oasis, Iraq, Middle East

In the darkest of hours, faith will guide you home.

Ethan paced up and down his apartment floor, unravelling Richanti's betrayal, piece-by- piece. He was struggling to find a motive that made sense but, so far, had found none that fitted the 'jigsaw puzzle'. Nonetheless, he knew what he must do. His apartment, unlike most of the others, was located next to an industrial centre.

Here, Richanti had recreated a replica of the Murray Institute. If the redbrick walls had gone, its essence was the same. As ever, it was filled with research graduates, part of Ethan's faculty, and a cocktail of chemical smells.

The lab was funded entirely by the Demran Corporation, of course, but it seemed that what Ethan had interpreted as entrepreneurship and philanthropy was actually just an attempt to control him.

Richanti had always restricted unauthorised trips back in time "to protect humanity". Well, that was what he said. Ethan was no longer so sure. Richanti had something to hide; and the more Ethan delved into the situation, the more he discovered just how much Richanti had to hide.

Being of a different nature entirely, Ethan wanted truth and justice. He had been manipulated into contributing the essence of his skills to the Oasis: the most sophisticated 'death camp' in modern times. But Richanti had been present in his life right from the outset of his career.

From the time he popped up in Golden Gate Park, right through to the Oasis, Ethan had been exploited; and he was angry about losing so many years of his life in this way. All the same, anger was not what drove him, now; it was curiosity. What was so secret that Richanti wanted to restrict time travel? Also buzzing around his brain like a regular blip on the radar was the question, exactly who was Jean? Then it dawned on him.

"Jean..." he thought, "No it can't be, surely?"

She was much older now, but he could see the similarity. The decades distort your looks and time erases your memory, but, once prompted, the human capacity to recall is incredible.

"It *is* Jean!" Yes, it's the same girl - now woman - that he had met during Freshers' week at Berkeley. His mind spun again. Surely, it couldn't possibly be her? But then, if it was her. Richanti had wanted her out of the way desperately. Then again, how did she get to be in Berkeley with him in the first place?

Ethan thought some more.

She worked at the University; it was conceivable that they had met there and she had travelled back in time in one of his experiments, he guessed, but she seemed even more important to him than a colleague; that was his instinct.

That Jean was good, and Richanti was evil, was certainly clear. He had to find out more. He walked into the corridor linking his apartment to the laboratory. Every good inventor has a back door to every experiment and Ethan was no exception; the machine was programmed to always take commands from its creator. He had a notion to go back in time and follow the clues from there.

He was in a plain white room with a metal box inside. There were no obvious panels, power, buttons, knobs, or flashing lights of any kind. The secret lay in the skin of the machine, which contained thousands of tiny dots; similar to the pixels on a computer screen. And it only *appeared* to be metallic in nature.

Ethan defocused to reveal the 'stereogram' image. The letter 'M' emerged from the ether. Ethan then changed his focus to the time just before he met Richanti for the first time with Jean in Golden Gate Park. He saw the bridge in the background and the lights of Sausalito beyond. The two of them were standing on the edge of the park just a few minutes before Richanti and the green station wagon turned up. He saw a kaleidoscope of colour in his mind.

There was a flash of pure white light and he was gone.

Ethan found himself in Golden Gate Park; another déjà vu moment, with Jean by his side. He had a few minutes yet. Twilight came upon them as they were walking to the top of the hill on the edge of Golden Gate Park. They moved slowly towards the bridge, watching the twinkling lights of distant Sausalito and the prison island in the Bay all illuminated in a rhythmic wave. Ethan turned to Jean.

"It *is* you." The moment confirmed what he had suspected for a while; he was starting to piece the jigsaw together.

Jean was startled. "Of course it's me." She sensed the change in him. He was like another person; not a boy with boyish ways, but a man. She was puzzled. He was not supposed to be aware of her intent.

"Who are you and why did you travel back in time to be with me? To influence me?"

Jean wasn't expecting to be challenged, quite the opposite, but this was an interesting turn of events. Then, it had been an interesting day. She went with it.

"You won't believe me, it's quite bizarre," Jean remarked with a hint of bemusement in her tone. She, too, was older than she seemed.

"Try me, you might be surprised."

"I'm your cleaning supervisor in 2012."

"Cleaning supervisor?" Ethan did a double take.

"I discovered your time machine and knew I had to travel back in time to ensure you invented it so that you could defeat Richanti. It sounds implausible, I know, but there it is. The rest I really don't understand; only that Richanti tried to tempt me and that's how I came to be back here. Other than that, I'm as muddled as you are."

Jean took a sharp breath and continued, "But we haven't got much time." She was agitated, expecting the green station wagon and men in suits coming from nowhere. Safe for the moment, thought, she added, "Well, I know about *that* part. It's Richanti and his motives that I'm worried about," she said in a rush.

"We have time; we have as much time as we need," said Ethan confidently. He had an idea and held out his hands. Jean placed hers in his. "Hold tight and focus. Let's go back to the point in time, at the lab, when you first connected with the machine. Do you remember where and when that was?"

It was less than 24 hours ago for Jean; and she was going home.

Jean and Ethan focused together.

The machine burst with a kaleidoscope of light and they were gone.

They materialised in the anteroom, which ran to the left of Professor Murray's desk back at his Birmingham research institute. The room was dusty and full of books. They hid behind one of the numerous book shelves and waited for their other selves to turn up.

It was an odd sensation to see Ethan's double enter the room. First, he opened the door to his office, then he unlocked the ante room and created a path to the lab door and his precious time machine. He then disappeared into the lab, evidently hiding somewhere within its numerous rooms and corridors.

Next they saw Jean appear. She looked sheepish; on the one hand highly inquisitive and obviously driven by this, but her gait showed she lacked confidence.

The parrot observed, "Here we go round the Mulberry Bush."

Ethan whispered, "He's led you." Then he thought again and corrected himself. "No, I have. I've led you to the machine but you think you've stumbled across it." He was beginning to understand.

Jean was distracted from his meaning by seeing herself in the same room - a novelty, like 3D-TV - and her eyes were focused on the retro outfit that she was wearing, rather than the significance of her actions.

"Why would he do that?" she asked herself. Jean saw the situation in a very different light to Ethan.

"It's about destiny," he smiled a little wryly. "It's your future; at least, it's one of your futures. There are many different possibilities, but certain events, which are like signposts at a crossroads you have to pass through, simply are; and always will be. So they can't be changed.

"Remember, time doesn't exist, Jean. Our whole future is played out to the end of the multiverse itself. If the possibilities and different journeys in our lifetimes are many, they are not infinite; whoever created our *multiverse* had to create limits by providing a framework and direction for certain events."

As Ethan rattled on, Jean chuckled, and tried to smother the noise; it escaped in a fit of giggles. He looked sharply at her.

"It's all right," she gasped. "I just remembered our first meeting at Berkeley. Please go on…!" Jean smiled mischievously, "Just as I said then."

Ethan smiled uncertainly; and then flashed-back on himself. "OK," he grinned, "got you.

No stopping him now, Jean realised.

"So, you see, each of us has a destiny to fulfil. We all get to a crossroads that has to be worked through, personally. Only then can we move forward to new possibilities, new experiences, or an entirely new life.

"In everyone's life, there's usually one major lesson to be learned and one test to be passed. Everything else is fluid and random. It's simply a question of what *your* particular journey involves. Ultimately, we all get to the same place; and we all learn the same lessons but in our 'own time'.

"Then again, no matter how much power, success or intelligence you possess, nothing can interrupt key elements of your destiny… *kismet*, as they say in oriental countries."

Jean looked at him blankly for a moment.

He continued, "You could say *my* destiny was to build the time machine and preserve the human race from extinction. Richanti, on the other hand, is apparently blind to destiny. He's too confused by power and material things. He'd be absolutely distraught if he found out that his life was merely about learning a simple lesson.

"Nothing can change that; no matter how much he tries to manipulate the time line or me... or you, for that matter. And your destiny's caught up with mine. If we're to find out why and how, we need to go a little further into the future from this point; less than a week, is my guess."

"Precession will force many of us to realise our life lessons prematurely; each of us must realise our destiny right now, in fact. Many of us because we won't be around in a few days' time. We have a gun to our heads; and only a few hours left to resolve the mystery of our lives."

Ethan paused to see if Jean was following his argument.

"What choices might you make differently, Jean? What would you really like to learn? Many people never understand destiny. It's only on their death bed that the enormity of their defeat becomes clear. They have failed in their one, major task: that of finding out who they are; and what they're here to resolve."

She had long ago noticed that many people only blossom when faced with adversity. Even so, she still asked Ethan, "Why can't people live the life they want to lead without the threat of losing their life?"

Ethan considered his own walks 'in the wilderness' and changed his train of thought to accommodate her. He was piecing his own jigsaw together, too, but there was still something missing. How did it end?

"This is the tricky part. Do you see anything in the future? Anything out of the ordinary... not a memory, but a vision of something that you have not yet lived"

Jean's memory was sharp, but she wondered about her disconcerting dreams.

"Funny you should say that, I had a dream earlier today... well, decades into the future, actually. I was slumped over my desk at work, half-asleep from exhaustion. It seemed odd but there was a man looking at me and I think the man was you; and then we were together, but we looked broken and desperate."

"That's it."

"Hold my hand and focus for me on the future, focus on your dream."

The machine gave out a ripple of white light and the two of them vanished.

Drip, drip, drip... Water was running in from the street above and Jean could hear the noise of traffic. It was dark and wet. The scenes before they reached this point evoked the US: everything was supersized and everyone was frantically busy. Inside, where they were, there was an odd, musty smell that Jean associated with the Customs Hall in Arrivals at JFK - the cleaning polish they used, maybe. But that was not where they were.

Before them was a caged room. It looked like some kind of stock room and was piled high with office consumables. They could hear people talking; they could hear themselves talking!

"Well this is a great way to end it all, crushed by a Manhattan office building and embalmed in printer ink. The historians of the future will have a field day trying to work this one out after the quake destroys us," Jean remarked drily. Her piquant sense of humour always came out in a crisis.

"Never say never," Ethan replied, always the optimist.

"Well, I'd just like you to try and get out of this one."

"Have faith. I have a plan. I need to get to the Oasis and intercept Richanti. We only have a few hours left."

"The Oasis, what's that?"

"It's Richanti's idea of paradise in the Middle East. He'll have recruited for it by now and filled it with the super-rich and the famous."

"Well supposing you get us out of here, what will you do?" The question's not what I would do, Jean clarified for herself. She reiterated, "What would *you* do?"

"What will *I* do?" Ethan threw the question back at her. "Remember what I said about our life paths being intertwined. The only path that will succeed is one that has you, me and Richanti in it."

There was a short silence while Jean took Ethan's remark on board, then she sidetracked.

"What about Ocean? She'll be outside this Oasis place."

"What about her? I promise you, Ocean's just fine. She's resourceful enough to find a safe place and she has the dossiers I sent her. She'll make sure the rest of the human race gets to know the truth. And Fitz will look after her. It doesn't matter any longer what the world thinks of *us*. Everything's going to change beyond recognition, anyhow."

"Fitz?" Jean asked, frowning in puzzlement.

"Yes, Fitz. Another Demagodran mongrel child. Richanti's not even aware that he has a son who is part of the Demagodran bloodline, let alone that his son has the heart of an angel."

This time Jean remained silent, but she was beginning to smile.

Jean and Ethan looked at each other, and listened intently to the other Jean and Ethan talking.

"I've heard enough," Ethan remarked.

In perfect sequence came Jean's, "I don't understand."

"You don't have to. It's all about the journey. You have a hurdle to cross; and that's all you need to know. It's enough for you to simply be in the Oasis; the rest will become clear to us. Let's get out of here. We need to get to the Oasis, fast.

"There's one other thing we can do right now, though, to help ourselves… "

He smiled.

"What's that?"

Ethan reached out for the cage door and pulled back the deadbolt. As the latch slid back, there was a grinding noise. With a sense of urgency he grabbed Jeans hand and focused intensely on the Oasis.

"Quick we need to leave, back to the Oasis; to the beginning and to the end."

The machine gave out a pulse of white light and they were gone.

-/-

"What was that?" Jean heard the deadbolt being slid back. She walked to the cage door and gave it a push. It opened. She was astonished, but deep down, somehow not altogether surprised.

"Have faith," Ethan smiled at her. The two friends hugged. They knew what they must do: the Oasis awaited them.

Chapter Thirty Nine

Friday, 21st December, 2012
Ethan's Apartment, The Oasis, Iraq, Middle East

*And though I have the gift of prophecy, understand all mysteries and all
knowledge and power,
without love, I am nothing.
Corinthians 13:8*

With Armageddon just a few hours away, Jean and Paula were preparing for the party of their lives, and Jean felt a ton lighter, having shared her secret with Ethan. Before her intervention, he was unaware of the dark side to the Oasis.

Right on cue, there was a knock at the door. Jean opened it to Ethan, who looked suave and elegant in a tuxedo and a brocade waistcoat. He admired Jean's sea-green silk trousers and matching tunic and – at Jean's behest – fastened the clasp of her necklace carefully for her. It was a silver chain with a peace symbol in jade. The two of them hugged.

Paula was surprised by the affection and wondered how they managed to bond so soon. She swept forward, looking a million dollars. She really had 'got' the Oasis look with her beautifully-cut but simple, black cocktail dress. The tiara and diamond drops were just a little over the top, though. Naturally, she had the champagne on ice.

"It's strange," she remarked. "Yet another bell boy has gone missing." She pondered the situation for a moment, wondering why management kept swapping them. Jean knew something, she was sure of that. Paula picked up everything: she was a survivor; and good at it. She always knew when she was being played and hated not knowing everything.

"Come on!" Paula interrupted Jean and Ethan's embrace. "Champagne to celebrate life!" Timing was everything, she thought.

"You two look a little sheepish," she added. "What have you been up to? And where have all the bellboys gone? They're dropping like flies."

Ethan and Jean looked at each other; she was very close. Jean said with a rueful expression, "You're right, but you wouldn't believe me if I told you."

Ethan interjected, "It's better that we don't tell you; not right now." He searched for an answer that was evasive but not a put-down.

"We need you to shine; and to look relaxed and natural tonight," Ethan said diplomatically. "What you do will be important, so we don't want to burden you with distractions... but I promise, before the night's out, we'll fill you in on everything. Please trust us, it's *really* important."

Paula looked unconvinced but flattered. "Okay, but knocking off bellboys must be an offence even in the Oasis." She couldn't have been closer to the truth.

Ethan smoothly changed the subject. "I have a job for you, Paula; an important one. We're all at the private party tonight, but not actually on Richanti's table, and we need access to him. Can you find a way to make it happen?"

Paula was more than a little pleased with the prospect of entertaining Richanti. She loved celebrities, and her mind soon wondered to how exactly she would fulfil her mission. With Paula now preoccupied, Ethan turned his attention to Jean.

"Jean, I need to do something before we go. These files must go to Ocean. I need someone I can trust on the outside; and Ocean seems to feel right. Is that okay with you?" Paula, the keeper of the iPad, overheard his request and passed the tablet to Ethan.

"It's funkypunkfish@gmail.com" she advised as he jotted down his email to Ocean.

"Dear Ocean, although you don't know me, I am a good friend of your mother's. I am sending you this in the event that we might not make it through the day. The story is a long one, but once you read this file, you will understand that everything written here is for real.

"You are in danger, too; by association. Tell nobody your location and trust no-one. Release this information to the distribution list in the file if you have not heard from us by tomorrow morning. I know you are fearless. Keep faith with your gut feelings and you will find there is nothing you cannot do. I hope we meet soon, Ethan."

Ethan looked up. "There, done. It's a matter of security for everyone, just in case. We can't afford to lose the sight of the truth again and those files are not just security for Ocean, they may provide just the head start she needs."

Paula was tapping again on the iPad.

"What are you up to now?" Jean was beginning to regret Paula's bond with her new toy. Without answering, Paula did as she was asked and dropped it into the designer handbag she had procured for the evening.

After the first glass, to Jean's surprise, Paula declined to finish off the remaining Champagne, saying "I need to keep my head on if you want me to be an Ambassador to Richanti." Ethan realised Jean had been right about Paula. They could rely on her.

He went to the exit and opened the door, bowing with a flourish to his feminine company. Despite the seriousness of the event, he was ready for some fun; always the optimist.

"Let's go to the party, then? We don't want to be late for civilisation's end."

"Do you really think it will end?" Paula asked, a frown creasing her forehead.

"I don't *think* it will, I *know* it will," Ethan replied crisply. "I've been studying Precession all my life. Before the day's out, this planet will be a very different place. Life will never be the same again."

Looking at Paula's stricken face, he added kindly, "You can't always predict change but nor can you stop it. Life changes. If you're not ready to change when the time comes up, someone or something will force you to change.

Jean found herself amused at the way Ethan kept cool at all times. Once, she didn't understand it, but now she realized that she probably appeared cool to others as well. She might be apprehensive, but not fearful. She had conquered her fear a long time ago. It never served her well and she had given up worrying about the future. By getting on with the business of living, she had learned her life lesson and become happier for it: the worry and doubt, the crutches of alcohol and food that she had used to mask her unhappiness had consumed her so much that she finally decided to let it all go.

"Yes, let's go," Jean said. "I'm looking forward to this. Richanti needs a good talking to and a little bit of justice."

The three friends - now in accord - drained their glasses. They were ready for the unknown.

-

The journey to the Great Ballroom was a short one; a steady climb upwards to the highest point in the Oasis city, which overlooked the desert beyond. An occasional farm could be seen and, further in the distance, a metropolis of jagged skyscrapers stained the blue horizon.

Central to Oasis was a glass dome, built up like St Bride's Church in London's Fleet Street, a veritable wedding cake of tiers and balconies with a spiral staircase sweeping through the middle, which had become a catwalk where revellers could display their couture before taking their seats. The seating dictated some sort of hierarchy in the millionaires' club. At its apex, a small group of tables formed Richanti's private dining room. The place was busy and Paula was in her element. Like a peacock, she proudly made her way to the bottom of the spiral and started to ascend.

The tiara and matching accessories made the impact she had desired and heads were turning. Someone started to clap. Paula loved the attention so much she went down the stairs and back up again to rousing applause. She paused. Jean and Ethan, not wanting to spoil her moment, began to climb the stairwell after her. They reached the apex and Jean recognised Richanti instantly. They were greeted by a waiter handing out Bellinis. Ethan picked up two, handing one to Jean and the other to Paula, then he picked up another for himself.

"That's him," Jean confirmed to Paula. "Do you recognise him from the newsreels?" Jean looked at Richanti and pitied him. She thought she would feel anger, but it was simply pity; and there was a connection there: she could also feel his pain. She had an amazing instinct and her reading of Richanti was no exception.

Deep in thought, she was pondering her instincts and wondered what they might mean when Richanti looked over at Jean. He looked directly at her and their eyes met.

Paula replied, "Yes. Handsome, isn't he? Much more dashing in person. TV makes people look all washed-out."

"This is going to be a doddle, leave it to me," Paula said.

She mistook Richanti's glance as interest in her, but then, that was Paula all over. Maybe her lesson was to learn a little less self-obsession. As she walked straight towards him, Jean and Ethan watched.

I don't know how she does it." She explained to Ethan that Paula always had that unbounded confidence; she was always able to work her way into any situation and maximize her opportunity. 'Projection' she called it.

While they waited for Paula to secure an invitation to Richanti's table, they sat on a chaise longue looking over the view towards the sun, which due to set.

As they did so, Jean thought about her own role on this special date; a role which was likely to make history. Although she had no idea what she was heading into, she knew she would never be the same again. What was her destiny? She wondered.

"History... we're making history today," Jean murmured, verbalising what was on her mind.

Ethan never satisfied with just one interpretation, remarked, "Strange word, 'history'. As it relates to the past, this moment has happened already; it's just our perception of it that lags behind."

"Do you think the other Jean and Ethan made it here?" Jean asked Ethan.

"Without a doubt. It's like a party that everyone has an invitation to. Whatever kind of life you're living, you're all invited to attend this crucial change in the octave of earth's history. Everyone's life paths are converging and will become *one* for a brief moment. Remember what I said about crossroads. Everyone has to pass through them and the event is fundamental to everyone's destiny.

"Our other selves will be here, for sure."

"We helped them didn't we?" asked Jean, comforting herself with the good work they had already done."

"Yes we did, but you'll never get the credit for it. They will probably try and explain it or, at best, see it as a paranormal activity: ghosts and spooks."

Jean's ears pricked up. "You mean that ghosts are real; you're just seeing another dimension, another lifetime?"

"Yes. Like errors in the computer program of life, they occur infrequently; but the very possibility of them occurring can never be eradicated fully as the errors, the pauses in the octave, are part of the whole design. The impossible can occasionally happen."

Ethan took Jean's hand. "I'm glad I'm here with you," he smiled.

Just then, a handsome young member of staff came over to them

"Places have been set for you at Richanti's table..." He said this in a slightly awed tone and continued, "If, of course, you *would* like to be his guests for the evening." Ethan smiled his thanks.

"Well so far so good!" Ethan was pleased things seem to be going their way. "Now for the best part."

Before he could speak again, there was an odd sensation... a slight wobble. They were so high up, they could see the movement against the horizon. The sensation was like a train going under their feet a few levels below; and with it, a slight rumbling. One more Bellini and they would have missed it.

Ethan didn't miss it, though.

"It's started, it's real. The structure is holding out better than I hoped. Did you feel it?" Ethan sounded mildly excited.

"I thought it was the drink," Jean replied wryly.

"No, that was an earthquake; and quite a big one if we could feel it."

They continued their walk to Richanti's table.

Ethan asked, "Do you notice something else? There's no media, here. Whatever is happening out there is being sanitsed. He's cut out the media and will provide his own version of history. Self-sufficient as the Oasis is, he has complete control of us here. This is a complete, self-contained bubble. We just see what he wants us to see; no questions wanted."

Jean understood. As for the earthquake, she looked onto the horizon in the distance... the city seemed to have changed, microscopic as it was. But then she had 20:20 vision. The shape of that faraway city seemed different. Obviously, some of the structures had collapsed. Ethan was right, it had been an earthquake.

Ethan was pensive as he looked at Jean. "There's something you need to know, Jean."

She was not sure what was real anymore, so much of what she knew had changed in the last few days. Nonetheless, she was ready for anything. Fearless, she welcomed the challenge. "Go on, try me. It sounds like bad news."

"No, not bad news, although I'm not sure how today will end, but there is something you need to know. It was something that was said, about Fitz. Remember 'mongrel of a Demagodran bloodline'. The files I sent to Ocean have all the details of the members of the Demagodran; a society with Richanti at its head. The closest members seem to be family members. He's experimented with genetics, too: an alien bloodline and genetic programming; and Richanti's the result of the programme, himself, Jean."

"Okay, how does that affect me?"

"You're part of the programme, Jean. You're a reject from the Demagodran programme."

"A reject from the programme, alien bloodline..." Jean needed time to take it all in. She mulled it over in her mind. Then the penny then dropped. It was a bigger shock than suddenly being part of an alien bloodline.

"But that means I'm Richanti's sister. Surely you can't be right about that?"

"I'm afraid it's true. Once I saw the horror of the dark side to the Oasis, I hacked into Richanti's files. He had been remiss and broken his own rules. He thinks he's on top but he's weak; and he's made mistakes. He thinks he's won.

"Remember that I designed most of the technology here. It was easy to gain access. I have files on all the children. Fitz is a discarded baby of his breeding programme, as were you. Most of them were, let's just say, 'disposed of'.

Jean had known for a while that her father was not her biological father but had never really questioned who was. Richanti as her brother was a bit on the nose, though.

"Yes, it's true that you're Richanti's sister and Fitz is your nephew; and that makes Ocean first cousin to Fitz."

"Why tell me all of this, now?"

"I think it's important. Your insight and your talents aren't random. They're real. You have insights into others, as does Richanti, and they help you circumnavigate your path in life. What's more, they help you to understand others life paths too.

"In addition, you have the gift of prophecy, which is ever so slightly ahead of the curve guided by your instinct… And one more thing. When 'the show' starts, I've reprogrammed all the security access so that those in the lower levels can access the rest of the Oasis. I have also released thousands of people not yet processed or murdered.

"I can't guarantee what the outcome will be but at least this place will have some chance of an equal and fresh start. I can't live here the way it has been, can you? Whatever happens, those poor people will be set free… although to what fate I have no idea."

"Alien bloodline, long lost brother, baby survivors from breeding programmes…! Jean's head was spinning. It all made sense to her, though; it explained the strange instincts she had had.

"These instincts…" Jean faltered a little. "Can you tell me more?"

"In my opinion, you should let them guide you as if they were *facts*. We all have a dose of alien genes but you have a full set. As it happens, Richanti has used his for evil and he'll come unstuck.

"And then there's the age we are living in, of course. As we headed towards this date, those of us who were open to it have been practising with our instincts and letting them guide us. Frankly, I'm not sure how the time machine works; only that it helps enhance powers that we already possess. It's an odd thing that the same machine, same experiment, didn't work six months ago. There's something about 'now,' about this time, that is not only important, it is probably unique in the universe.

"Here we are on December 21, 2012, at the zenith of the experience: looking directly down the centre of our galaxy into the eye of the black hole that gave birth to everything we can see. I just tapped into it. I believe this time will pass and, as the window closes, those of us who fail to learn will miss the opportunity to transcend to a greater level than we have lived on in the past. As the physical world we are used to fails, the human race has the opportunity to evolve and save itself; but this possibility is only available to those who want to make that journey… and who buy a ticket?"

Jean trusted Ethan, he had been straight with her and given her all of the information, good or bad; it was up to her now.

A waiter interrupted them. "If you'd like to make your way to your seat Madam, Sir, dinner is being served." Ethan thanked the waiter and looked at her. She signalled to him to go up ahead of her. Everyone except Jean was now seated. Paula was chatting away to Richanti but he wasn't really engaged. He glanced up at Jean and, for a brief moment, his piercing eyes looked straight at her. There was a place for her to sit between Richanti and Ethan. Jean made her way forward. Her whole life's experience had been leading up to this moment, it seemed. Richanti stood as she came to the table. Fearless, confident, she took her seat.

Richanti sat down, and leaned over to whisper in Jean's ear, "I know all about you, more than you would imagine," he paused, "sister." Jean was intrigued. She processed his opening line, thinking on her feet; of course, he would know. If Ethan can access the information, then Richanti most certainly can. She was glad Ethan had been straight with her and she had a plan.

"Ah but I'm the bastard, Richanti. By all accounts, that means I got the lion's share of the talent."

Richanti laughed. "Well done, my dear."

She realised why she was here, the chosen one: he wants an ally. He actually thinks that she is going to fulfil that role for him. He made an assumption that, because she has alien blood, she has his values, too. He couldn't be more wrong.

There was another tremor. The building swayed more than before and, this time, the quake didn't cease, although the building seemed to withstand the liquidation of the earth's crust below them.

Richanti piped up. "The main feature, my dear; come out onto the balcony with me."

Jean and Richanti stepped outside. Richanti pressed a button on the door ahead and the vast, single glass panel slid back to reveal Oasis city and then the open desert beyond.

"A blank canvas, "Richanti said.

"What do you mean?" Jean asked.

"The world is about to change beyond all recognition. Only a few will survive: thousands not millions or billions. There are a million souls in the Oasis. In a few years it will be safe enough to expand beyond these walls and, then, the whole planet is mine.

"I thought I was one of a kind until you turned up this evening. Of course, anyone can have a child; it's a child with 'the gift' which is so rare: the gift of prophecy. You see the future clearly, don't you?"

"I do," Jean replied as she considered her position. She knew he wasn't going to like the answer, but she would tell him anyway. "I see the future very clearly," she said, "but I see the future without you in it. You have a debt to pay for what you've done and the grief you have caused. I know the secret of the Oasis and..."

Richanti looked at her. He was coldly emotionless, and had processed her reply, but refused to give her a reaction. Instead, he changed the topic of conversation.

"Can you see the split in the crust beyond us, see the changes in level? The whole region is sinking and there's a line on the horizon."

Jean went along with what she knew either to be denial or, more likely, quick calculation of a plan. She could see his mind processing the information she'd provided. Jean had a plan of her own and it was a royal flush against Richanti's full house: he couldn't win. It was too little, too late for Richanti.

Meanwhile Richanti continued, regardless of the niceties. "A tsunami, the largest ever created, is pushing up the Indian Ocean and this whole region will become an isthmus. Africa will be cut off from the other continent by miles of a new sea; and here we will no longer be an Oasis but an Atlantean city."

The sirens started. It was a warning that the city had started to seal itself by converting into a submarine and water-tight haven. Richanti started to make his way to the doors, which were starting to close." Jean failed to follow, which confused Richanti.

She asked, "What about your son, Richanti?"

Richanti slowed. He was interested. It was the first sign of any emotion from him. "What do you mean, my son?"

"You have a son," Jean pressed home, "and I have a daughter. They are together. They'll build a new life together.

"I don't believe you."

"Does Fitz mean anything to you?"

Richanti stopped in his tracks. "Where? How did you?"

The doors were nearly sealed. A few metres more and they'll be sealed forever. Jean contemplated a move but she was beginning to understand her destiny. She didn't need to learn anything else. She was done. She was a giver, a lover, a mother, fearless and, most of all, happy. There was nothing else that she needed, or needed to be or to have; she was just Jean. She was ready for death but Richanti was not. She saw the sadness in his eyes.

"They took him away from you didn't they? They took your son away from you and you thought he was dead. It's a lonely situation to be in have everything and yet nothing; and it's even worse to have everything and then have it taken away from you. Look."

The doors closed and were sealed forever behind them. Richanti turned round angrily and demanded that they were opened, even knowing that was impossible. As he hammered on the glass, everyone watched from the safe side; some uncertain how to help; and most reluctant to try.

At the bottom of the ballroom, thousands began streaming up from the lower levels of Oasis: the service staff and the condemned had come to watch the end. Jean saw Ty and Mario leading the crowd. She was relieved that they had survived.

Richanti saw the influx of people and, for the first time, felt remorse over his master plan: a grave error of judgement and a very poor substitute for the feeling he really craved.

Jean was calm and collected as she watched as the man before her lived his last moments, but also learnt at high speed. He had craved a connection, craved love; and found none. That was what he had to learn and it was his weakness at the end.

"It doesn't matter, now," Jean observed. "With all your power and knowledge, the one thing that was denied you is what so many have in abundance and you hated them for it. Nobody wins in the end, Richanti. You could have had the love of a whole planet if you'd played your cards differently."

"How can you be so calm?"The Tsunami had reached the outskirts of the city and the swirling sea was rising fast below them.

"It's not the end; not for me anyway. My journey has just started." Jean smiled at him with compassion and forgiveness. He had finally understood that without love there is nothing; and nothing else really matters. Jean closed her eyes and, as she did so, thought of her daughter and her new friend.

The machine gave out a brilliant white light.

A rogue wave rose and engulfed her, picking her up like a statue and accelerating her skywards. Her expression remained unchanged: content, calm and confident.

Richanti scrambled to save himself and, as he struggled, it was torturous to watch his body forced up against the glass of the dome, the apex of his achievement. For a moment, his ghostly expression hovered against the window pane. It was an empty expression as his whole life flashed ahead of him. He had amounted to nothing but had learnt much. Then the current carried him downwards and he disappeared from view.

They were both consumed by the sea.

Who knows on what final journey it would take them on? Only the realm of imagination coupled with the elusive element of time will reveal the answer; and that's another story.

Epilogue

Friday, 21st December, 2012
Firle Beacon, Sussex, England

The process of creation and destruction is how we grow.

"Creation and destruction is the way we move forward," Ocean remarked as she looked out over the Sussex Downs rising in front of her. The sun should set soon. There had been mini quakes all day, each one a little stronger than the last. The tremors were like a woman in labour, becoming more frequent, sharper, as they pointed to the moment when a new life is born.

She was pondering Ethan's manuscript and his eloquent synopsis of the end of days. The answer was in the small print. There were very few parts of the UK, with its precarious position on the edge of the Atlantic, which would not be swamped by the coming Tsunami.

The distance of the South of England from the deep trenches of the Atlantic Ocean meant the effect from Tsunamis would be limited here, whereas a huge bore was predicted in the Channel with the Tsunami taking out most of the West Country, the West Coast of Scotland and flooding the industrial north as far as Manchester.

A greater danger, however, would come from the cold. The Eurasian tectonic plate would squeeze the Downs up a couple of hundred metres and the change in latitude would deep freeze everything almost instantly. The Arabian plate was sinking beneath it, turning the Sahara and Middle East into an extension of the Atlantic Ocean. They were safe here for the short term but, longer term, their odds were slim.

Fitz and Ocean had decided to move to the safer, high ground at Firle Beacon, a few miles away from the hedonistic rituals going on at Michelham Priory. This year, the partygoers were intent on revelling until their final moments; and the event promised to be the best yet. Most of them, of course, were in denial about the portents in the press.

With her cousin by her side – yes, her cousin: fate was a strange thing – Ocean felt confident; and their shared heritage was certainly one explanation of how they managed to gel quite so quickly. They were in tune with each other from the beginning; although they had not been nurtured together. They had been brought up very differently: their lineage more like those of lab rats that had escaped, both the offspring of genetic experiments.

Fitz looked at her, still seeing a young woman, but one cloaked in much wisdom: a modern Boudicca. His eyes widened to range beyond Ocean, although she remained central to his view. It was early evening, and surprisingly mild; he could see for miles. He knew, even if he couldn't see it physically, that Beachy Head lay to their left, with Eastbourne far below it, and to their right were the ever-twinkling lights of Brighton. Ahead, the blue of the Channel waters danced pink in the sunset and the green edge of the hills framed his vivid mental picture of the South Downs.

It was surprisingly warm for the lead-up to Christmas. In fact, it had been sunny all day long; and along with revellers everywhere, there were families taking their kids to the beach.

"Okay, so it's the end of the world," he remarked laconically. "We're looking into the centre of the Milky Way or some such thing and your mum and my dad are battling it out while we chill out," he said. That definitely got her attention.

He liked having her attention; that was a compliment to her. Lacking guile, he added simply, "Right here is exactly where I need to be; living in the present with you by my side."

Getting bothered about things he could not control had never been his weak point. Even on the edge of a holocaust, he remained calm. Why worry about what you cannot control?

Maybe it was the fact that he had been given everything and it had not really made him happy. His expectations of others were low and this attitude served him well. If he could make it through the night, he would be the happiest man alive. It is what you gain, rather than what you lose that is important.

Ocean drifted in on his musings. "What do you think my mother and your father will have to say to each other?" She answered her own question with a merry laugh, "She'll flatten him, and iron him out without ever losing her temper. My mother might look as though she's led a simple life but, I can tell you, she has integrity and courage; and she is fearless.

She added thoughtfully, "It's a powerful combination. If he has a weakness, she'll find it, which is not to say that she doesn't have issues. She's like all of us in that regard. All the same, it's what she is striving to be that defines her."

Fitz observed that Ocean was obviously her mother's daughter, admirably so. He wondered what he had inherited from his father and listened carefully to her next remark.

"He'll have a weak point," she stated," and all Jean will do is point it out. That might just give her the edge she needs."

Fitz listened, absorbing what she said with the air of a thirsty man. She looked into his eyes. "Extraordinary lives are about the last few percentage points, don't you think?" He grinned appreciatively.

Ocean also grinned and loosened up a little. "Don't mind me. All the same, the last few percentage points come, for most of us, after we've mastered the hard stuff only to fall at the last post. Excelling, I think, is about finding the smallest things in ourselves that hold us back from greatness."

As Ocean paused, Fitz stepped forward with a new question. "And what of this gift of prophecy you have or, to put it another way, of unusual insights into events? Do you actually have it?"

Ocean said, "If you'd asked me that before I read Ethan's manuscripts, I'd have said no. Now, I'm not so sure. I've always seen things but I assumed that everybody else saw the world the same way. When you think about it, we're all guilty of making that assumption."

"We all have our own reality, which involves talking to each other in words that may or may not describe a situation accurately. How accurately, may depend on our integrity. Inside, though, we each live in our own secret world; a world that we show to few, if any other people."

"Hoo boy," Fitz said grinning. "Did you learn philosophy in another life or do you just make it up as you go along?"

Ocean looked sheepish. "There are exceptions, of course. You're one of them, Fitz. Whatever is going on inside gets verbalised immediately. There's a direct connection between your head and your mouth, that's your weak point." She summed up, "It gets you into trouble but, at least with you, what you see is what you get."

Fitz smiled. He sensed she liked that in him; it was a firm foundation in a world full of people with two faces. His sense of timing dictated that he hold her and he grabbed her from behind, pulling her to the ground in a playful embrace.

"We'd better make the most of the time we have left, just in case," he laughed with the fresh excitement of a child. Yes, a child again with childish ways, if only for a moment.

Ocean got the message and submitted gracefully to Nature...

There was a flash of white light and a playful hum...

He kissed her and, as they melted together in the moment, one thing led to another. She understood what she was doing. Her instincts had taken over and she was creating a future for herself, binding herself to Fitz with a child. It will be a new bloodline and, if the genetics are to be believed, it will be an interesting mix. On this occasion, however, the pairing was conceived of love.

Fitz sat up, and looked a little dazed. "Ocean, did you see that white flash?"

"Hmmm," she replied lazily, "I think the universe is on our side."

They both lay back exhausted, staring into the twilight above them. An eerie silence descended and Ocean wondered where all the birds and animals had gone. They had better follow them... Then the rumbling came again; this time, it didn't stop.

Ocean looked across The Downs towards Brighton. What she saw was not precisely in front of her eyes, but it was an alarmingly accurate picture. The largest buildings went first, felled like match sticks. Strange rifts appeared as ancient weaknesses in the strata were suddenly exposed. They seemed safe for now in the wobbling grassland as there was nothing to fall on them and nothing to fall into, but the sea in The Channel in front of them had started to boil.

She thought about this pre-ordained moment: picturing the earth's oscillating cycle with the sun stunting growth and the winning civilization striving for a level of understanding of the universe to save itself from destruction, the timer being close on 26,000 years. Had 21st century man won or lost?

Other civilizations, it seemed – some technically more sophisticated than theirs - had survived, in part but most of their works, the Sphinx with its great library being one notable exception, had perished. So if they survived the night, there was the prospect of building-up a new civilization and a fresh start.

She felt warmth in her belly. They say that a woman can pinpoint the moment of conception. A click in her brain signalled a fresh spirit starting its journey within her. She knew what was to come. She saw the future, too: insight was a powerful thing. To know there was a way through gave her hope for the days ahead. How hard it might be to survive she could not see; but survival was indeed hers if she desired it.

She put her clothes back on, shivering a little at just the thought of the coming cold, and handed Fitz his clothes as he was apparently transfixed by events he, too, could see. He put his clothes back on quickly.

"Whoa!" Fitz cried out. "Look at that!" Like a scene from an action movie, a vast wave was making its way down The Channel, spreading out into the coves and estuaries of The South Coast like the tide sweeping onto a rocky beach, following whatever channel it could find.

"It must be 50 metres high!" Fitz shouted, the adrenalin pumping through his blood. He watched as the wave took everything in its path with a crest of dirty, twenty-first century detritus running ahead of the wake, tumbling like a washer on spin: perhaps a fitting metaphor for the failures of a civilisation as it died. The wave passed Brighton and wiped out what was left of the city, with the pier being swept up in its path and tossed about like a toy.

Then an offshoot of the main tsunami, at first a shallow ripple, building up to a wave with its own crest, flowed up the estuary at Newhaven and onto the Downs, and made its way towards them at lightning speed. The situation was no longer a scene from a movie but a very real threat. The water flow took out field after field, the foam of plants and trees ripping ahead of the wave towards them. Closer and closer it came, pushing on relentlessly, destroying everything in its path. It was almost upon them and they could see the head of its crest.

"Quick!" Fitz pulled Ocean to her feet. Holding her hand tight, he commanded, "Come with me." They were near an iconic communications tower and Fitz lifted Ocean bodily, pushing her upwards. He followed, encouraging her to move rapidly. "It must be twenty metres or more above the level of The Downs," Fitz explained in a quick gasp. "It might just be the edge we need."

They accelerated up the ladder provided for maintaining communications equipment. Fitz had his eye fixed firmly on the danger behind them, but thankfully, it was slowing and flattening out, running either side of the Beacon; taking the path of least resistance. Fitz forced his body against Ocean's, and locked her in against the ladder.

"Hold tight for the impact!" he shouted. The wave hit them and a tree smashed against the side of the tower. As it buckled, they were forced forward but the tower remained intact. The water rushed below them, over the edge of the ridge into the valley below: a waterfall of destruction racing down the hill to the smallholdings at its foot. The wave joined with its brothers and they watched as a neighbouring town was taken out ahead of them: a medieval 'toy town' now, with its castle, the only building intact.

The surge was short lived, however, and the water on the high ground quickly dissipated as quickly as it arrived leaving a muddy, black moonscape in its wake. The tremors continued unabated. Fitz and Ocean could feel the tower vibrating below them.

"That was close." Fitz relaxed his grip a little.

Ocean corrected him, "That was the easy part. What comes next is harder".

As they started to descend to ground level, he looked up at her and asked in concern, "What do you mean?"

"If Ethan's manuscript is to be believed, the rumbling you can hear is the earth's crust moving rapidly and a realignment of the poles. It is going to get darker and colder. We probably only have half a day before everything starts to freeze and darkness descends for a year or longer. "

Fitz started to laugh.

"What's funny?"

"My father's now the most powerful man on the planet and I'm going to be deep frozen in a bunker for a year while he lives in seven star luxury."

"A bunker?"

"Yes bunker, C9: a WWII relic. It is not far from here. You'll be safe there. It was adapted for The Cold War so I guess it's coming back into fashion."

Fitz looked about and spotted an upturned 4WD in one of the fields below them. He exclaimed in delight, "Perfect! That's the advantage of living in this part of the world. He set off at a run, turning to say, "Follow me, please."

Ocean happily followed Fitz down a dirt track, which was streaming with channels of water running off the hillside above. They reached the bottom and managed to navigate into the field that they had seen earlier.

"Can you get this to work?" Ocean asked uncertainly. The beat-up Range Rover seemed intact but had a number of dents; and had recently been submerged in the deluge of salt water. The interior looked okay though: slightly damp but with almost pristine leather throughout. Incredibly, none of the windows had been smashed.

"Yes, no problem," Fitz responded. He found a large piece of wood and pushed it under the side of the vehicle, pushing down on it. The vehicle righted itself, coming down with a bounce. He opened one of the doors and released the bonnet catch, which popped up. After a few minutes of messing around with the wiring, the engine roared into life.

"One of the advantages of prep school; well, the prep school I went to anyway, and that was hot-wiring cars." The two set off. Understandably, the going was slow, but the vehicle handled it well. After an hour, they had traversed the few miles to Crowborough and the C9 bunker. The journey was completed in an eerie silence, aside from the 4WD's chugging noise. Luckily, they were travelling mainly through the countryside and were spared the horror of the towns and cities close by. They knew there was little time and they needed to act quickly to find shelter and supplies.

"Here you go!" Again, Fitz was looking as pleased as Punch.

Built into the side of a hill, an ominous, grey cement-funnelled entrance bridged a large communications tower. Above this, on either side, were ventilation units. A path led into a dark doorway.

Ocean piped up. "So this is it, home."

"The inside's more exciting than the outside, I would imagine," he grinned. "It's huge inside."

The two left the 4WD and made their way to the entranceway. A large iron door blocked their path. There was a panel to the side. This appeared to have been used recently as the cover was broken off. There was a red light flashing and a camera appeared to be pointing at them.

Fitz pushed the button on the panel and looked into the camera. "Two survivors. Let us enter, please. We want safe passage to Cloud Nine."

Ocean looked at him. For the first time, she had doubt in her eyes. She thought she had read him, but something was not quite right. She was wary of surprises and turned inward to reflect on the past few hours.

She saw her mother engulfed in water, Richanti with her, and a whole crowd watching. A bright light burst into her mind bringing a three-dimensional vision of her mother.

Jean was talking to her. "It's up to you now. Show him trust and he'll repay you with trust. People aren't intrinsically bad, remember, they're just made that way. I'll always be with you, but it's up to you to deal with the everyday stuff, now."

Ocean didnt like the sound of that. She tried to ask a question but Jean had gone.

"Cloud Nine?"

Fitz replied, "That's my name for it. I haven't been completely honest with you, Ocean." Fitz was quite serious, now; she sensed a shift in him.

Ocean felt wounded and went quiet. Trust was so important to her and she didn't give it lightly. She wondered what might be behind the door and felt very scared of being alone in an unknown situation for a moment. Then she composed herself. After all, Jean had somehow just verified that Fitz could be trusted. So she had better do that and follow him with trust.

The door started to open and she heard voices beyond. It was the beginning of a new journey.

Afterword

A testament within a book.

This book is inspired by a true story. The events and characters within it are almost entirely fictional but they could not have existed – even in the realms of fantasy – without the experience of a little boy with blue eyes and blonde hair.

The boy was a likeable chap. He was one of the lucky ones. He had great parents, enjoyed a decent education lived in a wonderful home. Given a head start from birth, by the age of 26, he had grown into an enviable self-made success.

He soon learned, however, this was a grotesque hoax. You see, inside where it counts, he was entirely devoid of *substance*. He was empty, a sham, and longed for some intangible quality that was desperately missing. It wasn't long until he was forced into painful if inevitable changes: he lost his business and his partner; and many of his friends deserted him in one fell swoop. It was only then, however, that he truly found himself.

He took a new lover. He adopted a fluffy cat and a faithful dog. He moved on. With a bag of clothes and a laptop to his name, he started to rebuild his life. Einstein famously said, "The definition of insanity is doing the same thing again and again and getting the same results." A habit some can relate to.

That little boy is, in fact, me. Although the little boy with blue eyes and blonde hair, with everything going for him, has long gone, I am literally still the same person: the same organs, the same flesh, the same blood. But where it matters – between the ears – I'm brand new. Remnants of my old self still remain; the habits and niggles, for instance, but essentially I'm a different person. I'm refreshed; reborn.

This novel is the culmination of a five-year journey that began with the implosion of my personal life.

Since so much went wrong, I was forced to take a long hard look at myself. I asked myriad questions and found many answers but, more importantly, I kept asking them. This is sacrosanct. We must keep moving: "kill or be killed" and "change or be changed." It really is that Darwinian.

The questions are ones we can all find time to ask, and we owe it to ourselves to do so! Self-evaluation and self-esteem are symbiotic. To feel good about ourselves, we must know about ourselves.

There are some questions that we can answer easily, such as, "Who do I want to be?" and "What makes me happy?" But there are others we cannot answer easily, such as "Why are we here?" and "What is 'my mind'?"

The latter is of particular interest to me and it's a recurring motif in the novel. We still have no real understanding of our own minds, spiritually or scientifically, but our minds are clearly one of the most important aspects of our existence. I urge you to follow your mind's dictate. Other people are there for support, but not instruction. Do your own bidding and reap the rewards. Share with others but don't be controlled by them.

I believe there's a better way to live and that's why I wrote the novel. I didn't have any ambition to become an author but happened upon the idea of writing when I found how expressive and rich language can be.

It provides a clear outlet for pure, unadulterated thought; and it is a beautiful process. What makes it an even more poignant and powerful a tool for me is that I was denied access to writing in my youth. Born with dyslexia, I've always struggled with English grammar. And yet, with perseverance, I've managed to complete a novel – a manifestation of pain and learning – for all to enjoy and ruminate upon. Believe me, there's nothing you cannot do!

Now allow me to say a few words on the world as we perceive it. As I write, everything is in turmoil. Third-world debt, global inequality and the deepening socio-economic divisions between poor and rich have fuelled wars of words and violence. We carry the world on our shoulders; and I seek to lighten the load carried by you, the reader, in assuring you that your life can be what you want it to be. In other words, macrocosmic conflict can be up-ended with a simple personal revelation. Yes; every single individual can contribute to lightening the load for all. This is something I beg everyone to take on board.

The world's turmoil is surely at tipping point. At the Winter Solstice, when the Mayan Long Count reaches its denouement, many believe that the world will end. Although Modern Mayan people say they do not believe this will happen, I took this as the starting point of my novel.

Although I certainly do not wish to make any vast statement about the world ending, I do believe there are lessons to be learned for this time from both science and spirituality. Each throws some light on the Mayan mystery connected to December 21, 2012; but nobody knows for sure what will occur.

There is no point in dismissing theories just because they are unattractive. Although we know a good deal about the world, there is so much more that we don't know. It is no time to be complacent; rather, it is crucial to be as open-minded as possible. Therefore, the notion of moral renewal is something I'd like to put forward for this year.

As the solstice approaches, the need for spiritual growth seems utterly relevant. Imagine what we could do collectively if we shared our experiences with each other. We could achieve so much more as a tighter, more altruistic unit. We really are micro-organisms of the million-petalled flower of existence. It's time to celebrate this.

So, dear reader, may I thank you from the bottom of my heart for choosing this book from the plethora of literature you could have chosen. I hope I can help bring about the changes you seek; and that life will reward you with what you want – once you know what it is that you *truly* want. Just keep questioning!

My aim has been to capture your imagination with the idea of taking action and exploring the options that are open to you. Take charge, I urge you, and start to direct your own life.

Written particularly for the youthful and young at heart - those who are at the beginning of their life's journey - this book also extends a hand to those further on in the journey of life; to anyone who still wishes to live life to the utmost.

By design, some concepts in this book aim to provoke unexpected thoughts through metaphor and association with characters and situations therein. This was done to encourage you to reflect upon your own life.

We all live in a reality of our own making but few of us really understand *who* we are. The first step is to cultivate and keep an open mind. Become one of those extraordinary individuals who not only dream their own dreams but also are brave enough to live their dreams to the full.

It does not matter where you came from, who your parents were, or what your background is. Let the past go. It is not your future; and any control that you have over your future comes from living in the present. Remember, it is always easier to blame someone else for your own shortcomings or difficult experiences; but that would be a lie, would it not?

We have proved that our bodies operate in a very small spectrum of temperature; are sensitive to specific wavelengths of light; and that we require carbon and oxygen to sustain ourselves. In comparison to other fields of science, however, we have made little progress in developing our understanding of the mind. In fact, we have only scratched the surface of the mind's potential.

A decade or so ago, we were carving up monkey brains in the name of science but understanding the mind is not as simple as looking under the bonnet of a car and pointing out which bit does what. Although we now identify the brain it is the most complex machine known to man, we remain bio-chemical machines; ones that mainly work on automatic.

Nature, however, is the ultimate development unit. One thing Nature always does is to make use of all the resources available to her in the environment.

If a property of the universe enables communication across vast distances, nature has probably made use of this in our evolution in some form or another. So if the quantum mechanics theorists are right; and if we reflect our environment perfectly, our DNA will contain unexplained elements that we have yet to explore.

As designed by nature, we may simply be superior machines. The extra, unpredictable element is consciousness. Consciousness comes when the complexity of the machine allows us to take charge of the body and mind; and direct our own future and development.

Although the concept of collective consciousness as described in this novel is as yet unproven, I believe it accounts for many of the inexplicable factors of our time.

This theory led me to interview individuals with different views of the world to mine. Some focused on ghost sightings, conspiracy theories and psychic experiences. Along the way, I talked with UFO spotters and born-again Christians. I also observed alternative healers and psychokinetics at work. Their experiences were very real to the individuals concerned.

Now, if their experiences were fact and not fiction, surely that raises questions about how the world really works? Their views and insights certainly raised questions for me. At that time - such is the law of synchronicity - I discovered that an astronomical event associated with Mayan culture held a warning for us all. *Predication 2012* was the result.

Adrian Gilbert, co-author of *The Mayan Prophecies,* states, "The Biblical prophecy of the 'opening of the bottomless pit', which is followed soon after (in Revelation 21) by the appearance of a 'New Heaven and a New Earth', *is* connected with the Mayan Prophecy..."

The Mayans *did* prophesy the astronomical alignment we now know as Precession over a thousand years ago in their long count calendar.

Unfortunately, the invading Spaniards destroyed all but four of the Mayan books. These may have given further advice on the matter. Nonetheless, drawing from their verbal traditions, the Mayans are adamant that the winter solstice date does not mean an apocalyptic event. They regard it - correctly - as a cyclical matter.

What is extraordinary is that the early Mayans were able to pinpoint with accuracy the exact date of an event that occurs only once every 26,000 years.

Many researchers in the field have decided from their studies of Precession that it is, potentially, a time of transition and the beginning of a new era. Wouldn't it be great if 21 December 2012 became an opportunity for renewal of our society rather than a curse?

So what is needed to move forward from the brink of economic, ecological and moral collapse in 2012?

As the winter solstice draws near, mainstream scientists and journalists alike pour scorn on the idea of a looming crisis. Conversely, others who have researched the matter seriously are talking of a 'crucial tipping point' for Earth. The Bible, the Koran, the Jewish scriptures, the Hindu Vedas and seers such as Edgar Cayce, Nostradamus and the anthroposophist Rudolf Steiner converge along similar lines.

It is also worth considering the development of humankind and the world as a living entity in its own right. Of those pursuing this approach to human history, James Lovelock, an independent scientist and environmentalist, is a notable proponent of Earth as a living body. Regarded as one of the main leaders in the development of environmental awareness, Lovelock has written several books on *The Gaia Theory.*

Bringing an alternative perspective to climate change is the internationally renowned *New York Times* author and geologist, Gregg Braden. A pioneer in bridging science and spirituality, he suggests that "scientific evidence proves beyond a reasonable doubt that civilisation is at least twice as old as previously believed."

Braden refers to a discovery in Caral, Peru, that "goes back to between 5,000 and 6,900 years ago." He notes that Götekli Tepe (Turkish for "hill of the navel") dates back 11,550 years. "Even the Sphinx could be between 9,000 to 11,000 years old."

Additionally, he points to a "virtual library of our planet's history" contained in ice cores drilled from Vostok, Antarctica, in June 1999. These "give us a continuous window for 420,000 years into the past..."

What is of particular interest is that the data "offers a powerful key for understanding the climate of the past and determining whether or not what is happening in our world today is beyond the range of *normal cycles.*"

If civilisations have vanished in the past, can we learn from myths - such as Atlantis - rather than laughing them off as fantasy? Myths may well be based on factual circumstances.

Elsewhere, the archaeological remains of a lost city have been discovered 36 metres (120 feet) underwater in the Gulf of Cambay[i] (Khambat), off the western coast of India. Moreover, carbon dating suggests they are 9,500 years old. Another such find is the 8,000 BC site of Yonaguni[ii] - underwater pyramids.

In the UK, on New Year's Day, 2012, BBC Two showed Neil Oliver exploring a newly discovered 5,000-year-old temple on Orkney. Built 500 years before the iconic monument of Stonehenge, it was *buried* complete about 5,000 years ago. The temple find has turned the map of ancient Britain upside down.

Finally, it's important to disclose that not all of the experiences shared in the following pages are inspired by things that happened to me alone: some are shared, and some of the ideas that inspired my writing actually happened to others. It is to these people I am truly grateful. The counsellors, coaches, and conversations are the genetic make-up of my re-birth. I owe them more than I can say. So what is the truth about the world in which we live, start to listen the answer is within you, the world is changing, change or be changed, remember there is nothing you cannot do.

[i] Adrian Gilbert, December 21st 2012, P309. *Is This the End of the World as We Know It? The End of Time, The Mayan Prophecies Revisited,* 2006, Mainstream Publishing Company (Edinburgh) Ltd. ISBN 1 84596 098 X

[ii] James Lovelock, *The Gaia Theory, The Ages of Gaia and The Revenge of Gaia.* He is also Doctor Honoris Causa of several universities throughout the world

[iii] Gregg Braden, *Deep Truth: Igniting the Memory of Our Origin, History, Destiny, and Fate,* published by Hay House, September 2011: ISBN 978-1-4019-2919.

www.ingramcontent.com/pod-product-compliance
Lightning Source LLC
Chambersburg PA
CBHW070916130626
46555CB00001B/163